Taming
the
Wind

Books by Tracie Peterson

www.traciepeterson.com

House of Secrets • *A Slender Thread* • *Where My Heart Belongs*

LAND OF THE LONE STAR
Chasing the Sun
Touching the Sky
Taming the Wind

BRIDAL VEIL ISLAND*
To Have and To Hold
To Love and Cherish
To Honor and Trust

SONG OF ALASKA
Dawn's Prelude
Morning's Refrain
Twilight's Serenade

STRIKING A MATCH
Embers of Love
Hearts Aglow
Hope Rekindled

ALASKAN QUEST
Summer of the Midnight Sun
Under the Northern Lights
Whispers of Winter
Alaskan Quest (3 in 1)

BRIDES OF GALLATIN COUNTY
A Promise to Believe In
A Love to Last Forever
A Dream to Call My Own

THE BROADMOOR LEGACY*
A Daughter's Inheritance
An Unexpected Love
A Surrendered Heart

BELLS OF LOWELL*
Daughter of the Loom
A Fragile Design
These Tangled Threads

LIGHTS OF LOWELL*
A Tapestry of Hope
A Love Woven True
The Pattern of Her Heart

DESERT ROSES
Shadows of the Canyon
Across the Years
Beneath a Harvest Sky

HEIRS OF MONTANA
Land of My Heart
The Coming Storm
To Dream Anew
The Hope Within

LADIES OF LIBERTY
A Lady of High Regard
A Lady of Hidden Intent
A Lady of Secret Devotion

RIBBONS OF STEEL**
Distant Dreams
A Hope Beyond
A Promise for Tomorrow

RIBBONS WEST**
Westward the Dream
Separate Roads
Ties That Bind

WESTWARD CHRONICLES
A Shelter of Hope
Hidden in a Whisper
A Veiled Reflection

YUKON QUEST
Treasures of the North
Ashes and Ice
Rivers of Gold

*with Judith Miller   **with Judith Pella

LAND OF THE LONE STAR ★ BOOK THREE

TRACIE PETERSON

BETHANY HOUSE PUBLISHERS
a division of Baker Publishing Group
Minneapolis, Minnesota

© 2012 by Tracie Peterson

Published by Bethany House Publishers
11400 Hampshire Avenue South
Bloomington, Minnesota 55438
www.bethanyhouse.com

Bethany House Publishers is a division of
Baker Publishing Group, Grand Rapids, Michigan

Printed in the United States of America

Library of Congress Cataloging-in-Publication Data
Peterson, Tracie.
    Taming the wind / Tracie Peterson.
        p.   cm. — (Land of the lone star ; book three)
    ISBN 978-0-7642-1050-1 (hardcover : alk. paper)
    ISBN 978-0-7642-0617-7 (pbk.)
    ISBN 978-0-7642-1051-8 (large-print pbk.)
    1. Texas—History—Fiction. I. Title.
PS3566.E7717T36 2012
813'.54—dc23   2012013116

Scripture quotations are from the King James Version of the Bible.

The internet addresses, email addresses, and phone numbers in this book are accurate at the time of publication. They are provided as a resource. Baker Publishing Group does not endorse them or vouch for their content or permanence.

Cover design by Jennifer Parker

Cover photography by Mike Habermann Photography, LLC

12   13   14   15   16   17   18   7   6   5   4   3   2   1

To Dr. Dennis Maier
an extraordinary surgeon who has
a great sense of humor and bedside manner.
God bless your work!

I t is a lovely place for a horse farm," Carissa Lowe told her
sister. She glanced around the lush, green acreage. The
serenity found here spoke to her in a way the city hadn't. "I
can certainly see why Brandon loves it so."

"Well, I love it even more now that you and Gloria have
decided to join us. I'm glad that Mother and Father decided
to go north to see Uncle Robert. The trip away from Corpus
Christi will do Mother a world of good."

Carissa glanced to where her nearly two-year-old daughter, Gloria, played happily with Laura and Brandon's little
boy, Daniel. At a year and a half, he cautiously explored his
environment, while Gloria had seemingly no fear whatsoever. Even now she was trying to climb the rail posts of the
nearest fence.

"Gloria, get down from there," Carissa called. "You know

you aren't supposed to climb the fence." In the distance she heard the low rumble of thunder.

"You too, Daniel," Laura added. The child looked at his mother momentarily before refocusing on the fence.

Carissa went in the direction of her daughter and caught up to her before Gloria could renew her efforts. "It's nap time," she told her daughter.

"No nap! No nap!" Gloria declared with great insistence.

"You too, little man," Laura said, grasping her son's hand.

Daniel wiggled to get away, but Laura held him fast. Carissa stroked her daughter's blond hair and smiled as she calmed. "Just take a very little nap, and then we will go see the new horses."

Gloria clapped her hands. "Horsey. I wanna see horsey."

"After your nap," Carissa assured. Thunder rumbled once again, and Carissa looked beyond the trees to the billowing clouds on the horizon. They didn't seem particularly threatening or dark, but apparently a storm was brewing. "I suppose it's going to rain," she told her sister. Clapping had become Gloria's new means of communication, and she gave a hearty applause at the comment about rain.

Laura lifted Daniel to her left hip. "We'd best get the laundry off the line in a hurry."

"If you'll take the children, I'll get the clothes," Carissa replied. Laura nodded and swung Gloria onto her right hip.

"I'll be there to tuck you in, Gloria. Just get on your bed and wait for me." Carissa leaned over to kiss her daughter's head, then hurried to retrieve the laundry basket.

She couldn't help but smile as she thought about her child. Thunder and winds never seemed to disturb Gloria, and Carissa couldn't help but wonder if it was somehow related to the fact that Gloria had been conceived and carried amidst great strife and trial. Daniel often cried during storms, but not Gloria. Storms were just a way of life for Carissa and Gloria.

There were just a few dresses and shirts to contend with, so Carissa pulled them quickly from the line and placed them in the basket. There was a nice table on the back porch where she could dump the load and come back for the towels. She worked quickly and barely beat the rain as she pulled the last of the towels from the line. By the time she made it back to the house, the rain began to pour in a fury.

She left the towels on the table with the other things and made her way to the room she shared with Gloria. To her surprise, the child was already asleep, and Carissa couldn't help but sit down beside her for a moment. It was a miracle the child had ever been born. Gloria's father, Malcolm Lowe, had thrown Carissa down a flight of stairs when she was only a few weeks pregnant. She'd been certain she would miscarry, but when she didn't, Carissa thought of the unborn child as her consolation for a miserable marriage. A short time later, her husband again threatened her life.

Though she'd fallen for his charms as they courted, Malcolm had revealed his true nature once they'd wed. With the Union Army after him, he'd done his best to slip from their capture by kidnapping Carissa and Laura, figuring to use them to keep the law at bay. He also planned to kill them both for interfering in his plans. Later, when surrounded by soldiers, Malcolm attempted to escape by water and ended up throwing Carissa into the Gulf off the shores of Corpus Christi, in order to distract his pursuers. But that distraction had been short-lived. In the end, Malcolm had perished from wounds given him by the soldiers. Laura, too, had nearly drowned, but Brandon had saved her. Tyler Atherton had been responsible for rescuing Carissa.

When Malcolm nearly succeeded in ending her life, Carissa found little to live for, she was so devoid of hope. But the growing life inside of her compelled Carissa to live . . . and Gloria was the beautiful result.

"You are more than my consolation," she told Gloria, kissing the sleeping girl. "You are the very reason I rise in the morning."

Daniel was fussing, and Carissa knew her sister would have a difficult time calming him, especially with the constant rumble of the thunder. Laura would no doubt be a while, rocking and singing the boy to sleep.

Carissa quietly exited the bedroom and walked to the front-room window to look out on the storm. Thunder rumbled again and again while the rain steadily fell. *Just a spring storm,* she thought. Hopefully there wouldn't be any hail or tornadoes to contend with. She sighed and watched a bit longer at the window.

She had never intended to live here on the farm with Laura and Brandon. For the last two years she'd resided with her parents in Corpus Christi and quite happily vowed to remain there. Well, perhaps *happy* wasn't a word that Carissa could associate with her life. She had never felt all that close to her mother and father, and she knew full well that the fault was her own. Widowhood and being a mother had softened her heart in a way that made Carissa regret her actions in the past.

With Malcolm dead at the hands of the army, Carissa was grateful for her parents' care and accepted that widowhood would be her lot in life. In fact, she cherished it. She never again wanted to have to deal with a deceiving husband.

Instead, she would use her days to be a good mother and perhaps improve her relationship with her parents.

Of course, despite her resolve, the men didn't keep from calling. She had never suffered for suitors. But after Malcolm, Carissa was wary of any man save her father, brother-in-law, and Tyler Atherton—and in truth she hadn't had many dealings with the latter. After he had saved her life, Carissa had seen very little of the man, and it was just as well. Something about Tyler's gentle manner touched her heart in a way she would just as soon forget. She reasoned she only felt drawn to him because he'd saved her life. It seemed a sensible explanation.

It was best, Carissa determined, to remain on her guard where men were concerned. She'd thought she'd known Malcolm so well, despite the fact that he always told her his business was to remain his alone, and that she should refrain from asking too many questions.

Carissa could never quite understand his insistence until the truth came out and she learned that for Malcolm, the War Between the States had never ended. Brandon once told her that it hadn't ended for a lot of people. Even now, nearly three years after Lee's surrender at Appomattox Courthouse, folks were still at war. At least their own personal war.

Fortunately, Carissa's family were Union supporters. So, too, were many of the families in their social circle of Corpus Christi. There were plenty of Confederates, but also a good number of people who simply supported Texas rather than siding with either the North or the South. Carissa knew that Tyler Atherton had fought for the South, just as her husband had. But where Malcolm had been made hateful and bitter by the war, Tyler was sad and regretful. She much preferred the latter's way of thinking. She couldn't see how either side had truly won anything, given that families had been set against each other and hundreds of thousands of lives had been lost.

I'm only twenty-one, she thought, *yet already my life feels as if it has concluded.*

"You seem awfully quiet," Laura said, entering the room. "I suppose you're thinking deep thoughts."

Carissa startled at the comment. "I was, actually." She smiled. "Did Daniel finally settle down?"

Laura smiled. "Yes. He was very tired and despite the storm, he nodded right off. I hope this next baby is a little . . . calmer," she said, putting her hand to her growing abdomen. "But no matter. August can't get here soon enough, and I'm so glad that you're here to help. Already I feel as though I've been carrying this one forever."

"The baby will be here before you know it." Carissa forced a smile and went to the sewing basket. "Besides, I thought the doctor told you that you might well expect to deliver in July."

"I know. But July or August, I wish it were sooner."

Carissa nodded, knowing just how confining a pregnancy could be. "I'll work just a little while on this mending, and then after the storm passes I'll start the ironing. I think I'll iron on the porch. Maybe the air will be cooler after the rain."

"I've been thinking we're going to need to make some new curtains for the upstairs bedrooms once Brandon finishes painting them. Goodness, but there is so much work to do on this place. I had thought it to be in perfect condition until we actually moved in. It seems my list of things to do only grows."

"Still, it's very nice." Carissa picked up one of Brandon's shirts and began to fix a loose button. "And I am grateful that you are allowing me to stay all through the spring and summer. I had no desire to travel with Mother and listen to her rant about all the injustices of the world and instruct me in mothering Gloria. My patience has been wearing thin."

"I'm sorry she's so hard on you."

Carissa paused in her work. "I suppose I deserve it. I've been hard on her . . . so I'm trying to use our time together to mend some of the tears in our past."

Laura met her gaze and nodded. "I'm glad you're here all the same. I missed you so much, Carissa. Leaving Corpus Christi wasn't easy for Brandon or me. I truly loved teaching, though when the Freemen's Bureau took over education issues for the former slaves, our little school became obsolete. I suppose it was for the best, since I was expecting Daniel, but nevertheless, I do miss teaching."

Laura walked to the window. "Looks like the storm has passed. It's raining very lightly now." She dropped the curtain back in place. "I'll get the irons heating and then start supper." Laura took a few steps, then turned back. "I'm hopeful that once the horse farm begins to support itself, we'll be able to at least hire a good cook."

When Carissa said nothing more, Laura left the room. It wasn't Carissa's intention to slight her sister, but she had no desire for conversation and pleasantries. For the last two years Carissa had been longing to find peace of heart, but that peace seemed to elude her. At night when she slept . . . if she slept . . . she continued to have nightmares about all that had happened in her brief marriage to Malcolm. She silently wondered if the bad memories would ever leave her.

Mother had always told her daughters that dwelling on lovely things would cause bad thoughts to disappear. Carissa

. never found it to be completely true, but always tried to embrace the practice. Yet even now as the storm faded and Gloria slept, Carissa struggled to think of the good things in life.

I'm safe, and I have a beautiful daughter. Father and Mother have blessed me with a monthly income, and I needn't worry about finding a new husband, unless Mother gets a bee in her bonnet—which she has been known to do. Carissa sighed and tried again to think positive thoughts. *I have a home here for the time, and it's a beautiful place. And I have the love of Laura and Brandon, as well as Mother and Father.* Why wasn't it enough?

She thought momentarily of Tyler Atherton. He was a compassionate man; even in their early acquaintance, when Carissa had been self-centered and immature, Tyler had been patient and kind. She couldn't help but wonder how he was doing. Brandon mentioned that he lived not so far away on the Barnett ranch. Tyler's own family property had been confiscated for his having served with the Confederate troops. She thought it unfair, as did William Barnett, Tyler's good friend. Barnett had immediately gone to plead on Tyler's behalf, but so far it hadn't rectified the situation. For now, Tyler worked and lived with him.

A knock sounded at the front door, and Carissa jumped to her feet. They weren't expecting anyone, so when to her surprise she opened the door to find Tyler Atherton, it was almost as if she'd conjured him up and set him at her door.

"Mr. Atherton." For a moment she couldn't think of what else to say. Finally she stepped back. "Won't you come in?"

"Thank you," he said, pulling his hat off. Water sprinkled Carissa's face and gown. "Oh . . . I'm . . . I'm so sorry." He slapped the hat against his thigh to release more water. "The

rain has stopped, but I'm afraid I rode through the worst of
it." He pulled off his rain slicker and threw it over the porch
rail. "At least most of me stayed pretty dry."

"If you came to see my brother-in-law, you're too late. He
isn't here. He rode out to someone's ranch to look at stock.
He should be home for supper." Carissa smiled and tried
to sound nonchalant. "And if you came for supper . . . well,
you're early."

He laughed. "I did come to see Brandon, but that can wait.
Perhaps you'd grant me the pleasure of your company and
tell me how you've been. It's been a very long time since we
last met. I ran into Brandon at the mercantile the other day,
and he mentioned that you'd be staying the summer."

"Yes, that is the plan. Mother and Father traveled to Chicago, then plan to go abroad until September. I chose to come
here to be with Laura and Brandon. I believe I can make
myself useful to them."

"I'm quite certain you will be very helpful." He glanced
over her shoulder. "And what of your . . . daughter?"

"She's sleeping. Perhaps if you're here when she awakens,
I can introduce the two of you."

"I'd like that." Tyler smiled in that warm, casual way he
possessed. Carissa had always liked his smile and couldn't
help but return it.

"Why don't I have Laura come speak with you about Brandon." She stepped back from the entryway. "You can wait for
her in the front room." Carissa motioned for him to follow.

"Why don't I just sit here with you and visit while you
sew?" he questioned, nodding to the shirt she still held in
her hand. "I don't need to bother Laura."

Carissa looked at the shirt and then back to Tyler. "I

suppose . . . for just . . . just a while," she replied. "I plan to iron clothes as soon as the irons are hot. Now that the rain has stopped, I thought I'd do so on the porch, where the breeze after the storm might keep things cooler."

"That's fine." He stepped past her into the room. "Where are you sitting?"

She hesitated. Visiting with Tyler Atherton wasn't exactly what she'd expected, but she crossed the room and took her seat in a small but comfortable chair. Tyler wasn't far behind. He grabbed a larger wing-backed chair and pulled it close.

"So . . . how are you?" she asked, trying hard to focus on her stitches rather than on Tyler's tanned face.

"Well enough. I don't know if you heard or not, but I'm stayin' with Will Barnett and his family." He paused, seeming to carefully weigh his words. "The government took away my ranch."

"I had heard something to that effect. I think it's wrong of them," she added quickly. For some reason it felt important that he know her thoughts on the matter.

"I have some cattle that I've been running for a few years with Will's, so at least they are still mine. William's also fighting to get my ranch returned, but it isn't looking great."

"I'm sorry to hear that." And she was, even though it had nothing to do with her. "Can you sell some of the cows and buy new land?"

"The government isn't all that inclined to help an ex-Reb. That's why I'm dependent on William for help. If all else fails, he thinks he'll buy the ranch, then sell it back to me."

"That's quite generous . . . and kind." She looked up again and had a harder time looking away. "He must be a very dear friend."

"He is. We've been working together since the war ended, and our cattle herds have grown considerably. This last year we moved them north on open range to avoid tick fever. Now our plans are coming together to drive them to sell in Kansas."

"Why can't you sell your cows here, Mr. Atherton?"

"Whoa, right there. You call me Tyler, and I'll call you Carissa. We've gone through too much to start puttin' on airs now."

She nodded. "I suppose you're right."

"And second, cows are females and I have both males and females. My plan is to drive the fattened males—the steers—to market in Kansas because the prices are ten times what I can get here in Texas. William wants to do likewise, and we have another friend, Ted Terry, who also wants in on it. That's why I came to talk to Brandon today. We're going to need a good wrangler. Having someone to handle the horses is critical."

"Well, Brandon would definitely be able to do that job. He has a way with horses that I don't think I've ever seen before . . . unless, of course, it was my sister's abilities. I've never seen anyone quite like Laura dealing with a horse."

"And what of you? Do you also have a way with horses?"

Carissa shook her head. "I haven't ridden in years."

"We should rectify that," Tyler said, grinning. "I'd be happy to take you out. This is some mighty fine land for riding."

"I doubt you would be quite so happy after spending a day picking me up off the ground and listening to me complaining about all my aches and pains." She shrugged. "But one can never tell."

"Why, Tyler Atherton, I didn't know you were here," Laura said, entering the room.

"I only just arrived." He got to his feet. "I came to see your husband, but I understand he's out."

"Yes, but he's due back anytime. Won't you stay and join us for supper? I'm not the best cook in the world, but I am learning. In fact, Carissa has taught me quite a few tricks."

Embarrassed by her sister's praise, Carissa put aside the sewing. "I'm going to gather the clothes for ironing." She left before either could protest. She hated to admit it, but Tyler's presence flooded her mind with painful longing. She had loved the attention of boys when she'd been younger. When Malcolm had paid her court, she felt like the belle of Corpus Christi. Men used to fall at her feet if she so much as gave them a second glance, and now she wanted nothing to do with them. But at the same time . . . she was lonely for a man's attention.

"What in the world is wrong with me?" she asked as she made her way to the back porch. "Haven't you been through enough, Carissa?"

She began sorting through a tableful of dried but wrinkled clothes. *I must be a glutton for punishment,* she thought. *To feel things I swore I'd never allow myself to feel again. What a troublesome woman I've become.*

"Would you like some help?"

She looked up, feeling almost frantic at the sound of Tyler's voice. "That isn't necessary."

"I know, but I'd like to help you if I can."

Carissa wadded a calico gown into a roll and stuffed it in the basket. "I'm perfectly capable. I might not be able to ride horses, but I can keep a house. You might as well rest and wait for Brandon. I'm sure Laura will fix you some refreshments."

"She's already offered," Tyler said, reaching out to take

hold of one of Brandon's shirts. "I told her I can wait until supper and that I'd just as soon come out here and talk with you. She seemed relieved."

Like I would be if you'd leave.

"So I was thinking we might go riding on Saturday. Would that be acceptable to you?"

Carissa mashed another gown into the basket and frowned. "I . . . well . . . it is hard for me to make plans. With Gloria, I'm never certain what I'll be able to do."

"So you named her Gloria? That's an unusual name." He placed the carefully folded shirt in the basket atop the wrinkled gowns.

"I suppose it is," Carissa replied. "I wanted something that sounded pretty, and happy. You probably think me silly, and I couldn't blame you if you did, but it's from the Bible when the angels were praising God. Carlita, our maid, was singing a song one day, and I kept hearing her say, 'Gloria in excelsis Deo.' I asked her what it meant, and she said, 'Glory to God in the highest.' Only in the Latin, they say *Gloria.* I thought it made a sweet-sounding name."

Tyler nodded. "I think so, too."

Carissa didn't know what to say after that, so instead went to pick up the laundry basket. But Tyler wouldn't allow her to carry it.

"I plan to talk with you while you iron, so I might as well carry this for you."

She bit her lip, wondering how she could tell him that she didn't want to talk to him. All that they shared between them was in the past, where she wanted it to remain.

"The world feels new after a rain, doesn't it?" he asked, looking at her intently. Then, as if he knew her thoughts, he continued. "Makes me want to leave the past firmly behind me, and concentrate only on what's ahead. To a brighter future."

Carissa gave a brief nod, then tried to ignore the way his glance seemed to steal a look all the way into her soul.

Tyler looked up as Brandon finished the supper prayer. "Thanks for having me. I hope it's not too much of an inconvenience."

"No inconvenience at all." Brandon smiled and handed Tyler a platter with fried chicken. "Always room for one more."

He helped himself to the crispy chicken and held the platter while Carissa took a portion, as well. "I hope you'll still feel that way after I explain why I've come."

Carissa took the platter and passed it to Laura. "I think he will. My brother-in-law always seems to enjoy a challenge."

Laura looked at Carissa with a strange expression. "A challenge?"

Tyler intervened. "Yes, I have to say this will be a challenge. William Barnett and I are putting together a cattle drive with another rancher. We'd like to ask you to come along as our wrangler and handle all the horses. We'll probably have at least fifteen men for the drive, and with the cook wagon and reserve mounts, there will probably be some seventy to eighty horses."

"A cattle drive to where?" Brandon asked.

"Kansas." Tyler took a bowl of grits and helped himself to a healthy portion. He followed that up with thick chicken gravy and waited for Brandon to digest the news.

"How long would a drive like that take?" Laura asked before Brandon could speak. "We are due to have another baby in August, in case you were unaware."

Tyler smiled. "The drive . . . if we can get everything in order, will start the first or so of April and we should be back by July at the latest, maybe even sooner. We've heard good reports from the forts along the way, and rivers are crossable for the most part. Those that are still running high will be down considerably by the time we reach them. The boys have already rounded up most of the herd for branding and such, so we're well on our way to bein' ready."

"What about Indians? I presume we'll have to travel through Indian Territory," Brandon said, still not looking at his wife.

Tyler frowned. "Well, that's the worst of it as far as I'm concerned. Comanche killed my father and some of his men. I'm none too inclined to want anything to do with them; however, there are new rail pens in a town called Abilene in Kansas. That's pert near straight north of here, not quite five hundred miles. So in order to take the shortest route, we'll have to deal with the Indians."

"Five hundred miles in the saddle, eh?" Brandon asked, shaking his head. "Not sure I'm ready for that kind of riding."

"We take it slow. The cattle graze along the way. We don't want to run the meat off of them."

Carissa looked at Tyler. "How many miles would you travel each day?"

"Anywhere from ten to twelve. We don't push for more than that usually," Tyler said, meeting her worried expression. "It's already becomin' a well-established trail and shouldn't be all that rough. The hardest part will be finding good grazing if there's already been a lot of other drives through the area."

"So we're looking at about fifty days, more or less," Brandon said.

"That's a good average," Tyler admitted. "Then there's the ride home. It goes quicker, but it's still five hundred miles." He grinned. "So we figure about ninety days."

"And what benefits would there be for my brother-in-law?" Carissa asked.

Tyler laughed. "She would make a good businesswoman. The drovers are gettin' about thirty-five dollars a month and can bring some of their own cattle if they have them. Your cut would be considerably more because a wrangler gets better pay. Of course, you'd have to be able to shoe and doctor up any animal that needed attention. The trails are hard on the mounts."

"I'm sure they are. However, I am capable of doing both," Brandon assured.

"We'd take care of feeding you and providing the equipment needed," Tyler added. "The pay is one hundred dollars a month due to you after the beeves are sold in Abilene. And that includes payin' you for the return trip. Will said, too, that if we get a really high price for the beeves there will be bonuses for everyone."

Brandon's eyes widened. "That's a lot of money. Far more than I would have expected."

Tyler laughed. "You'll earn it. You'll also need a couple of other men to help you with the horses. William's got some good men who can help, but you'll no doubt want to meet them and get to know them. That's why I'm here. William was hoping that if you're of a mind to join us, you might come on over next Saturday for a bit of a meeting. Bring the family. Hannah—that's Will's wife—plans to prepare a feast for everyone."

"Sounds like a good excuse to get together," Brandon said, glancing to Laura. "What do you think?"

"I don't like the idea of you going away and traveling off through Indian land, but I realize we could use the money, with another baby on the way." She looked at their son and smiled as he stuffed a piece of buttered corn bread in his mouth. He managed to mash more of the bread between his fingers than he actually got in his mouth.

Tyler couldn't help but grin at the boy. He seemed so happy with his accomplishment. But it was Gloria Lowe who truly held his attention. He turned toward the little blond-haired girl. She sat very manageably on her mother's lap while Daniel was in a feeding chair between his mother and father.

"I don't think it would hurt to at least hear what William has to say," Brandon finally replied.

Tyler nodded. "He'll be glad to hear it. Ted Terry, too. They want to get under way as soon as possible. You'll get a chance to meet Ted and his wife, Marietta, on Saturday. They own a large ranch to the west and north of Will's. And here's something else to interest you even more: You could buy additional horses for your farm in Abilene."

"I was just thinking on that, but maybe not in the way you were," Brandon admitted. "I was thinking that I could have my father ship some of his stock to Abilene. I could pick them up at the rail station and bring them back with us to Texas."

"See there, already thinkin' like a true Texan. Never make a trip for one purpose if you can do it for three or four."

"You said there are forts along the way?" Laura questioned. Tyler could hear the worry in her voice. "Yes, ma'am. The army is keeping a good eye on the Indian nations. The renegades are still likely to raid, but the army is working to keep them contained."

"We'd heard that the Kiowa attacked earlier this year. We were told it happened just before we arrived in the area," Laura replied.

"It did, and it wasn't all that far north of here." He couldn't hide the anger in his voice. "It was much like when they killed my pa. Renegades attacked, robbed the place, burned everything, and killed those in their way. Only three men managed to survive the attack on our ranch. In the case of what happened in January, I'm told some of the women and children were taken hostage. No doubt to be traded."

Laura shuddered. "To whom would they trade . . . people?"

"Other tribes. Mexican bandits." Tyler shook his head. "Seems there are always those who are looking to take a slave no matter the color of their skin."

"How awful," Carissa said. "Do they always take hostages?"

"No, not usually. It's more likely they kill everyone. That's how it was at our place . . . at least that's what they tried to do." Tyler picked up his chicken and began to eat.

"But I thought you said your mother and sister were alive. At least I thought I remembered you telling me that once. Were they not on the ranch when the Indians attacked?" Carissa asked.

"They are alive. Thankfully they were in Dallas with me and my grandfather when the Comanche attacked the house. I thought eventually we'd all return to the ranch, but Mother decided to go east to live with her cousin after my grandfather passed on. She said Texas made her far too sad. My sister, Lenore, married and now lives in Georgia. I was sorry to see them go, but now I'm just as glad they did. Since the government took my land, I'm hardly in a position to support them, but I do try to send my mother a little money. Hopefully after this cattle drive, I can send her more than just a little."

"Seems a complete injustice that they should rob you of your home," Carissa said, shaking her head.

"They figure me for a traitor," Tyler replied. "Truth is, I never planned to go to war in the first place."

"Then how was it you ended up in the Confederate cavalry?" Brandon asked.

Tyler shrugged. "It's a long story. Even my pa wanted to stay out of the war. He was of a mind like Sam Houston— that Texas had no business goin' to war. After Pa died, my grandfather and I fully planned to rebuild the ranch." He fell silent. "The war put an end to that. First because it took me away from the ranch. Then because my participation took the ranch away from me."

"But what about the Homestead Act?" Laura asked. "Couldn't you get another place that way?"

Brandon shook his head and answered before Tyler could. "No, he fought against the United States. They won't allow him to have land. At least not here. I don't know for sure how they're doing it elsewhere. You have to sign a paper stating that you never bore arms against the United States."

"As I told Mr. Atherton . . . Tyler," Carissa began, "I think it very unfair that he should be treated that way. I wish there was something we could do to help him."

"Well, we will just have to put our heads together and see what can be accomplished," Brandon replied. "I have good friends who served with the Union and some are in fairly high places now. Perhaps they might help."

"William is doing his best to help me," Tyler said, trying hard not to let the bitterness well up. First Indians had taken what he loved, and now the very government he was supposed to swear allegiance to had stolen his land.

"If Texas were to revert to being a republic again, you might easily be able to get your land back," Laura suggested. "As I understand it, there are many who want exactly that. They feel slighted that Texas has not yet officially been allowed back in the Union."

"We aren't like other states," Tyler admitted. "Never will be. This state is made up of folks who know what it is to have to fight for their very existence. Texas isn't for the faint of heart. Even so, I doubt we'll ever see a return to our republic days. I doubt Texas will ever be like it used to be."

⌒

The next morning Tyler awoke in William's house to the smell of side meat and coffee. He smiled and quickly dressed. Hannah was in the kitchen with Juanita, her housekeeper and cook, when Tyler strolled in. He made an exaggerated effort to draw in a long deep breath.

"Sure smells good in here."

"Morning, Tyler," Hannah said, motioning to the stove. "Coffee's ready."

He grabbed a mug. "I think this may well be my favorite

time of day. I'd all but forgotten what it was like to have a woman in the house. Camping on the battlefield doesn't exactly allow for the comforts of home."

"No, I'm sure it doesn't." Hannah turned with a platter of scrambled eggs and grits. "If you take a seat, I'll bring you some breakfast."

Tyler quickly complied. He was happily focused on putting away a second helping when Will joined him. "Wondered if you were gonna sleep away the day."

William rubbed his right leg, as he often did since taking a war bullet. Mornings seemed worse for him, and stiffness caused his limp to be more pronounced. "I wasn't sure you'd be up this early. By the time I went to bed last night, you still weren't home."

There was a hint of disapproval in William's voice and that only caused Tyler to laugh. "I wasn't out whoopin' it up, if that's what you're worried about. I had dinner at the Reid farm. I think Brandon is going to do the job for us."

"He'll come on the drive?"

Tyler nodded. "So long as you can have him back by August. He's got another baby due then."

Hannah joined them, bringing a plate of corn bread and one of side meat. Juanita followed behind with the coffeepot. She quickly refilled Tyler's cup and then turned to William's.

"So I'm not the only one expecting," Hannah said with a smile.

This was news to Tyler. "You're gonna have another baby, Hannah?"

She blushed and nodded. "Yes. As best I can figure the baby will come in October, possibly as early as September."

"Well, congratulations. That's mighty fine news." Tyler

reached over and gave William a slap on the back. "Mighty fine."

"We're pleased," Hannah admitted. "And now we know there will be new young ones. I like having more and more children in the area. That's how you settle a community. Families are the best way to civilize the land."

The clock chimed six, and Tyler finished the last of his grits. "Guess I'd best get out there and make sure the boys are gettin' those last few details ready for the drive."

"I'll be out shortly," William replied. He rubbed his thigh again. "Need to get my leg limbered up."

Tyler took up a piece of warm corn bread and cut it open. Without being prompted, Hannah forked a piece of side meat and held it out to Tyler. He grinned and grabbed the greasy piece with his fingers.

"You know me pretty well, don't you?" He stuffed the meat between the pieces of corn bread. "Sometimes I'm mighty sorry Will got your attention first."

Hannah laughed. "William would probably tell you that life with me is not all that you might imagine." She cast a quick glance at her husband. William's expression was one that suggested he knew better than to speak on the matter.

Tyler decided it would probably be best to head on out before further comments could be made. "I'll see you at the pens."

He headed out the back door and crossed the yard to the horse barn. Cutting through the structure, Tyler continued through the maze of outbuildings to the first of three large pens. The boys were standing around talking to one of the greenhorns.

"So you fellas don't have enough work to do, is that it?" Tyler asked.

"No, boss. We were just telling Newt here about steer sliding," one of the men replied. His expression was quite serious.

Tyler eyed the man who'd formerly been under his command in the Confederate army. "Now, John, you know it's not fair to expect a new man to know everything. Especially not one that hailed from the city."

Newt Clapton was seventeen at the most. His small, wiry frame made him look even younger, and there was something about his naïve nature that the men couldn't resist playing pranks on.

"So it's true?" Newt asked, his eyes widening. "You really have to learn to slide under a steer? I ain't never heard of it."

For a moment Tyler thought of exposing the hoax and then thought better of it. The boys were just having fun. "To work this ranch you have to learn a great deal you've probably never heard of."

"Boss is right," Grubbs continued. "You never know when you'll find yourself in the middle of a bad situation. I've seen many a man trampled by steers for lack of knowin' how to escape 'em."

"And that's why you learn steer slidin'?" Newt asked, looking uncertain.

"That's right," one of the other hands said with a serious nod.

Andy Dandridge, Hannah's brother, came to stand beside Tyler. "I had to learn it," he told the greenhorn. A shock of white-blond hair blew over his left eye, prompting Andy to push it off his face in annoyance.

"Andy's learned just about everything a fella can learn on a ranch. You should probably pay close attention to him. He's gonna be on the drive north with us."

The seventeen-year-old didn't seem too pleased to yield to a mere boy. Tyler, however, knew that Andy Dandridge had skills that nearly equaled any man on the place. William had taken Andy under his wing after marrying Hannah, and the two were inseparable. William was even allowing Andy to put his studies aside and join them on the drive. Andy was to be one of the paid drovers, and Tyler thought this was just fine. Hannah, however, was harder to convince.

Newt looked back at the men. "Well, I guess if I need to learn this steer sliding, I'd best get busy. What do I gotta do?"

Grubbs crossed his arms. "First ya gotta get used to slidin'. Sometimes it's hard to master. We have a fella practice slidin' in the dirt first. No sense having any obstacles in the way until you get that down. Andy, why don't you demonstrate how a fella should slide."

Tyler smiled as Andy quickly jumped the fence and jogged across the now empty pen. "You want to lead with whatever leg you favor," Andy called. Then without further ado, the boy took off running. About twelve feet from the fence, Andy stuck out his right leg and hit the dirt. Just as he reached the fence, Andy grabbed the bottom rail and used it to pull himself under. He skidded across the remaining distance and came to rest at the feet of the greenhorn.

"It's just that easy," Grubbs said, nodding in approval. "But like I said, I would just try slidin' for now. You can practice that anywhere. When you get the hang of it—you can try it with the fence."

Andy got to his feet and dusted off his backside. "It ain't hard once you get a feel for it."

Tyler and the other men nodded. Newt frowned. "It doesn't

look all that easy. I thought for sure you were gonna hit your head on that fence."

"I have before," Andy admitted, "but that's why you gotta practice. When you ain't workin', you need to be practicin'."

"The boy's got that right," Grubbs said as the other men nodded. Tyler turned away lest his smile cause the greenhorn to question the validity of their statements. He'd seen this trick played on more than one new man. It was just the boys' way of having some good-natured fun, and God knew that by the time they reached Abilene, they'd all be in need of diversion.

arissa sat down for the first time that day and decided a
bit of rest was in order. She'd risen at five that morning
and now seven hours later was more than ready for a bite of
lunch. She looked at Gloria, who was happily playing with
a collection of wooden thread spools that Laura had been
saving.

"Are you hungry?" Carissa asked, kneeling down beside
her daughter.

"I want cookies," Gloria said, immediately putting the
spools aside.

"How about some soup and bread first, and then cookies?"

Gloria frowned and looked at Carissa in a most serious
manner. "I like cookies."

Carissa smiled and pushed back the child's blond ringlets.
"I do, too, but the soup is hot and ready for us to eat. Let's
just have a little and then we can have cookies. Come on."
She got to her feet and lifted Gloria in her arms.

Brandon and Laura had taken Daniel to town for his first real pair of shoes, so Carissa and Gloria enjoyed a bowl of vegetable soup from the big pot of it Carissa had put together that morning. Laura had promised to return as soon as possible, so Carissa had busied herself with baking and cooking most of the morning.

"Cookies now, Mama?"

She looked at her daughter and nodded. "Yes. We can have cookies now. Why don't we take them outside? It's so nice, and you can play before nap time."

"Don't want a nap, Mama. I'm not tired." The blue-eyed angel looked up at Carissa as if expecting a reprieve.

"Well, you may not be tired, but I am. I want you to take a nap for me. But first, we play. Go find your ball."

Gloria scampered off, and Carissa went to the cookie jar. Choosing four sugar cookies, Carissa wrapped them in a towel and tucked them in her pocket just as Gloria returned clutching a gray-black ball as if it might get away from her.

Carissa led Gloria outside and down the porch steps. "Let's play over here," she suggested, leading Gloria farther away from the house in case the ball managed to get out of control. The last thing Carissa wanted to do was clean up a broken window.

They rolled the ball back and forth at first; then Gloria decided it was time to start throwing. She was awkward at best, and Carissa couldn't help but laugh. She chased down the ball and gave a weak toss to her daughter. Gloria tried to catch it, but got scared and backed away. The heavy rubber ball fell with a bit of a thud and landed near the child's feet.

"Please, I want cookies now," she said, looking first at the ball and then back to her mother.

"I do, too." Carissa pulled a cookie for each of them from the towel in her pocket. "Here you go."

Gloria clapped her hands and then took the cookie. "What do you say?" Gloria asked.

Carissa had to laugh. She'd been trying her best to teach Gloria the necessities of saying *please* and *thank you*, but the child always managed to turn it around when it came time to offer thanks.

"Thank you," she said, nevertheless. "When someone gives you something . . . you say *thank you*."

Gloria nodded and started to run back to where she'd left the ball. Carissa called out, "Gloria, what do you say?"

It sounded as though a sigh passed from the child's lips. "Thank you." Her statement suggested that she was well aware of protocol, but had lost interest in the game.

Carissa walked around the yard, keeping Gloria in sight. It truly was a lovely farm. Someone had mentioned that it belonged to a Confederate-supporting family prior to the war. She felt sad at the thought that her family had somehow displaced another; after all, that's exactly what had happened to Tyler. She supposed it might be different if this family had left of their own free will. But if not, how grievous it would be to put a lifetime of hard work and dreams into a place, only to have it taken from you.

The sound of Gloria's laughter caught her attention. The little girl was crouched on the ground, looking at something. Carissa couldn't see that there was anything for her daughter to be amused with, and after a moment, Gloria was off and running again.

Carissa turned at the sound of an approaching horse. She put a hand to her forehead to block out the sun in an attempt to see who was coming. To her surprise it was Tyler. He gave a wave and Carissa found herself waving back without thinking.

"I was hoping you might want to go riding with me today," he said, bringing his mount to stop about ten feet away. He walked the horse the rest of the way to the hitching post and tied him off.

"I can't. Laura and Brandon are in town, and I wouldn't have anyone to watch Gloria." The little girl came running to join them.

"I could hold her. She could ride in front of me."

"Tyer," Gloria called. She was unable to manage the *L* in his name. "Tyer, I got cookies."

"Yum," he said with a grin. "Wish I had cookies."

"Mama give Tyer cookies," Gloria demanded.

"Gloria, his name is Mr. Atherton." Carissa saw the hopeful look on Tyler's face and forgot her rebuke. She reached into her pocket. "I just so happen to have two right here. If you need more, we will have to return to the house." She handed the cookies to Tyler and replaced the towel in her pocket.

"Sugar cookies are one of my favorites. Did you make these?"

Nodding, Carissa felt rather self-conscious. "Esther taught me a long time back. You remember her, don't you?"

"I do. She was one of your family's slaves."

"Not a slave. Esther was paid to help. After I married, she taught me to cook."

"And iron," he added.

Carissa remembered him watching her iron and nodded. "Yes."

"Apparently you take instruction well. Hopefully you'll be

just as good at ridin'." He gave her a wink and glanced to where Gloria was playing. "Well, since you don't seem to be of a mind to go ridin' just yet, what say we just sit and talk?"

Carissa glanced at the porch. "We can sit up there. I have some crocheting to work on."

Tyler followed her, as did Gloria. "I want to play, Mama."

"Then go and play. We aren't going in just yet."

Gloria clapped her hands and hurried away as if fearful that her mother might change her mind. Carissa settled into a chair on the porch and picked up the bag she'd left there earlier.

"So what are you making?" Tyler asked. He leaned back on the porch rail.

"A tablecloth," she answered, holding up a square. "Of course it will have a great many of these pieces worked together eventually."

"Pretty," he said before biting into the cookie.

"I hope it will be. It's a gift for Laura. Her birthday's in August, and I wanted to give her something special, with her expecting the baby about the same time."

"When's your birthday?" he asked with a grin.

Carissa didn't think much of it. "November thirtieth."

"Good, then I'll have some time to figure out a present for you."

She looked up in surprise. "You can't get me a gift, Mr. Atherton."

"You promised to call me Tyler." He looked at her and shrugged. "And I can get a present for anyone I choose."

"But . . . well, it wouldn't be appropriate for me to accept a gift from you." She lowered her face so that he couldn't see her embarrassment.

"I think it's perfectly appropriate to share gifts with anyone you like," Tyler countered. "Especially a friend. And we are friends, aren't we?"

Carissa tried to focus on her stitch. "You saved my life, so of course we are friends."

"A fella has to save your life to be your friend?" he asked in a teasing tone.

Realizing she hadn't seen Gloria for several minutes, Carissa glanced up. The child was playing happily not far from the house. She tried to concentrate on her work, but all she could think of was the day Malcolm had tried to kill her. Her hands froze as the images flooded her mind.

She could very nearly feel the rocking of the small boat where Malcolm had her bound. He'd already committed murder earlier in the year and apparently had no conscience where such a thing was concerned.

"Carissa?"

She closed her eyes at the sound of Tyler's voice. It reminded her of when he'd revived her. She had nearly drowned when Malcolm had thrown her overboard. He had figured it would delay or distract the navy officials long enough for him to make his getaway. Instead, gunfire had erupted, and Malcolm had been killed.

"Carissa, are you all right?"

She lifted her head, but her eyes were still closed. "Sometimes," she whispered, "I can't help remembering."

"I know. Me too." Tyler's voice was gentle.

Her eyes opened at this. "You? Why would you think about that day . . . about Malcolm throwing me in the water?"

"Because I was afraid you would die. I was afraid Laura would die."

"You were sweet on my sister, as I recall." She hoped the change of subject would push the memories from her mind.

Tyler chuckled. "I was sweet on most young women back then, except for you. You were already taken."

Carissa remembered her silly girlish notions and behavior with regret. "I was quite self-centered then. You must have thought me completely annoying. It's a wonder you bothered to rescue me."

Tyler sobered. "Everyone deserves a second chance, don't you think?"

For a moment she considered his words. She did like to believe that second chances were available for those who needed one. She had tried to give Malcolm a second chance . . . and a third . . . and a fourth.

"It is God's way," she replied. "Although back then I wasn't overly concerned with God's way or anyone else's but my own."

"Back then, I suppose I wasn't all that concerned with His ways myself." He shrugged. "William and Hannah have helped me to draw closer to God. To learn what it means to forgive and forget—at least where some things are concerned. I'm still workin' on others."

"I wish I could forget."

Tyler started to say something, then stopped abruptly and turned. Carissa couldn't figure out what was going on. She looked at him oddly and started to speak, but he held up his hand.

Gloria had ambled over to the fence line and Carissa could see that she was once again trying to climb the posts. Without warning, however, Tyler bounded off the porch and pulled his pistol at the same time. "Rattler!" he cried, the single word sending a chill through Carissa.

The following gunshot was deafening, and poor Gloria immediately broke into tears. Carissa ran after Tyler and scooped up her child. The snake, indeed a large rattlesnake, lay coiled and dead not a yard away. Hugging Gloria close, Carissa calmed the child.

"It's all right. Tyler killed the snake. It can't hurt us now."

"Tyer, that gun is loud."

"It has to be," Tyler replied. "That way it scares little children away from ever touching it without permission. Promise me you'll never touch this gun."

Gloria stopped her tears and nodded. "I pwomise."

Carissa checked Gloria for any sign of a bite. "The snake didn't hurt you, did he?"

The child shook her head. "I not hurt, Mama. Let me go."

Reluctantly, Carissa lowered Gloria to the ground. She straightened as the little girl ran back to where she'd left her ball. A wave of dizziness altered the horizon, and Carissa felt herself falling. Tyler easily caught her and just before she fainted dead away, Carissa was certain she heard him call her name.

⁓

The sound of a carriage could be heard approaching as Tyler climbed the porch steps. "Tyer carry Mama!" Gloria announced as the Reid family pulled to a stop in front of the house.

Laura and Brandon both looked shocked as Tyler turned to reveal Carissa in his arms.

Brandon quickly jumped from the carriage. "We heard the gunshot. What's wrong?"

"I'm afraid it was just a fright," Tyler announced. "I had

to kill a rattler before it could strike Gloria. Carissa made it through that and then fainted dead away."

Brandon helped Laura from the carriage and took their son from her. Laura immediately rushed to Tyler's side. "Bring her in the house. I'll get the smelling salts. Brandon, please see to Gloria."

"Unca Bwandon, Mama's bein' silly," Gloria said, clapping her hands.

He smiled as he lifted her. "Sometimes ladies are very silly."

Tyler placed Carissa on the front-room sofa and stepped back, reluctant to move very far from her side. Laura returned with a tiny bottle and pulled the stopper. She waved the salts under her sister's nose until Carissa began to come around.

"Oh dear," Carissa said, struggling to sit up. "I've done it again, haven't I?"

Tyler smiled. "It wasn't the first time I had to catch you before you hit the ground."

She looked at him and nodded. "Thank you." She closed her eyes and then, as if all reason had returned, she snapped them open again. "Where's Gloria?"

"She's with Brandon," Laura assured. "I'm sure she's showing him the snake."

"Oh, it was so horrible. She was so close to being bit." Carissa shook her head. "I'll never let her play by the fence again."

"Why not?" Tyler asked. "It's not like snakes limit themselves to the fence line. You gonna keep her from playin' outside altogether?"

"If it keeps her from harm, I will." Carissa struggled to sit up. "That's my duty and desire. I must keep her safe."

"But no one is ever completely safe from harm," Tyler replied gently. "That's why we need God."

"Well, God should have kept the rattlesnake from getting so close to Gloria," she said, her tone clearly irritated.

"How about just praising Him because He provided someone to hear the snake and then kill it?" Tyler could see that she wanted no part of reason and logic, but he couldn't help himself. "I figure it this way, Carissa. You pray for Gloria's safety, and God made provision for her. Doesn't much matter who He used to do the providing—does it?"

"No, but I just . . . well . . . I'm afraid." She shook her head. "I couldn't bear it if she were to get hurt because of my neglect."

Tyler nodded. "I don't think you have to worry about that, Carissa. You won't ever neglect that little girl. But neither will you always be able to keep her from harm. You need to remember that. Otherwise you might drive yourself to madness tryin' to be perfect. It ain't gonna happen in this life, so you might as well face facts here and now. God's got our days numbered. Yours . . . mine . . . Gloria's. There's nothing we can do to add on more or cause it to be less. It's in God's hands."

She looked at him for a moment, and Tyler saw something in her expression soften. Had he been able to get through to her? Her next words left him with mixed thoughts on his success.

"It may be in God's hands," she replied, "but don't forget: God gave us hands, as well. We have a responsibility to right wrongs."

Her words penetrated something deep inside him, and Tyler found his mind going back to when he first learned of his father's murder. He had vowed to hunt down and kill every last Comanche in an act of revenge. That hadn't happened, but not for a lack of desire. Had it not been for William's council, he would have stayed in the army to fight in the Indian Wars. He would have had a sense of satisfaction in killing those who had killed his father and friends—at least he told himself he would have. For so long he'd been able to put that anger aside and forget about revenge. Now Carissa's innocent words only served to stir up that need for vengeance—a need that Tyler feared might not go unresolved.

"So much for forgiving and forgetting."

4

"**B**randon suggested a dog," Laura commented some days later.

Carissa looked up from kneading the bread and nodded. "Tyler did, too. In fact, he said he'll bring one from the Barnett ranch when he comes to see us next time. Apparently they have a pup some nine or so months old. He says the dog knows to sound the alert on snakes."

Laura massaged her neck a moment, then continued pumping the butter churn. "I swear, I never knew so much hard work went into life. We were quite spoiled with our servants. When I think of our large house and all the work required to keep it clean, I have to say I feel quite guilty."

For a moment the life they'd known back in Corpus Christi flooded Carissa's memories. It was almost impossible to think of the girl she'd been without cringing. "I was so selfish then. I had no idea of the labor that went into ironing a gown or preparing a bath."

"Or making butter," Laura said with a laugh. "It just appeared on the table, so I thought it must be quite simple."

Smiling, Carissa nodded. "The bread, too, just appeared. Although I knew that it had to be baked. I loved the way the aroma of freshly baked bread filled the house."

"It was so rare to have white bread during the war, and even now flour is so expensive. Oh, how I long for Cook's fresh-baked rolls. Do you remember those?"

"I do. They were so light." Carissa started separating the dough into round balls. "Do you want me to make another batch after these are set to rise?"

"No, that should be enough to get us through the week," Laura replied. "We'll need some things to take with us to the Barnett get-together. I was thinking maybe a cake or a couple of pies."

A glance at Laura told Carissa she was growing weary of the churn. "I can finish up the butter, and then bake a cake if you like."

Laura eased back against the chair. "I'm so tired of late. I'm sure it's because Daniel has had me up more nights than not. I don't know why his sleep has been so disrupted, but it's wearing me out."

Carissa had just finished with the bread and was wiping her hands when she heard the sound of a carriage or wagon pulling into the yard. "Who could that be?"

Laura shook her head. "I'm sure I don't know."

"Here, I'll take over, and you go and see," Carissa said, moving to the butter churn. She started the pumping process and could feel that the butter was thickening nicely. "This won't take long."

Soon Carissa could hear Laura chattering away with another

woman. It was only a few moments before an older woman appeared in the kitchen at Laura's side.

"Carissa, this is Mrs. Terry. She lives on a ranch to the northwest of us."

"Pleased to meet you," Carissa said, glancing back to the butter churn. "I would rise, but I just got seated."

"Don't trouble yourself," Mrs. Terry replied. "I was visiting my neighbor Hannah, and I heard that your sister and brother-in-law had taken the old Lawton farm. I'm glad to see that someone is livin' here again."

"Whatever happened to the former owners? I heard that they left before the war was over," Carissa said.

"They lost two boys in the war—early on," Mrs. Terry began. "Then the youngest boy and Mr. Lawton signed up and left Gladys and their two daughters behind. There were all sorts of land schemes going on during the war, but somehow Mrs. Lawton managed to keep the place running. Unfortunately, her husband and son were injured. They managed to make their way back, but the ugliness and loss of war had really hurt them. Then entrepreneurs, trying to grab up as much land as they could, descended. Before Ted and I even knew their dire situation, the family loaded up and left for California. Mrs. Lawton was a broken woman, I must say. This farm was her pride and joy."

"I can see why." Laura gestured toward the window. "It's quite beautiful, and it's obvious that a great deal of work went into the care of the ranch. Why, the flowers and fruit trees alone must have taken considerable time and attention. I hate that we should benefit from their troubles."

"Gladys would be glad that it went to a family like yours." Mrs. Terry paused and smiled. "I've heard such good things about you all from William and Tyler. I'm so glad to have the chance to meet you both before tomorrow's fixin's. It'll be a noisy affair with all the children playing and the menfolk discussing their cattle drive."

"We were just talking about that," Laura said. "I thought perhaps I'd bring a cake or a couple of pies. What do you think?"

Mrs. Terry shook her head. "Save yourself the trouble. I brought over a wagon full of food, and Hannah and Juanita—that's Hannah's housekeeper and cook—were already hard at work. Food is one thing we won't lack for, so just come as you are."

"Doesn't seem neighborly not to bring something," Laura said, glancing at Carissa.

"My mama always said bring a smile and that's good enough." Mrs. Terry grinned. "There will be enough future gatherings where you can furnish food. For now, just come and get to know everyone."

Mrs. Terry then glanced out the window. "Now I need to be gettin' to town with the mister. He's out front speaking with your husband, but he'll want to be off soon. Why don't you come out and say hello," she told Laura.

Carissa chimed in, "Go on and greet him for me, as well. This butter is nearly done, and it won't be long before the children are awake. Then we'll be hard-pressed to get anything done in an orderly fashion."

Once they'd gone, Carissa allowed the steady rhythm of the churn to calm her. The notion of everyone gathering the next day at the Barnett ranch had set her on edge. She pictured everyone laughing and sharing their stories—husbands, wives, children. And there would be Carissa—on the outside.

Alone, with a child . . . and yet dependent on her family. She knew many war widows had already remarried, but Carissa had no desire to give her heart away again.

A fleeting image of Tyler Atherton touched her thoughts. He seemed so kind and generous, but then, so had Malcolm before their wedding. After the ceremony he had almost immediately shown his irritation and lack of patience with her. It had been hard to realize just how much Malcolm had fooled her—fooled everyone.

"Well, it won't happen again," she said aloud, shaking her head. "Never again."

Tyler sat down at the supper club with his former men. At one time they had fought together for the South, and now they were just struggling to eke out a living. Thanks to William they all had jobs and pay, but Tyler wanted a place of his own with his own men to help work it.

"My, my. It's good to see you again, Tyler," Ava Lambert purred, sashaying around the back of his chair.

"Ava. The boys and I decided it might do us well to hear you sing tonight," Tyler said with a smile.

The proprietress—and entertainer—nodded to the men. "Show starts at nine, like always. You boys get your supper ordered? I have some of the best beef steak you could ever sink your teeth into. Melt in your mouth—guaranteed. Fresh in from Dallas." Her words were enticing and low, but it was her expression that had most of the men in the place eating out of her hand.

"We'll have a round of 'em," Tyler declared. He turned to the men. "Ante up, boys, I ain't footin' the whole bill."

Ava laughed and touched Tyler's shoulder. "I see you put on a clean shirt for me. I'm honored."

Tyler laughed. "I put on a clean shirt most times I come to town for supper. Seems only polite to leave the dirt back at the ranch."

"You gonna have any dancin' tonight, Miss Ava?" Isaac Sidley asked. The youngest of the men, Sidley had joined Tyler's unit when he'd been not more than fifteen. Of course he'd lied about his age, and because he was a crack shot with a rifle, the army ignored their concerns. Now five years later, he still was barely growing enough stubble to shave.

"Not tonight," Ava said, touching the boy-man's cheek. "But don't you worry, darlin'—I'll keep your attention." Isaac blushed furiously and ducked his head to hide his embarrassment. Ava gave a deep, throaty laugh and moved away from the table. "See you in a little while, boys."

Tyler took the opportunity to ease Isaac's distress by introducing the reason he'd asked them to join him. "Y'all know we're puttin' together a cattle drive with Will Barnett and Ted Terry. We're gonna need drovers. Pay's decent, but the work will be gruelin' and dangerous. Since I have a good number of steers to put in the drive, Will and Ted said I could extend a job to you boys at thirty dollars a month. It's payable when we get the steers to Abilene."

"Texas?" John asked.

Shaking his head, Tyler eased back in his chair. "No. Kansas. It'll take us at least ninety days, and you'll be paid for all of it."

Grubbs gave a whistle. "That's ninety dollars. I ain't never had that much money to my name."

Isaac nodded, wide-eyed. "Is Abilene the new railhead west of the capital city?"

Tyler nodded. "It is. Ted's heard from friends that it's a good place to get the cattle to market."

David Bierman looked apprehensive. "I heard the trail goes straight through Indian Territory. That true?"

"It is, and as much as I'd like to avoid any involvement with those savages," Tyler replied, "it appears a necessary evil. It's nearly a straight shot north through what I'm told is friendly Indian country. If that's possible." He pushed down his anger and tried not to dwell on what had happened to his father. "The trip is across decent ground—a lot of good grazing and water on the way."

"Well, I've learned to rope and ride a fair sight better than when you asked me to drive cattle to Louisiana," Bierman replied with a grin. "I'm in."

"Me too," Isaac concurred. "'Ceptin' for Will's place, I ain't seen work even offered around here except for roundup. I was fixin' to head out west, maybe try my hand at minin'."

"This will be a whole lot surer than minin'. What about you, John?" Tyler asked.

"I was hopin' to be asked. Been hearin' some of the others talkin' about it. Sounded like a pretty good deal."

Tyler nodded. "I think it will be. Ted Terry has some men, and Will has his. Now I feel better knowing I'll have some of my own."

"This drive gonna help you get your place back, boss?"

Tyler smiled at the title. His men had always called him *Lieutenant* in the war, but he'd rebuked them harshly for any such comment these days. Such a comment could get a whole fight started before you could even blink. Thankfully, John had started calling him *boss* instead, and it just sort of stuck. Of course, they all hoped that one day they would be working for Tyler for real, instead of hanging around to see what kind of side jobs they could land.

"I have no way of knowing when or how or even if that's gonna happen. I do know that my plan is to sell off as many steers as I can so that if I need to buy back every acre of that property, I'll be able to. I owe that much to my pa."

"Well, you'll have our help," John replied. "Ain't a one of us here you didn't manage to keep alive in the war. We ain't forgettin' that." The other men nodded in a silent, solemn promise. "Besides, we'd all rather work for you in the long run."

The food came and just as Ava had promised, it was some of the best steak Tyler had tasted in a long while. They weren't given to eating a lot of beef these days, since most ranchers were busy trying to find ways to get their cattle to market. The war had created a hunger for beef in the bellies of the nation east of the Mississippi, and Texans were only too happy to deliver the product and make their fortune. Tyler could only hope and pray to be among their number.

At precisely nine, Ava appeared on stage in a daringly low-cut, sleeveless black gown. She had black satin gloves that encased her hands and most of her arms and around her neck was a cluster of rhinestones that twinkled when the light hit just right. Matching earrings dangled from her lobes and her hair was swept up with black ostrich feathers to complete the look. It was her signature look for performing—something she said she'd begun while in California, entertaining in San Francisco.

For some reason Ava had given up her life there and moved to Texas just the year before. She'd brought a small entourage with her—a prized chef and several maids, as well as a handful of musicians. She had thought to settle in Dallas proper, but real estate had been more reasonable in Cedar Springs, and everyone knew it would be just a matter of time before Dallas engulfed the little town anyway. So she built her supper club on the Dallas side of town and drew in a remarkably large crowd most every evening. Once word spread, people were known to come from as far away as Austin.

A four-piece band began to play softly, and Ava smiled and touched a hand to her carefully coiffed and decorated hair. Ostrich feathers fluttered in the air as she began to move and sway to the rhythm.

Tyler took a long drink of the hot coffee the waiter had just poured as Ava's melodious voice joined the musicians.

> "When the hours of Day are numbered,
> And the voices of the Night
> Wake the better soul that slumbered,
> To a holy, calm delight;
>
> Ere the evening lamps are lighted,
> And, like phantoms grim and tall,
> Shadows from the fitful firelight
> Dance upon the parlor wall,
>
> Shadows from the fitful firelight
> Dance upon the parlor wall."

The words startled Tyler. They were from an old Longfellow poem his mother had loved. "Footsteps of an Angel," wasn't it? He could almost see his mother sitting by the fireplace reading from her book of much-loved poetry.

" 'Then the forms of the departed enter at the open door,' " Ava sang, and the words chilled Tyler to the bone.

"The beloved the true hearted,
Come to visit me once more;

He, the young and strong, who cherished
Noble longings for the strife,
By the roadside fell and perished,
Weary with the march of life.

By the roadside fell and perished,
Weary with the march of life."

Tyler thought of all the young men he'd seen die in the war. It hadn't taken many battles to leave them weary. Truth be told, he was weary from the march of life. Weary that he should have to fight so hard to right wrongs.

Thoughts of the departed brought his father's image to mind. Howard Atherton had been the wisest man Tyler had ever known. He'd been generous and loving, too, and now he was dead. If only Tyler had stayed at the ranch that day. *I might have been able to save him.* Tyler shook his head. *Most likely I might be buried alongside him.*

Either way, I failed, Tyler thought as Ava continued the song. *I failed to be there when you needed me most, Pa. Failed to keep the ranch.* He sighed. All he had wanted was to make his father proud. His pa had always said that a man was no better than his word, and that his word had to be backed by actions. If a man gave his pledge to something—then it was up to him to see it through. Otherwise, what good was that man?

I made a pledge to avenge you, Pa, and I sure haven't seen that through. Tyler glanced at the ceiling, wondering if his father could hear his thoughts. Since the tragic death of his father and other Atherton ranch hands, Tyler had mulled over the idea of seeking out his father's killer. Osage McElroy was one of three men who'd survived the attack. The other two men had moved on, but Osage stayed. While Tyler was away at war, it was Osage and a couple of other trustworthy men who had kept the ranch running. Now they worked for Will.

A bitter taste was in his mouth, and Tyler quickly took another swig of the coffee. Osage had detailed the attack for Tyler. There had been a threat all week—it was one of the reasons his pa had insisted Tyler take the womenfolk and Grandpa Venton to Dallas for shopping and visiting. They'd be safe there with friends in case something happened.

The men thought they could handle the Indians, but they were ill-prepared. Lulled into believing the threat had passed, they put down their guard and were surprised just before dawn. It was easy enough to learn it was a renegade group of Comanche who'd killed his father, but no one knew for sure the name of the leader. There were all kinds of rumors, but Osage always said he'd know the man if he ever saw him again.

Ava's voice rang rich and smooth.

> "Uttered not, yet comprehended,
> Is the spirit's voiceless prayer,
> Soft rebukes in blessings ended,
> Breathing from their lips of air.
>
> Oh, though oft depressed and lonely,
> All my fears are laid aside,
> If I but remember only
> Such as these have lived and died!
>
> If I but remember only
> Such as these have lived and died!"

The music ended and the men in the supper club clapped furiously. Tyler let the words settle over him and ease the pain of his memories. *Oh, though oft depressed and lonely, all my fears are laid aside, if I but remember only such as these have lived and died!*

Of course, Tyler knew that God was truly the only help for his kind of sorrow. There was depression and loneliness to be sure, but also anger, hatred, and a sheer will to avenge. God alone had helped him calm the spirit of anger and revenge, but every so often, the beast reared its ugly head.

Tyler looked back to his plate as Ava bowed and then began a jollier tune. He couldn't help but think of Carissa and all that she'd endured. He wondered if she'd ever heard the poem. Perhaps he'd have to share it with her sometime. It was certainly the kind of verse she could appreciate.

He tried hard not to dwell on her, but he couldn't help it. Ever since he'd pulled Carissa out of the Gulf of Mexico, Tyler had found himself inexplicably connected to the young woman. Even during the last few years when he'd seen nothing of her, Tyler couldn't shake her image from his mind—nor the thoughts of the way she felt in his arms.

"And now she's here, and I'm going away."

"What was that, boss?" John questioned, leaning across the table. "You need something?"

Tyler shook his head. "No. Just thinkin' out loud."

Carissa sat listening as plans for the cattle drive were explained. William Barnett was in charge and led the discussion for the most part, though she saw him clearly defer to Ted Terry on more than one occasion. Tyler, too, seemed to hold a position of authority.

"We've talked to others who have made the trip," William stated. "There's good grazing along the way and plenty of water. The Indians who are settled in the area are friendly, and there are numerous army forts along the way just to make sure order is kept."

"Have you thought about other routes?" one of the men questioned.

Carissa had no idea who the man was, but he seemed to be one of Ted Terry's men. William didn't appear troubled by the question, she noticed. He nodded and pulled out a roughly drawn map.

"We looked into driving them to California or taking the

Goodnight-Loving Trail to Denver. We even thought about the older route up through eastern Indian Territory. But given the facts and the need to be back in time for the womenfolk, this is the shortest and easiest trail to take. With, I might add, the fewest complications."

"How many cattle are we lookin' to move?" someone else asked.

"At least twenty-five hundred," Ted Terry replied before William could answer. "Maybe a few more. William, Tyler, and I have contributed to this herd so the sale will benefit everyone. William and I are providing most of the gear and grub, but Tyler brings expertise and a few good men to the table, as well."

"We are also blessed to have a qualified horseman," William added, nodding toward Brandon Reid. "Brandon grew up on a horse farm in Indiana. He's taken on the old Lawton farm in order to raise some quality animals. He's agreed to be our head wrangler."

The discussion went on and on with every imaginable question being posed. Carissa tired of the details. Gloria and the other children were playing with Marty Dandridge, Hannah's ten-year-old sister, so Carissa had no excuse to leave. She glanced around the room until her gaze fell on an Indian shield hanging on the wall. The sight of it made her shiver. Why would such a thing be on display?

"That question brings us to the issue of food," William replied.

Carissa wasn't sure what question had been asked, but decided to pay better attention. A grizzled older man stood up.

"Name's Osage McElroy," the man declared. "Most of ya know me. I worked quite a few years with Tyler's pa. Then he was kilt, and for a time I took care of the place for Tyler. I can cook a fair bit. Ain't had no complaints, I might add." He grinned and rubbed his graying reddish-brown beard. "I've been workin' of late for Will Barnett, and he asked me to run the chuck wagon on this here drive. I figure to keep you boys fed well. There won't be any liquor, however, and if I find any on you or in the camp, I'll be forced to destroy it."

"And then you'll be fired, and you'll be forced to make your way back alone—even if we're in the middle of Indian country," William added. "We're gonna make this drive sober. There won't be any gambling, either, and on Sundays we'll have a time of prayer and Bible reading. If you have a problem with this, you'd best say so now and quit the drive." He waited a moment to see if anyone wanted to back out.

Carissa was surprised that no one offered so much as a protest. Maybe they'd all worked together long enough that they knew what to expect in the ways of do's and don'ts.

"Once we get to Abilene, you'll be paid, and you're free to do what you like with your money. You'll also be free to stay or return with us. We plan to make it an immediate turnaround so that I can be back in plenty of time for the birth of my second child. And while that isn't expected until nearly October, Mr. Reid here has a wife who's expecting in August."

Laura blushed and lowered her head at the comment. Carissa was amazed how easily such delicate matters were discussed in mixed company. Back in Corpus Christi such details would have been reserved for the women alone. If men ever discussed the topic at all, Carissa was certain it was only in passing references of congratulations.

"My point here is that what you do to entertain yourselves in Abilene will be your business. However, until then . . ."

He paused and looked around the room. "Until then, it will be mine and Ted's. We'll expect your word on the matter."

The men around her nodded and the conversation continued. Carissa listened to William discuss the route and what they could expect. He answered questions posed by Hannah and Mrs. Terry, then announced that Hannah's nearly thirteen-year-old brother, Andy, would accompany them on the trail.

"Most drovers aren't much older," William declared. "It's a hard business for an old man, but the young seem to thrive."

"Speak for yourself, Will," Ted stated. "I think old is just a state of mind."

"You may think otherwise after a week in the saddle," Marietta Terry said with a laugh.

William smiled and continued. "There will be no favoritism, if you're worried about that. But neither will I tolerate abuse of Andy for the sake of getting back at me. The same is true for any man. You'll earn your keep out there and if you do your best—you'll earn my respect, as well."

The meeting continued another half an hour or so until Hannah finally rose and put a stop to it. "It's nearly noon. We need to feed these boys," she told her husband.

There was a hearty round of approval for that comment, and Hannah smiled. "I think you boys will be pleased. Juanita has been cooking ribs all morning over the spit, so you're in for a real treat. She has a special sauce that will make you sit up and beg for more."

Tyler moaned. "She's got that right. Won't be able to put 'em down, and afterward we won't be able to stand 'cause our bellies will be draggin' the ground."

The men laughed and got to their feet as the ladies rose.

Hannah motioned to the men. "We have tables and benches set up outside for everyone. Make your way around back, and we'll eat as soon as grace is said."

She didn't have to instruct them twice. The men—especially the younger ones—hurried from the room as if their pants were on fire. Carissa marveled at the way they all but climbed over each other to empty the room.

"Guess they're hungry," Tyler said, coming alongside her.

She looked into his eyes and nodded. "I guess so."

"How about you?"

Carissa put her hand to her waist. "I am hungry. In fact, I'm really looking forward to the special ribs."

He laughed. "And well you should be. Juanita has many talents, but cooking is probably right there at the top."

"Maybe she can teach me a thing or two," Carissa replied.

Tyler took hold of her elbow. The move surprised her, but she didn't pull away. He guided her through the house and out the back door to avoid the rush of men out the front of the house. Carissa had smelled the aroma of the meat cooking all morning, but here the scent was even stronger.

She was surprised to see that Marty already had the little ones settled at a very small table off a ways from the activity. They were sitting quite well-behaved, in fact. Carissa could only wonder at how she'd bribed them. Daniel sat directly beside Marty completely captivated with something in her hands. William and Hannah's two-year-old son, Robert, seemed anxious to dig into the food on his plate, but kept his place. And to Carissa's surprise, Gloria had a napkin tied around her neck and had her hands folded in her lap. She made quite the angelic picture, but Carissa knew just what an energetic little spirit she could be.

Ted Terry blessed the food, and it wasn't long before everyone was eating their fill. The food had quieted the chatter considerably, but as the minutes passed and hunger abated, the conversation gradually picked back up.

Mrs. Terry sat at Carissa's left and pointed to an entire table of desserts. "See, you definitely needn't worry about that cake or pie you didn't bring." She grinned at Carissa. "If it's one thing we women know how to do right in this area—it's dessert."

"Maybe you can share some of your recipes with me sometime," Carissa replied. "I started learning to cook while in Corpus Christi. Growing up, we always had someone else to do that chore, but I actually find I rather enjoy it."

"I do, too. We have a wonderful woman who works for us—Teresa is her name. She can cook up a storm, but from time to time I like to put my hand in. I'll probably be bringing some dishes to the Barnett ranch just to help with feeding all of you while the men are gone."

"What do you mean?" Carissa asked.

Mrs. Terry frowned. "Didn't you hear them explain that you and your sister will come here to stay while the men are gone?"

Carissa shook her head. "But who will tend the farm?"

"Will and Ted have already seen to all of that. Your animals will board here, and riders will go to check up on the place from time to time. It's too dangerous otherwise. You won't have anyone to help you should there be an Indian attack."

"Is that likely?" She tried not to sound fearful.

"We don't expect trouble, but we do plan for it," Mrs. Terry replied. "Texas is still a wild country. Unlike the civilized states back east, we struggle to maintain order. The

Kiowa and Comanche are still on the warpath, and we have to be prepared."

"So we're to stay here at the ranch? How is that to work?"

"Well, Hannah and William have added a good deal of space to this house. Hannah has extra rooms to share. You and Laura can each have a room as I understand it. You and Gloria will be together, and Laura can be with her boy."

Carissa felt a little uneasy at having her life dictated to her. "I suppose if that's the only way . . ." She let the words trail off.

"Well, it's the safest way," Tyler said as he took the seat to her right.

His company surprised her, as earlier he'd sat between William and Mr. Terry. "I realize that I have little say in the matter, but it would have been nice to be consulted," she murmured.

He grinned. "Your sister said the same thing. Fact is, this is a much better choice for you. Hannah once did some favors for the Comanche, and they've been pretty good to leave this ranch alone. Doesn't mean they always will, but at least you'll have an extra element of protection."

"Hannah did favors for the Comanche?" Carissa asked, glancing down the table to where the petite blonde sat.

"She sure did. Just about gave us all a heart attack. She went off to help the Comanche in their camp when they came down sick with smallpox. I thought William was going to lose his mind in tryin' to find her. Kind of like when Brandon was searchin' for Laura in Corpus."

Carissa frowned. "I'd rather not be reminded of that time." She focused her attention on her plate and daintily picked up a rib. The meat was messy, but the flavor was well worth the trouble.

"I didn't mean to bring up bad times. We were just as desperate to find you, as I recall."

"Why did the Indians come to Hannah for help?"

Tyler seemed prepared for this question. "She had helped to save the life of the chief's son Night Bear, prior to their outbreak of the pox. After that, the word spread that she was a friend to the *Numunuu*. That's the name the Comanche call themselves. It means, *the people*. They gave her that shield you saw in the other room."

"I wondered why civilized folks would have something like that in their house."

"Night Bear sometimes has come to see Hannah in the years since. He has a fondness for her cinnamon sweet rolls." Tyler grinned. "But then, who doesn't?"

As the food dwindled and folks started pushing back from the table, Carissa went to take Gloria in hand. She could see that the child was nearly asleep on her feet. When she cradled Gloria against her shoulder, the little girl put her thumb in her mouth and closed her eyes.

Then a moment later Gloria pulled her thumb out. "I'm not tired," she insisted.

"Yes, I can see that you're wide awake."

Carissa nuzzled her face against Gloria's curls as her daughter fought to keep her eyes open. Nothing felt as good as holding her baby.

"You make a right good mama," Tyler said, watching her from a nearby tree.

"Thank you," Carissa murmured. "Though sometimes I fear she's missing out."

Tyler frowned and shook his head. "Why is that?"

"She's never had a regular life. The only father figures she's

known have been my father and Brandon." Carissa bit her
lip. Why had she said such a personal thing to him? Now he'd
think she'd opened the door to a deeper friendship.

But maybe that's exactly what I want.

Tyler didn't disappoint. "God has a way of filling in the
empty places, but I reckon not havin' a pa could be a hard
thing for a little one. Hard for you, too."

Carissa didn't know what to say. She wasn't entirely sure
if Tyler was implying that raising a child alone was difficult,
or that being a woman without a man was the problem. She
supposed that either way, he was right.

Carissa glanced at her now-sleeping daughter. "When
Brandon comes in from working, Daniel is always so excited
to see him. Now that he can walk—even run—he runs to his
papa, and Brandon lifts him in the air and plays with him."
Her voice sounded wistful, but Carissa couldn't help it. "I
know Gloria doesn't understand, although Brandon does his
best to include her. I've just started trying to keep busy somewhere else when I know he's due to come in. That way I can
keep Gloria occupied, and she doesn't have to feel so alone."

"Are you sure she's the one who feels alone?" Tyler asked,
his voice barely audible.

Carissa felt her brows knit together as she thought hard
for a moment. "I know she is. She asks where her papa is all
the time."

"And what do you tell her?"

"The truth, as best I can. I tell her he's gone away and
isn't coming back. I tell her that he was a very bad man and
we are better off without him—that he would only hurt us."

"Do you think that's wise?"

She glared at him. "To tell the truth? Of course I think

that's wise. I don't want her to be a fool like I was." She wished she hadn't offered that last remark, but it was too late.

"You weren't a fool, Carissa," Tyler said, reaching out to take the sleeping Gloria. "Malcolm Lowe was the fool. You were just a girl in love."

"Well, I'm not that girl anymore." She looked up at him. "I was going to put her down somewhere quiet."

"I know just the place," he said, cradling the little girl.

The sight of them together caught Carissa off guard, and she thought it one of the most precious and painful moments she'd ever witnessed. Words stuck in her throat as Tyler stepped away and headed toward the house. She wanted to cry, but knew it would do little good. Gloria did need a father, but unfortunately Carissa didn't need a husband. That complicated the matter rather considerably when it came to resolving her situation.

Days later, Laura and Carissa worked to pack up for the move to the Barnett ranch. Gloria seemed almost anxious, but Carissa assured her over and over that they were going to have fun.

"You will get to play with Marty and Robert and Daniel every day. Won't that be fun?"

Gloria clapped her hands, then pushed back a mass of blond curls. "I wanna play with Marty. She fixes my hair."

Carissa eyed her daughter with a raised brow. A hint of a smile touched her lips. "Well, I don't know how she manages to get you to sit still long enough to do more than fix a few tangles, but she does seem to have the touch."

Laura laughed. "I was quite impressed with the way she handled the children. Could be that with her helping out, we can get caught up on all of our chores for once."

"Yes, but so much of what we hoped to accomplish needed to be done here," Carissa countered. "Papering and painting can't be done from a distance."

"True, but perhaps we could slip away from time to time and come over here during the day."

Carissa shook her head. "I doubt that. Tyler said the whole idea of our staying at the Barnett place was to keep us safer. I can't imagine any of them would agree to the idea of our traveling back and forth. Tyler said it's a dangerous time for many reasons."

Laura frowned and continued placing several articles of clothing in a trunk. "Well, we can work on the curtains and rugs, and Hannah said she would teach us to make our own candles and soap. There's so much you and I need to learn in order to be proper ranch wives."

"I don't intend to learn it for the sake of being anyone's wife. Do you realize that I am old enough and qualified to take on a homestead? As the head of my household, I could sign on for a parcel, and I would have something like five years to fix things up. Maybe Father could help me with some extra money, and I could pay workers to do the building for me."

Laura looked at her sister in surprise. "You've given this quite a bit of thought."

Carissa nodded. "I read about homesteads in the paper a while back. I was thinking that with our family's loyalty to the Union, Father might be able to work a deal with the administration."

"It's just not like you, Carissa, to even know about such things . . . much less to be planning out your future dealings."

"I'm not the same person I used to be, Laura. I grew up. Nearly dying will do that to a person."

Laura reached out to touch Carissa's arm. "I didn't mean to cause you pain. You have grown up, and I'm sorry that you had to have your innocence ripped away from you. I would never have wished that for you."

Carissa had no desire to linger on the past. Instead, she placed a large stack of folded diapers near the trunk. "These are ready."

Laura took the diapers and packed them with the other things. She glanced up as she worked, and for just a moment her expression suggested she would revisit her earlier comments. Then her face relaxed. "Hannah said to just bring what we needed to wear. She has all the cooking things we'll need, as well as bedding." Laura straightened and put her hand to the small of her back. "I already feel displaced, and we haven't even moved."

"I know what you mean." Carissa reached down to take up Gloria's stack of clothes from a basket. "Which trunk do you want me to use for these?"

Laura pointed to a medium-sized wooden trunk that their parents had sent filled with supplies for Carissa. "Use that one. It will be perfect. Just put all of Gloria's things in it and you won't even have to worry about separating them out once we're at the Barnetts'. You can just use it as a clothes chest."

Carissa looked to where Gloria was busying herself with Daniel. The two seemed intent on building a tall tower with Daniel's wooden blocks. She couldn't help but think of how tenderly Tyler had cared for Gloria the day of the Barnett gathering.

The scene continued to play out in her mind, and Carissa felt a sense of longing at the memory of Tyler carefully cradling Gloria's sleeping frame. He had smiled and touched her golden curls as he carried her to the house. Carissa couldn't help but wonder at his actions and feelings. Most single men had little interest in children; goodness, many married men felt the same way! But not Tyler. He played with Robert and Daniel quite enthusiastically, as she recalled. So she couldn't say the attention was only for Gloria, although she found herself almost wishing it were. Gloria deserved fatherly attention. She deserved a father.

But that would require me to remarry, Carissa thought.

"Well, look there," Laura said from the window. "It's Tyler, and I believe he has a dog with him."

Gloria jumped up, knocking the tower over. Daniel began to cry as Gloria ran to the window. "I wanna see the dog." She pressed her nose to the glass. "Where's the dog? Where's Tyler?" Just then she spotted him and clapped furiously as she jumped up and down. "Tyer!"

"Let's go downstairs and greet him properly," Carissa told Gloria.

"You go ahead," Laura declared. "I'm going to try and comfort Daniel and rebuild the tower." She smiled and approached her son. "It's quite all right, sweetie. We can stack them all up again. Let Mama help you."

Carissa wasted no time. She lifted Gloria in her arms and hurried downstairs. She paused a moment at the hall mirror to check her reflection, then chided herself for being so silly.

"It's just Tyler."

"Tyer comin' with the dog, Mama," Gloria declared.

She laughed and nodded. "Indeed he is."

She opened the door and put Gloria down in order to pull it closed behind her. To her horror, the child went running toward Tyler and the horse. The animal reared slightly in surprise, but Tyler turned the beast easily and reached down to pull Gloria into his arms very nearly in the same motion.

70

For just a moment Carissa thought Tyler would fall from the saddle, but he quickly righted again and drew Gloria up with him.

Carissa had been about to call to her daughter, but fell silent as the pup began barking. She walked down the porch steps and shook her head. "Gloria, you know better than to ever run like that at a horse. What have I told you?"

"She was just excited." Tyler slid from the animal with Gloria in his arms. "But your mama is right, and you have to be extra careful with the horses, Gloria. Promise you won't run at the horse again."

"I pwomise, Tyer." She looked so contrite that Carissa could only smile.

"Good. Since that's settled, look what I've brought you, Gloria. Your very own dog."

"My dog!" Gloria said with her customary clapping.

Tyler laughed. "Yes. Yours and Daniel's. You'll have to share." He whistled for the distracted animal. "Come." The dog came quickly and sat at Tyler's feet.

Carissa studied the reddish-brown-and-white animal. He looked like one of the many cattle dogs she'd seen in the area. He looked up at her with the strangest pale blue eyes and began to wag his tail.

"I think he likes you both," Tyler said, putting Gloria down so that she could pet the pup. "He's about nine months old and already well trained. Andy's been workin' with him for some time."

"So the dog is his?" Carissa frowned. "I wouldn't want to take it away from him."

"Nah, he had a litter of five to train. Rusty here is the last of the bunch to find a home."

"Rusty, eh?" The dog perked and cocked his head at the sound of his name. "It suits him. He has a rusty-colored coat."

"Rusty," Gloria said, trying out the name. She put her arms around the pup's neck and hugged him close. The puppy received the affection in calm order, much to Carissa's relief.

"You'll have to keep teaching him to mind," Tyler told the little girl. "He knows how to sit and come. He knows his name, so when you call to him, he should always listen."

Unlike Gloria, who by now was giggling at the way in which Rusty bathed her face in licks. Tyler looked at Carissa. "What do you think?"

"I think he will make a fine pet—perhaps a fine guardian in time." Carissa watched as Gloria took off running, the dog on her heels and her laughter ringing out. "Thank you, Tyler."

"You are quite welcome. Rusty already knows about snakes. We made sure he would know to bark, but then leave them alone. That way you can teach Gloria that when Rusty barks and backs away, she needs to, as well. As they develop a friendship, I'm confident Rusty will protect her and Daniel quite faithfully."

"That's a relief." She put her hand to her eyes and looked to where Gloria was now rolling around on the ground with the puppy. "She's so fearless."

"Like her mother," he countered.

Carissa met his gaze. "Hardly that. I live in fear of everything."

His brows rose. "I find that hard to believe."

"Well, just because I endure doesn't mean I'm not terrified."

"Why don't we sit a spell on the porch and you can tell me about it." He moved to the porch steps without waiting for her to agree.

Carissa followed him and took a seat in her favorite rocker. Tyler sat down beside her and waited for her to continue. "Doesn't anything frighten you?" she asked instead.

Tyler nodded. "Sure, I have my moments. Sometimes my biggest fear is that I'll never see justice done for my pa and the men who died with him."

"That's not a real fear. You aren't seriously afraid of that—are you? I mean, do you lie awake at night and worry about it?"

His expression seemed to change in a flash. One moment he was tender and smiling and the next he was . . . well . . . almost angry. Carissa pressed back in her chair, afraid that perhaps she had said too much.

"I haven't had a decent night's sleep since my father was killed. I should have been there with him." He shook his head. "The killings were horrible. Then I went to war. . . . The things I saw there were enough to give me a lifetime of nightmares."

"I'm sorry. I suppose my words sounded callous, and I didn't mean for them to. It's just that I always figured men, being men, had little that caused them fear. Women seem so weak and helpless in comparison. We cannot vote or make doctrine in our country. We can't do business without facing a great deal of trouble and even then—more often than not we are refused. I find myself fearful of so much."

"I wish you weren't afraid," he told her. Tyler's expression softened once again. "I'm glad you'll be at the Barnett ranch while we're gone."

"I wish you weren't going away," Carissa said without thinking.

"Gonna miss me, eh?" He grinned.

She felt her cheeks grow hot. "I . . . well . . . I'm going to miss all of you. I feel safer when you're all here." She hurried to put the focus back on Tyler. "So what would justice for your father and his men look like to you? Would you want to see the Indians go to trial?"

He shook his head. "No. I would want to see them dead." His voice was cold, and the finality of his comment left Carissa chilled, as well.

"Would you . . . kill them yourself?" she asked.

He looked away at this point. "I would be glad to kill them."

His tone reminded her of Malcolm, and she shuddered. Were all men so filled with hate?

Laura came through the door with Daniel on her hip. The moment he saw the puppy, he was almost impossible to hold on to. Laura descended the steps and let him go. He raced across the grassy yard to where Gloria and Rusty were still happily engaged.

"Tyler, I see you brought us a dog," Laura said in greeting.

"Sure did. That's Rusty. Like I was tellin' Carissa, he's trained to come and sit. He'll need more training, but he's a smart dog and works fast. I think if the kids spend a lot of time with him, he'll be a good guard dog to them."

"He's also been trained to recognize the threat of snakes and to bark," Carissa declared. "Tyler said he'll bark and back away. That way we can teach the children that means danger, and they should move away, too, and get help."

"Good. That's something of a relief." Laura put her hand to her mouth to suppress a yawn. "I do apologize. I've been so tired."

"Why don't you go take a rest?" Carissa suggested. "I can watch the children and sew. They're completely enthralled with Rusty, and I don't think they'll be any trouble."

Laura paused, hesitant, but Carissa insisted. "Go. Go now while Daniel is busy and doesn't see you leave."

"Thank you. I think I will rest for a bit. If you'll pardon me, Tyler."

"Of course. I'm havin' myself a nice visit with Carissa."

A smile touched the corners of Laura's mouth, but she made no comment. For this Carissa was greatly relieved. She waited until Laura went back into the house before picking up the conversation. "I'm sorry if I upset you earlier. That wasn't my intention."

Tyler shook his head. "My thoughts are well-known around here. I hate the Indians."

"All of them?"

He drew a deep breath. "No. I suppose not all of them. Just the ones who murdered my pa and the ones who go on murdering white folks."

She nodded. "Why are they so angry? Why do they want us dead?"

For a moment he said nothing, and Carissa thought perhaps he wouldn't answer her. Finally, however, he spoke. "I suppose when I really think about it, they are mad because we've taken their land. We've forced them to leave their way of life and live on reservations. And we've broken just about every promise we've ever made to them as a nation."

"I suppose I would be angry in that case. Is it true that the army often goes on raids, killing the Indians en masse?" she asked.

"Where did you hear that?" He looked at her with a completely puzzled expression.

"I overheard some of the men talking the other day at the Barnett place. One of them said something about a massacre of Indians by the army. I think they said it happened during the war."

He nodded. "They were probably talkin' about Sand Creek. There was a big massacre there. I have to admit I don't know a whole lot about it. I did hear that those Indians had been causing a lot of trouble in the warmer months when they'd attack whites on the trails."

"And for that, they deserved to be massacred?" she questioned.

Tyler looked at her hard. "You haven't had to worry much about Indians down in Corpus—have you?"

She shook her head. "No . . . and I don't pretend to understand it all."

Tyler started to say something, then shook his head. "I suppose nobody really understands. Seems to me like somethin' could have been worked out a long time ago to let us all live together in peace."

"I'm sure wrongs have been committed on both sides," Carissa replied softly. "That's usually how it goes."

Tyler looked to where the children were playing and nodded. "I suppose that's true enough. Still, there have been a lot of unprovoked raiding parties in the last few years. The Comanche and Kiowa seem bent on puttin' an end to the white man's existence. They've murdered a lot of innocent settlers—children, too." He turned his gaze back on Carissa. "How would you feel if they killed Gloria and Daniel?"

The very thought caused her to stiffen in fear. She had heard accounts of babies being dashed onto the rocks and killed. She shook her head. "I wouldn't want justice," she finally said.

Tyler's brows drew together. "I don't believe you."

She shrugged and fixed him with a hard stare. "I wouldn't want justice. I would want revenge."

For a moment neither said anything. Carissa couldn't help but wonder if she'd angered Tyler by suggesting that his motives weren't justice as much as a desire for payback. A part of her wanted to further the statement and let him know that she certainly didn't fault him for wanting revenge. She could understand that passion—that need. Even if the very thought terrified her.

7

"I hope the rooms are to your liking," Hannah said as she opened the door to the first bedroom. "Carissa, I thought this might work well for you and Gloria."

Peering inside, Carissa found a small, but adequate, space. An iron-frame bed stood against one wall with a small oak nightstand beside it. Across the room was another larger table with a bowl and pitcher on top.

"It's very nice," Carissa said, nodding. "More than enough room for Gloria and me."

"I had Will put the bed against the wall so that you could have Gloria on the inside. That way she won't fall out at night." Hannah smiled and turned to Laura. "Come, and I will show you to your room."

Carissa wanted to follow after them, but didn't. She knew Tyler would be coming along shortly to help Brandon bring up her things, and she wanted a chance to talk to him. Besides, she hadn't been encouraged to join Hannah and her sister.

She walked to the edge of the bed and sat down. It felt comfortable enough. The mattress felt firm, but not hard. Carissa gave a sigh and closed her eyes for a moment. She was glad that Marty had taken the kids to play. Gloria had been so rambunctious that morning, and Carissa held little patience for her antics.

A noise drew her attention, and Carissa opened her eyes to find Tyler watching her from the doorway. "Sorry. I didn't mean to disturb your rest. You looked . . . well . . . you looked comfortable," he said, setting down the two trunks he carried.

"I was just enjoying the quiet." She got to her feet. "I had hoped to talk to you for a minute."

He straightened and smiled. "I've always got time for a pretty lady."

She frowned. "This is serious."

"Is something wrong?" His tone took on an edge, suggesting he was all business.

"It's just this . . . well . . . this whole Indian thing. I didn't want to say anything to Brandon or Laura, for I know it's already hard enough for Brandon to leave my sister in her condition."

"So what is it that has you worried?"

Carissa drew a deep breath and squared her shoulders. "I want you . . . I mean, I wonder if you would be willing to teach me to shoot. You mentioned it once before."

His stance immediately relaxed. "Is that all?"

"I know you men plan to leave in the next two days, so that doesn't afford us much time, but I want you to teach me what to look out for . . . what kind of signs we'd see if the Indians were going to attack."

"You probably wouldn't see any signs," he replied. "They're

crafty that way. They know the land and how to survive on it. I've seen bands pick up in the middle of the night and slip right past the army. If they decide to attack this ranch, you probably won't see it comin'."

"Then how are we supposed to protect ourselves?" she asked.

Tyler considered the question for a moment. "I'll take you out to shoot this afternoon. We can get a lot of practice in before I have to leave. Chances are you won't need to worry. Like I said before, Hannah has earned the respect of the Comanche. Word among the tribes is that she's a friend to the people."

"And so they've never attacked this ranch?"

"No. They've taken things from time to time. Mostly a few steers and some horses. Will lets them, however. He feels that if he shows a willingness to overlook small thefts, the Indians won't be inclined to make trouble."

His words gave Carissa little comfort. "You will be gone for a very long time."

"There will still be men here. Will's got a good right-hand man in Juanita's husband, Berto. And there will be others. You'll be well looked after."

"I couldn't bear to lose Gloria." Carissa's words were choked as she fought her emotions. "I couldn't bear to lose Laura or Daniel."

Tyler stepped rather awkwardly toward her and started to put his hand to Carissa's shoulder before pulling back. "I know, but don't go borrowing trouble. Things have been peaceful here for a good while. With the war over and the army forts resupplied, the days of the Indian wars will soon come to a close."

She trembled. "Do you really believe that?"

"I do. The Indians will either give up and go to live on the reservations, or the army will kill them. I don't see that there will be much in the way of compromise."

❧

Tyler tried not to dwell on his earlier words to Carissa as he showed her how to handle the Henry repeating rifle. "Hold it tight against your shoulder," he instructed. "It's got a recoil to it."

Carissa looked at him in confusion. "Recoil? Will it hurt?"

He looked at the petite woman trying hard to hold the rifle up and shook his head. "This is crazy. That rifle is almost bigger than you."

"I can handle it," she told him. He reached out to snug the rifle tighter against her shoulder.

"I've no doubt you can, but after a shot or two, you're gonna be black and blue if you don't keep that thing tight. Maybe it'd be better to teach you to fire a revolver."

She relaxed the rifle at her side and narrowed her eyes. "I thought you said the range is shorter on the revolvers. If I am to be useful, I ought to be able to shoot a rifle."

He laughed. "Honey, you'd stop any Indian in his tracks just by givin' him that look."

His comment obviously took her by surprise. Carissa's mouth dropped open, and she giggled. "My father always said I could freeze a man in his steps with that look. Maybe it will come in handy."

Hoisting the rifle back to her shoulder, Carissa nodded toward the cans Tyler had set up. "So now what?"

He came to stand behind her. "Sight in your target. Remember what I told you about this particular Henry."

"Pulls to the right," she said.

"So lean into it." He steadied her arm. "Squeeze the trigger."

To Tyler's surprise, she wasted no time. The rifle discharged and she held her ground. He grinned. The shot missed the mark, but she was still standing. Better yet, she was looking at him with a smile to match his own, despite the cloud of gun smoke that rose between them.

"Can I do it again?"

Tyler thought that if he hadn't already had feelings for Carissa, that simple statement would have won him over. "We can stay out here as long as you like."

After another few shots, Carissa commented on the heat of the barrel. "It's really warming up."

He nodded. "It'll do that. Some of the fellas in the war said they'd fire it in battle until it all but glowed red. Why don't we rest for a few minutes and let it cool down?"

Carissa handed him the gun. "It isn't as hard as I thought it'd be."

Tyler laughed. "You haven't hit the target yet."

"I will." She moved away to the shade of a sycamore and leaned against the trunk. "I'll do what I have to in order to protect my daughter."

He could hear the determination in her voice. How different she was from the flighty young girl he'd first met in Corpus Christi. It was sad, he thought. She had gone from one extreme to another.

"You know, there are other ways." He crossed to where she stood fanning herself with a straw bonnet. The air was heavy, and Tyler figured they were due another storm before the day was out.

"Other ways of protecting? Don't you think I know that?"

She sounded offended. "I came to be with Laura instead of staying in Corpus. I could just as easily have remained there, but I knew it would be safer for Gloria here. At least I had hoped it would be. I had thought about how calm and peaceful it would be away from the city. Now I have to worry about whether or not we're going to be attacked by Indians while you and the other men are off on some fool cattle drive."

Tyler was surprised at the comment. "You think this drive is foolish?"

She met his gaze and nodded. "I didn't at first, but once I started hearing about all the risks I changed my mind."

"We didn't make this decision lightly," Tyler said, trying to choose his words carefully. "When William first talked to Mr. Terry, neither was convinced this was the best plan. Then they talked to other folks who had made the same trip. They considered other routes, as well. You really have no idea all the planning that went into this."

"I suppose I don't," she said, her voice softening. She pointed to the sky. "It's starting to cloud up. We'd better get back to my lessons."

She started to walk past him, but Tyler reached out and took hold of her arm. "Carissa, you don't have to put that wall between us. I don't fault you for your fears, but I do want to help if I can."

"I know, but . . ." She fell silent, and though Tyler waited for several minutes, she didn't finish her thought. Instead she smiled. "Come on, I need to hit that target."

⁂

That afternoon, Carissa sat with Hannah, Juanita, and Laura to discuss the distribution of chores. They had barely started when Juanita's eighteen-year-old daughter, Pepita, joined them. She was quite the beauty, with long silky black hair and dark eyes.

"I'm sorry to be late," she announced, taking her seat. "Andy, he wanted to show me the new foal." She smiled and nodded to Hannah.

"That's all right. We just settled down to business," Hannah replied. "I took Mrs. Terry's advice when she was last here." Hannah handed a piece of paper to each woman. "She said we women would get along a whole lot better if we had a plan." She paused. "I know this is difficult, and I'm not fooling myself to believe it won't be hard without our fellas. The ranch is never the same with the men gone. However, there will be plenty of work, and we need to see to it that we benefit each and every family."

Carissa took the paper offered her and looked at the schedule. It seemed simple enough. Each day was listed out and the chores were given with one or two names beside each duty.

"As the gardens flourish we will have more work to manage, with weeding and canning and such," Hannah said, looking at her list. "But for now these are the main things we need to focus on. Juanita is in charge of the kitchen, but since we will still have some thirteen people to keep fed, what with us and our children and the remaining hands, she'll need help. So each day I've assigned one of us to work with her. Carissa, I remember you saying you liked cooking, so I hope you don't mind that I put you on cooking twice in the week. Pepita will double up as well and Sundays are less work because we try to prepare most everything on Saturday, so Juanita says she is good to work alone."

Carissa nodded, looking at the paper. She was assigned to Mondays and Fridays. "Looks good."

"Laura, you mentioned that you were quite handy with a needle, so I put you and Pepita on mending and sewing twice. Is that acceptable?"

"Absolutely," Laura replied. "I'm impressed that you've managed this so neatly. I think it looks quite orderly." Pepita nodded her approval.

Carissa studied the list for a moment. There were all the regular chores of milking, gathering eggs, gardening, washing and hanging out clothes, ironing, cleaning, cooking, and seeing to the children. But along with this were a few of the other tasks that normally would be assigned to the men, such as bringing in wood and water. She wondered why the remaining men on the ranch couldn't handle those jobs.

"Berto and his men will be busy with the livestock, keeping watch of the place, and other jobs that keep the ranch running in a smooth fashion," Hannah continued, as if reading Carissa's mind. "The men have been working hard to put up enough wood that we shouldn't have to worry about ordering any in or cutting it ourselves. However, we may find it necessary to split some of the wood from time to time."

"Berto say he would keep the wood split," Juanita offered. "He will see to it each night before bed."

Hannah nodded. "I really appreciate that." She flipped her paper over. "You'll see on the back that we will also have some of those chores that aren't done daily. We have soap to make, and I remember you saying that you were working on curtains and rugs for your new place, Laura."

"Well, I hardly expect you to help with that," Laura replied.

"We'll work together. You're helping me keep my ranch

running, and in turn we will help you keep your farm running. I have arranged with Berto to have a detail of men go over to the farm once a week to check on everything. The important thing will be to ensure that no one has broken in or caused mischief. They will tend the garden, as well, although they weren't too happy with that assignment." She laughed and shrugged. "Will promised them a nice bonus, and that softened the blow."

"I had thought maybe we could accompany them when they went to check on the place," Laura said.

Hannah shook her head. "I don't think that would be wise for several reasons. First of all, most of the folks in the area are going to know the men have gone on this drive. That's why it was important for us to come together for protection. There are often renegades other than Indians who would seek to cause problems. This is the wild frontier, and you have to keep in mind that the laws and restrictions that might be observed in the city are often overlooked out here. Not only that, but the war has changed folks. It's made criminals out of men who might otherwise have been upstanding citizens. William doesn't even want us driving into town. He thinks we'll be safer to just sit tight."

"For three months?" Carissa asked. "That seems a bit much. Why would we not be safe enough with some of the men accompanying us to town?"

"We could, but it is just more prudent to remain here." Hannah drew a deep breath. "It wasn't really to my liking either, but it puts our men's minds at ease to know we'll be safe here. Giving the men one less thing to worry about on the trail makes staying here seem a small sacrifice."

"She's right," Laura said. "Besides, in my condition, I'm

going to feel less and less inclined to travel very far. It's just not that comfortable."

Juanita spoke up. "The men will go to town once every two weeks for news and supplies, but if we need the doctor or the sheriff, they will ride for them."

Carissa looked around the room. So this was to become her prison in a sense. Maybe it would have been better to remain in Corpus Christi. She felt her sister's gaze on her and forced a smile. There was no sense starting this with complaints.

"What shall we do about church?" Laura asked.

Hannah was ready for this, as well. "We will hold our own service. Marietta Terry said she might even join us. I love to hear her stories about how the Lord has worked in her life."

"Well, it would seem that you've thought of everything," Laura said, nodding at the list. "I think we can accomplish a great deal working together like this."

"I think so, too," Hannah replied. "Like I mentioned before, as the gardens produce more and more, we will cook and can. We will share the bounty so that when the men return, you will take home food for your family."

Carissa had never known women to work together like this. In the city, her family and their friends had servants for such things. Joining Laura at the farm had given Carissa quite a shock at the amount of work that was required just to keep up with daily operations. She was glad that Hannah Barnett seemed to have a good understanding of what was expected of each of them. Her admiration of the woman continued to grow, and she couldn't help but hope that in time, Hannah would become a good friend. God knew that Carissa needed one.

"So if we're all agreed," Hannah said, interrupting her

thoughts, "I'd like to pray and ask God's blessings on our time together and on the travels our men will soon endure."

Carissa watched as the other women bowed their heads, then lowered her own. *God,* she prayed silently, *please keep us safe. Please keep Tyler and the others safe.* She paused for a moment to hear the words Hannah prayed, and then continued with her own prayer.

And, Father, help us both to learn to forgive and let go of the past. There's a lot that hurts me still, and I know it won't go away without your help.

"Guess we're headin' out tomorrow," Tyler told Osage. The older man nodded. "'Bout time."

Tyler leaned back against the fence rail. "I agree." But his heart wasn't nearly so fixed on the idea as it had been before Carissa Lowe had come to the area.

"You have everything ready?"

Osage gave him a look of disgust. "Have you ever known me not to be ready for a job? Your pa always knew he could count on me to have my work under control."

"I wasn't really questionin' your abilities, Osage—just makin' conversation."

The old man grinned. "I knowed it. Couldn't help givin' you a bad time of it since your pa ain't here to do the job."

"I miss him," Tyler said, looking off across the ranch. "I know he would have wanted to go on this drive. He always dreamed of bein' a big Texas rancher."

"You can carry on that dream."

Tyler looked at the older man. "I'd like to, but that's hard to do without a ranch. Doesn't look too favorable, either. Will's doin' all he can, but you know how folks feel about us Rebels."

"What I know is that folks are wrong. You deserve to have your land back. The boys and me are behind you on that. In fact, I'll do what I can to help you. I didn't bear arms against anyone, so maybe I can help you get the ranch back."

"Will says the same thing, but in truth it ain't the same. I shouldn't have to rely on someone else to get back what is rightfully mine."

"Oh, so now you're too good to have help, is that it?"

Tyler shook his head. "That's not it at all. I just . . . well . . . I want to have what's mine returned. I shouldn't need anyone's help to have that happen. It's Atherton land. It ought to be returned to an Atherton."

"Say, ain't that the judge hisself?" Osage asked, pointing.

Tyler's attention was drawn to the men coming from around the house. William was crossing the yard with a man that Tyler knew to be Judge Peevy from Dallas. "It is. Maybe he has news." Tyler pushed off the fence to go meet them.

"I'll get back to work, but you let me know what you find out, ya hear?"

"I will," Tyler said over his shoulder. He kept walking toward the two men. "Have you had some word about my claim to the ranch?"

"It's not good news, I'm afraid." Peevy rubbed his white beard. "I've met with resistance from every direction. Your service for the Confederacy is the biggest obstacle we're up against. The Republicans are not easily swayed to do anything that resembles aiding the enemy."

"The enemy, eh?" Tyler shook his head. "I could have figured that'd be the way of it. My grandfather might have wanted me to serve in support of the South, but my father didn't fight against the Union."

"Well, we aren't giving up just yet," William interjected. "Judge Peevy is working to tie this up as long as possible. He thought he might be able to work out something to at least get the property returned to your mother."

"It won't be easy," Peevy added, "but we're trying to fight this from every angle. But it hasn't helped that your mother moved away to live with her cousin or that your sister married a former Confederate major. Had they remained on the property, it might be a different story now. There might have been some sympathy for a widow. Even if she is a Southerner."

Peevy's comment only served to anger Tyler. "I thought the country was supposed to be unified now. I thought we were supposed to put aside the past and move forward."

"If you were on the right side of the war, that's true enough," Judge Peevy replied. "I'm sure life in the North goes on as it did before, except for the fact that they want to make the South suffer and pay for the war. I'd like to believe the past issues can be put aside, but frankly, there's too much bad blood to wash away."

"Perhaps if Lincoln had lived," Will began, "he might have been able to change the hearts and minds of the people. Especially those in Washington. His death has left a bitterness between the North and South that might never heal."

"William is right. Even those of us who supported the Union are looked upon as the enemy for simply living here."

"They don't understand the heart of the Texas people," Tyler muttered. "It never really was our war. We stood in support of our Southern brothers, but mostly we would have been content to reform our own country. Now we want to put the war behind us, and they won't let us."

"Be that as it may," Peevy countered, "there are those in control who can hopefully be counted on to help." He reached out and put his hand on Tyler's shoulder. "I want you to know that I will be working faithfully on this matter while you're away, but I cannot promise anything."

"In other words," Tyler said, balling his hands, "I could return to find the place sold and forever out of my reach."

William and Judge Peevy exchanged a glance, and then turned back to Tyler. Peevy nodded. "That's the truth of it, son. I'm sorry."

⌘

Carissa watched as a man of some means spoke with William and Tyler. "Who is that?" she asked as she and Hannah made their way back from the smokehouse.

"That's Judge Peevy. He's trying to help Tyler get his ranch back."

"It seems so unfair that he should have lost his home. Especially after his father died trying to defend it," Carissa replied.

Hannah paused and fixed Carissa with a smile. "You care about him—don't you?"

Carissa's hand went to her throat. "I . . . well . . ." She licked her lips and forced her nerves to steady. "I care about everyone here."

"But Tyler is special. I can see that."

Carissa didn't know what to say. The idea of admitting her growing feelings was something she wasn't at all comfortable with. Over and over she'd told herself that it wasn't sensible to care about another man. But at the same time, she feared for Gloria.

Hannah reached out to touch Carissa's arm. "He's a good man, and he cares about you and Gloria. I've not seen him show this much affection for anyone else. I think you should know that."

"But why?" Carissa questioned.

"The men are leaving tomorrow. It might be wise to tell him how you feel."

Carissa shook her head. "I'm not even sure I know how I feel—except for overwhelmed. So much has happened. Tyler saved my life, and in essence, Gloria's too. I will always feel a special connection to him because of that. But my husband was cruel. He's made it so that I don't feel . . . safe . . . with other men."

"Don't give him any more power over you, Carissa. The past can be put behind you. It's not easy, nor can I say that you'll never have to face certain fears. But for Gloria's sake, I'd encourage you to try. A woman without a mate has a hard enough time in this world. A woman with a child . . . well, I can tell you from the experience of raising my brother and sister that it only gets harder. I fell in love with William but had already decided I'd have to marry in order to see to their needs."

"But that's not a good reason to marry," Carissa said, shaking her head. "What about love?"

"I agree that love is important. It was very important to me, but many a marriage has started because of something other than love." Hannah paused as the men moved off toward the pens. "I know he cares about you. And, Carissa, I can't help but believe you care about him. I think love is growing between the two of you. I just want to encourage you not to let fear kill that love."

Carissa was momentarily offended by Hannah's frankness, but then realized it was exactly what she wanted in a friend. "I think I'm afraid of everything," she finally admitted.

"'Perfect love casteth out fear,'" Hannah countered. "That's from the Bible. God's love is perfect, and when we turn to Him, He can set us free from fear through His love. Laura told me that you haven't been long in seeking God's direction. Maybe while the men are on the cattle drive, you can focus on growing closer to God."

"I wouldn't know where to start."

Hannah smiled. "Maybe I can help. Would you like that?"

Carissa felt her chest tighten. "Yes, I think I would."

⁓

"I don't wanna sleep," Gloria said in protest.

Carissa knew her daughter wouldn't take a nap willingly, but she also knew that without the break, Gloria would be impossible at supper.

Taking a warm, wet cloth, Carissa began washing Gloria's face. "I know you don't want to sleep, but how about you just rest. You can talk to your dolly."

"I want Rusty."

"No, the dog has to stay outside." Carissa put the cloth aside and unfastened Gloria's pinafore. Gloria suppressed a yawn and danced around as Carissa worked to take off the apron and dress. Once this was done she pointed Gloria to the bed.

"You be with me."

"No, I have work to do," Carissa said, despite the fact that the idea was greatly appealing. She reached over to the nightstand and picked up Gloria's doll. "Here's your baby."

To Carissa's surprise, Gloria didn't argue. As was often the case, if she could get Gloria to be still for a little while, she usually yielded to her exhaustion. The girl yawned again and took the doll to her chest. Carissa pulled a sheet up to cover her daughter.

"You get some rest and when you wake up, it will be time for supper."

"I see Tyer, too?"

Carissa looked at her daughter for a moment, then sat down on the edge of the bed. "You like Tyler, don't you?"

Gloria nodded. Her lids were growing heavy, and Carissa knew she should just leave her child to go to sleep. Something kept her there, however. She thought of what Hannah had said about Tyler caring for her and for Gloria.

Reaching out, Carissa smoothed back her daughter's blond curls. To her surprise, Gloria spoke. "You like, Tyer, Mama." It wasn't a question, but rather a statement. Even so, Carissa felt that she could at least be honest with her child.

"I do like Tyler."

Gloria nodded again and closed her eyes. Her peaceful expression left Carissa with a sense of well-being. Her daughter was safe and happy. She really couldn't hope for more than that—could she?

Leaving Gloria to sleep, Carissa made her way to the kitchen. She spied Juanita and smiled. "I'm here to help you."

Juanita nodded. "I have two pork roasts in the oven. We will make corn bread and grits, gravy, and something sweet."

"Sounds delicious." Carissa took down an apron and slipped it on. Securing the ties, she went to the sink and washed her hands. "I know how to make corn bread and grits, but I'm not too good with gravy."

"Then I teach you," Juanita said matter-of-factly.

Carissa smiled and nodded as she turned to face the Mexican woman. "I'm ready."

They had barely started working when someone came in from the back. Carissa wasn't surprised to see it was Tyler. Somehow she had almost expected it.

"We could use something to tide us over till supper," he announced. "Would you happen to have any of your cinnamon sugar cookies, Juanita?"

"*Sí*, I have those and some of Miss Hannah's gingerbread. You want both?"

"Absolutely. Me and Osage are pert near starvin'." He looked at Carissa and winked. "We're workin' way harder than a man ought to work."

She couldn't help but grin. "You'd better hurry then, Juanita. We wouldn't want them to expire."

Tyler returned the smile and happily received a stack of cookies from Juanita. Next she went to a jar and pulled out pieces of gingerbread. Wrapping them in a dish towel, she admonished Tyler.

"You don't lose my towel." She brought him the bundle and handed it over.

"I wouldn't dream of it," Tyler promised. "In fact, if I had another set of hands, I wouldn't even take it."

Juanita shook her head. "If you had more hands, you'd just take more food."

Tyler laughed and moved toward the door. "She knows

me pretty well," he said, meeting Carissa's gaze. "You could learn a lot from her."

"That's the plan," Carissa declared.

This caused Tyler to pause, and Carissa could tell he wanted to know exactly what she meant by her statement. With a shrug and a hint of a smile, Carissa went back to where Juanita had started her sifting flour for the gravy. "I hope she'll teach me to make those cookies. They look delicious."

She risked a quick glance at Tyler and saw that he looked momentarily confused. He didn't let the expression linger, however.

"Thanks again, Juanita."

And then he was gone and the room seemed suddenly large and empty. She missed his presence. Carissa frowned. She had never felt that way about Malcolm. Not in the time they were courting, and certainly not after they wed.

"You don't need so much," Juanita said, interrupting her thoughts.

Carissa looked down at the huge mound of flour. "Oh, sorry. I was daydreaming."

Juanita gave her an understanding smile. "Dreams are good . . . and sometimes they come true."

That night Ted and Marietta Terry came to supper at the Barnetts'. Carissa helped to put the last of the dinner on the table before taking Gloria in her arms. She was used to holding Gloria for meals, but it wouldn't be all that long before the child could sit on her own.

"I don't know why Andy gets to go on the cattle drive and I got to stay here," ten-year-old Marty declared as she took the seat opposite Carissa. "I can ride better than he does, and I can lasso, too."

"Girls don't usually go on cattle drives," Hannah declared. "At least not unless they absolutely have to."

"Well . . . I have to," Marty said in protest. Her long blond braids, coupled with the pout on her face, made her appear years younger.

Hannah shook her finger. "That's not true, Miss Marty, and you know very well how I feel about you exaggerating things."

"Cattle drives are hard work," William added. "And you aren't going to have any of the nice things you have here at home."

"Besides, you're too little to go on a cattle drive," her brother declared. Andy plopped down in the seat beside his sister. "You couldn't handle a stampede or calm the herd in a storm."

"I wish you weren't going, either," Hannah said, looking at her brother. "You know how I feel about this, Andy. It's dangerous."

Will put his hand out to touch hers. "Remember we talked about this, and you agreed to stop fretting. Andy is nearly thirteen and that's plenty old enough to drive cattle."

"He's right," Ted said, helping Marietta to a seat. "Boys that young go all the time. They're hardy and better able to endure the trail. Why, when I was his age I could drive a herd of a hundred by myself."

"And walk on water when they came to river crossings," Marietta added to everyone's amusement.

Ted grinned. "Well, pert near. As I recall there was a time when you thought that highly of me."

She smiled. "I still do, Teddy. I still do."

One by one the others came to the table, and as Carissa settled into her seat, she found Tyler helping her. "Here, I'll hold Gloria." He swung the little girl up into his arms before Carissa could say a word.

She looked at him for a moment, seeing how pleased Gloria was at his attention. Tyler pretended to munch on the little girl's neck and Gloria squealed.

"She certainly seems to enjoy you, Tyler," Marietta said.

"She's my special friend. Aren't you?" he said, looking to Gloria.

"Yes. Tyer is my fwend." Gloria wrapped her arms around his neck and pretended to return the munching.

Tyler laughed and sat down beside Carissa. "I'll take her now." Carissa held out her hands.

He didn't even pretend to heed her instruction. "She's fine with me." Gloria quickly sat down on his lap and ignored her mother.

Carissa wasn't sure what to say, especially since it seemed everyone was now looking to see what her reaction might be. She lowered her gaze to the empty plate and folded her hands. Her discomfort seemed to stretch as she waited for someone to offer grace.

"Let's pray," William finally declared.

Carissa breathed a sigh of relief and closed her eyes. She felt so confused. Life used to be much easier—as a young woman, she would flirt and bat her eyelashes at any man who captured her fancy. She was the belle of the ball, and they all vied for her attention. Then Malcolm came along, and she thought he'd hung the moon and stars. He was so good at convincing her of his love. How could she ever trust her heart again?

"He said amen," Tyler whispered in her ear.

Carissa's head snapped upward to find everyone busily passing platters and bowls. She looked at Tyler and realized he was the only one watching her. She gave him a weak smile. "I'm afraid I'm rather tired."

"I don't doubt it. You were hard at work every time I saw you today."

Taking up the bowl of grits, Carissa put a portion on her plate and held the ladle up. "Would you like some grits?"

He smiled and nodded. "I sure do. And I wanna top it with

some of that good pork gravy." He looked to Gloria. "How about you, little gal? You want some grits?"

Gloria clapped her hands. "Grits are good. I want grits."

He laughed and turned back to Carissa. "You heard the little lady."

Carissa pointed to her plate. "She can eat off my plate."

"Or mine," he said as if it happened every day.

Ted Terry interrupted her thoughts. "I heard from our buyer in Abilene. Prices are on the rise. There's a big demand for beef out of Chicago and New York. Our buyer feels confident he can get us top dollar. The sooner we can get there, the better. I have a feeling once word gets around, every man and his brother will be pushing beeves north."

"So we might make more than forty a head?" William asked.

"That's what I'm thinking," Ted said, helping himself to some of the pork roast. "Maybe even as high as fifty."

"That would bring us well over a hundred thousand," William said, looking to Tyler. "Depending on how many head we lose, it might well bring us close to . . . a hundred and twenty-five thousand dollars."

"That's amazing," Marietta said, shaking her head. "Three years ago we couldn't give those animals away. I remember Ted selling five steers for ten dollars."

"Apiece?" Carissa asked casually.

"No, for all five," Marietta replied. "Two dollars a head. The war made it impossible to make any decent wage."

"She's right about that," Ted agreed. He took two large pieces of corn bread and passed the platter to Tyler. "But now the entire world is starved for beef. The King ranch down Corpus way is shipping them out as fast as they can. I heard tell that Mr. King is going into the meatpacking business, as well."

"Wouldn't that require a lot of money, to keep the beef from going bad?" William asked. "I know they ship in ice cars on the rails, but our rail system isn't the best."

"King could be planning to send his beef out of Corpus on ships," Brandon offered. "Packing a freighter full of ice would probably keep easier than a railcar."

"Possibly. All I'm sayin'," Ted continued, "is there are gonna be a load of opportunities for us in the future. I believe we can join our efforts to accomplish great things."

"I am certainly all for that," William replied.

Carissa noted that Tyler remained silent. She wondered if this was due to his uncertain future. She wished there was some way to offer him comfort. She wished her father and mother weren't bound for Europe. Her father had many good friends among the former Unionists. Perhaps he could have helped Tyler get back his land.

"So did you ladies plan for how you will go about living together?" Marietta asked.

Hannah nodded. "We did indeed. We took your advice and made a list for each of us. The chores are shared among the women. We may even find ourselves with time to just rest and take it easy."

"That'll be the day," William said with a snorted laugh. "I think the only time you sit still for more than a minute is at meals, and even then you're up and down so much I very nearly get seasick."

Chuckles sounded from around the table. Carissa watched as Hannah blushed and shook her head. "The only way to get things done is to do them."

The meal continued in a pleasant, almost celebratory, spirit. Carissa listened to the men discuss the need for extra lassos and gloves. Marietta suggested taking a stack of wool blankets in case the weather turned cold.

"You can never tell about the weather. I've heard tell of snow in Kansas even into May. Best you go prepared," she told them.

Hannah mentioned a new quilt pattern that she got in the mail, and Marietta and Laura seemed more than a little interested. Twice Carissa tried to take Gloria from Tyler, but neither the child nor the man showed any interest. She fretted that this arrangement somehow signaled to the others an intimacy she was not yet ready to concede. But by the time dessert was served, Carissa finally began to relax and realize that no one thought it strange that Tyler and Gloria should share the meal. This seemed even more apparent when Ted took young Robert Barnett from his high chair and bounced the boy on his knee.

The women cleared the table when everyone was done, and Marty took the children to play for a bit before bedtime. Carissa offered to help with the washing up, even though it wasn't her night, but Hannah waved her off.

"Go talk to Tyler," she suggested in a whisper.

Laura was standing close enough to hear and raised a brow in question. Carissa shrugged and moved toward the back porch. Laura wasn't willing to be dismissed so easily.

"What did she mean by that? Is there a problem between you and Tyler?"

Carissa paused at the back door and shook her head. "No. Not really."

"Then what did she mean?"

Meeting Laura's concerned expression, Carissa drew a deep breath. "Hannah thinks that Tyler has feelings for me."

"Well, that's nothing new. I've felt that way for some time."

"She thinks I should tell Tyler that I have feelings for him," Carissa confessed.

"And do you?"

Carissa carefully weighed her response to Laura's question. "I don't want to have feelings for someone who may well die on this fool cattle drive." That was easier to say than to explain her own fears regarding Malcolm and the past.

"What?"

"The drive is dangerous," Carissa said, looking Laura square in the eye. "I know that my words might offer you more to worry about, but cattle drives are dangerous and passing through Indian Territory is just asking for trouble."

"So you can't have feelings for Tyler because he might die?"

Nodding in her discomfort, Carissa continued. "Yes. I've already endured so much, Laura. To risk my heart again seems foolish."

"Well, I suppose this means that you will no longer have feelings for Gloria or Daniel."

"What? Don't talk crazy. I'll never stop having feelings for them."

"Well, children die all the time. Sickness comes and they are too little to fight it off."

"That's not the same, Laura. This is something the men are choosing to do. They are choosing to risk their lives."

Laura nodded. "I see. Then you won't be able to love me anymore."

Carissa was growing quite frustrated. "What are you saying? Of course I love you."

"But I chose to have another baby. Women often die in childbirth. So since I chose to risk my life, you cannot have feelings for me."

Carissa could see Laura's point. Her shoulders dropped a bit in defeat. "All right, so life is a risk and giving one's heart is a part of it. But it doesn't stop me from being afraid."

Laura stepped forward and hugged her close. "No one said that it wouldn't be hard. Loving someone isn't the easiest thing I've ever done. I hope you won't let your fears, however, keep you from true happiness. Not all men are like Malcolm. In fact, I'm certain Tyler Atherton is nothing like Malcolm Lowe."

"I agree, he isn't." She bit her lower lip and tried to make sense of the moment. Finally she glanced back at Laura. "I suppose I should talk to him. I mean, he's shown such kindness and affection toward Gloria, and I know she needs a father."

Laura shook her head. "Don't just extend your heart to Tyler in order to get Gloria a father. You need to make certain you can love him all for yourself."

At the mention of loving Tyler, Carissa felt her chest tighten. "I think I need to pray on this. I'll speak to him in the morning." And before Laura could say another word, Carissa pushed past her and went in search of Gloria.

The next morning proved to be pure pandemonium. Ted's horse spooked and threw him, and the doctor had to be sent for. Carissa stepped up to cover for Hannah in the kitchen, and by the time she was free to go in search of Tyler, she was shocked to find him otherwise occupied.

A carriage was parked at the end of the walkway, and as William led the doctor into the house, Carissa caught sight of Tyler helping an attractive young woman down from the driver's seat. Ducking back quickly, Carissa's first thought was to leave as Tyler escorted the woman toward the house. But she couldn't help but pause just around the corner of the house and listen to what was being said.

"I heard you were going on this cattle drive, and I knew I had to see you before you headed out. Since Dr. Sutton needed a ride, I thought I might as well be the one to give it."

"That was mighty kind of you, Ava. I'm sure the doc appreciated the help."

"I missed you coming to see me last night." Her voice grew husky and sultry. "You nearly broke my heart, you know. I had my best meal ready, too. Just the way you like it."

He laughed. "Well, you know how much I enjoy your food, Ava. Between you and Juanita, I'm hard-pressed to choose the best."

"Well, I hope that my company puts the choice into proper perspective," the woman replied. "After all, Juanita is happily married . . . while I am . . . well . . . still waiting to be."

Tyler laughed. "Oh, it won't be that long before you're walking down the aisle."

"Well, it'll be at least a few months or more." Her tone was coy and playful. "That seems like a very long time if you ask me."

"Now, Ava, I know you've got plenty to keep you busy."

Carissa felt her stomach churn at the woman's shrill laughter. She said something in a raspy, low voice, but Carissa couldn't make out the words. She did, however, hear Tyler's reply nice and loud.

"That would definitely keep you busy, Ava."

Feeling as though she might be ill, Carissa tried to move away but found her feet frozen in place. They were teasing as if courting. She'd been such a fool. Of course Tyler had a sweetheart. He had lived in this area for some time and no doubt had known this woman for a while.

"I brought you some spice cake to take on the trail. I know it's your favorite."

"That was mighty nice of you, Ava. I'm sure I'll enjoy it—as I always do."

"Well, since you couldn't be there to enjoy it last night, I figured I would send some with you."

"Hello, Ava," Carissa heard William Barnett say as he joined the couple. "You are looking lovely today. Tyler tells me that you cook like a dream and sing like an angel."

"You should join us sometime for supper. You could bring your wife. I met her once at the mercantile. She's quite a beauty."

"I think so," Barnett replied.

His presence seemed to break the spell and Carissa slipped off toward the back of the house, her heart racing. She'd come so close to making a fool of herself! Hurrying past the horse pens, she saw a strange sight. Several men were gathered around, cheering on another young man as he ran and slid under the bottom post of the fence.

"You done it, Newt!" Andy Dandridge called. "You're gonna be good at steer slidin'."

Carissa frowned as the dusty young man jumped up and searched for his hat. Steer sliding? What in the world was that?

"Come on and do it again," someone called.

A cheer went up and the young man climbed back over the fence, hat in hand, and made his way to the other side of the pen. For a moment Carissa was tempted to pause and watch, but she feared having to speak if one of the men noticed her. She spied Marty and Gloria playing with the new baby goats in a smaller pen attached to the far side of the barn and made her way to where they were.

"See the babies, Mama," Gloria said, running to the little gate. "Come see."

Carissa carefully entered the pen and was immediately set upon by six baby goats. "Where are their mamas?" she asked Marty.

"Juanita is milking them. The kids are being weaned, so we're playin' with them to keep them busy."

Carissa knelt in the dirt and straw. A small brown-and-white kid immediately came to her, looking for a treat. She smiled, trying hard to put aside her embarrassment at what had just happened. She hated herself for very nearly yielding her heart—especially to a man whose interest obviously lay elsewhere. She felt tears come to her eyes and buried her face in the soft fur of the baby goat. The animal protested, causing Gloria to giggle. She came to her mother's side and patted Carissa's back.

"You squeezin' him too tight."

Releasing the kid, Carissa looked at her daughter's happy expression and wanted to cry all the more. She had thought Tyler might make a good father for Gloria.

"Marty, can you take these inside for me?" Juanita said, bringing two pails from the barn.

"Sure," the girl said, getting to her feet. She bounded over the fence as if she were one of the boys and grabbed the buckets. Glancing over her shoulder, she looked hesitant. "I'll be right back."

"Go ahead," Carissa said. "I'll take Gloria with me to do chores."

She started to get to her feet as Marty made her way to the house. But Gloria nearly pushed her over backward as she raced to the gate, calling the one name Carissa had hoped to avoid hearing.

"Tyer! Tyer, you come see the babies!"

"I'd rather come see you," he declared and reached over the fence to pull Gloria into his arms.

Carissa straightened and got to her feet, dusting off dirt from her skirt as she stood. She kept her gaze fixed on the dust smudges to keep from having to face Tyler.

"You two look like you're havin' a good time."

"We played with the goats. You can play, too."

"No, I'm afraid I have to go. I just wanted to come tell you to be good for your mama until I get back."

Gloria wrapped her arms around Tyler's neck. "Don't go away."

Carissa tried hard to be strong. She walked toward the man and her child. "Gloria, stop it now. Tyler has to go."

"But he can stay," Gloria declared. She pulled back and took Tyler's face in her hands. "I wuv you, Tyer."

Her daughter's words hit Carissa hard. She swallowed back a sob that seemed to work its way up from her very soul. She hadn't ever thought to give her heart to another man, and surely she hadn't really given it to Tyler Atherton. But if not, then why did this hurt so much?

✑

Tyler had never known such joy as when Gloria Lowe declared her love for him. He supposed the only thing that might have made the moment perfect was if her mother had done the same. Instead, Carissa was acting rather aloof—almost put out with him.

"I love you, too, darlin'," he told Gloria. He glanced at Carissa and smiled. "It's good to see a lady who knows her heart."

Carissa all but snapped back, "Well, it seems to me there are a lot of women around here who know their hearts."

Tyler laughed. "That's true enough. You should hear Marietta in there. She's threatened to all but shoot Ted if he doesn't stay in bed. The doctor told him he's dislocated his hip and might have even broken it. He can't go on the drive."

The stern look on Carissa's face melted away to concern. "Oh no. That's awful. I hope he'll be all right."

"Ted's a tough character. He'll get on just fine—especially since Hannah has informed him that he and Marietta will remain here until he's healed. That man will get more attention and fussin' than a fella could ever want."

"Still, I know he had his heart set on going with you to Kansas."

Tyler watched Carissa for a moment. Something about her seemed different—almost hard. Was she upset about his leaving? Did he dare to hope that she was going to miss him?

"Come on, Gloria. We need to get our chores done." Carissa stepped from the pen and secured the latch.

"I wanna go wif Tyer."

Carissa came to take the girl from Tyler's arms, but Gloria wanted no part of it. "Now don't make a fuss," Tyler told Gloria. "If you're good for your mama, I'll bring you back a present."

"A pwesent?" she asked in awe. "And a pwesent for Mama?"

Tyler watched as Carissa's cheeks reddened. She ducked her head as if embarrassed, but Tyler thought it endearing. "Of course I'll bring a present for your mama. What do you think I should get her?"

Gloria shook her head. "Don't know."

"Come on, Gloria. I need to get to work." Carissa all but ripped the child away from him.

Tyler frowned. "You know it can wait. Why don't you tell me what's really botherin' you."

Carissa shook her head. "I've just got a lot on my mind. It's a busy morning. You all are leaving, and I have to think about our safety. I'm still not a very good shot, after all."

114

"So you're worried about Indian attacks, is that it?"

She straightened and met his gaze. "Of course. What else would there be?"

"Yeah, I guess that's enough, huh?" He tried not to care that her words sounded cold and indifferent to him. "But I think you'll be just fine. Even Doc said that there hasn't been any word of problems lately. I think the army has probably got them on the run."

"Good. I hope so."

Gloria began wiggling to be put down. "There's Marty. I wanna go play."

Carissa let her daughter go, and Tyler couldn't help but use the opportunity to speak. "I think you shouldn't worry so much. You told me that your faith in God is stronger than it has ever been. I think that's what you have to focus on now."

She seemed puzzled for a moment, almost as if trying to interpret what he'd said. Tyler started to say something else, but Carissa spoke up. "Hannah has offered to help me study the Bible. I think I shall do a lot of focusing on God. Now if you'll excuse me."

"I'll be leavin' in just a few minutes," he said. "I wanted to be sure and tell you good-bye."

"Good-bye," she replied and walked toward the barn.

Tyler couldn't help himself. "Wait a minute. That's it?" The night before she'd seemed so receptive to his attention. She'd let him feed Gloria and sit beside her as if they were a family. Now she acted as though he ought to be in quarantine.

Carissa turned and looked at him with a frown. "Was there something else?"

He crossed the distance between them. "I don't know—you

tell me. You seem angry. Did I do something to upset you, or is this just about the cattle drive? I know you don't think it's wise."

"I don't, but no one really asked me what I thought," she replied in a curt manner. "They never do."

"Don't let your fears turn you bitter," he said with a touch of a smile to soften the comment.

She seemed stunned and shook her head. "I'm not bitter."

"I didn't say you were," he began. "I said don't let fear make you that way. It's an easy place to go, believe me. I know firsthand."

"Tyler!" Ava Lambert called as she rounded the corner of the house.

Tyler turned and waved. "I'm over here."

"Will said to find you. I think he's ready to head out." She joined him and smiled at Carissa. "I don't believe I've met you yet. I'm Ava Lambert."

Tyler didn't wait for Carissa to reply. "This is Carissa Lowe. She's Laura's sister."

"Oh yes, I met her in the house," Ava said, still smiling. "It's nice to meet you, Carissa. I'm sure we'll be the best of friends."

Tyler saw Carissa stiffen and her brows knit together. "I'm sure, but for now I need to go. Have a good day." She hurried away and disappeared into the barn.

"Well, she doesn't seem to like me," Ava said with a bit of a pout.

"She's a troubled soul," Tyler said, frowning. "She's been through more than you'd know."

Ava's expression softened, and she put her arm through Tyler's to lead him back to the house. "There are a great many wounded souls in the world, Tyler. Her heartbreak isn't the first, and it certainly won't be the last."

"I suppose not," Tyler said, "but her heart is mighty important to me."

Ava shook her head. "I don't think there's enough of her heart left intact, Tyler. You might want to reconsider. After all, I got enough heart for the both of us."

He shook his head. "Ain't nothin' to reconsider."

❧

Carissa joined the others just as the men were mounted and ready to go. She took Gloria from Marty's care and hoisted the child to her hip. She wanted to run for the cover of the house, but knew the women would question her afterward as to why she wasn't there to say good-bye.

Laura stepped forward with Daniel in her arms. "Please be careful," she told Brandon as he leaned down for one last kiss.

Carissa envied her sister. Brandon loved his wife more than life. He tousled the hair of his son and smiled, and the look on his face was so intense that Carissa almost felt like an intruder. Brandon glanced over at her.

"You take good care of her, Carissa. Don't let her do too much."

Carissa nodded and tried her best to smile. "I'll sit on her if I have to."

He laughed. "I know you both to be determined and stubborn women. Good luck."

The others also exchanged their farewells. Carissa glanced around for Ava Lambert but found she wasn't there. Neither was the doctor or his carriage. Apparently they had already gone.

Tyler drew up on his horse and smiled down at Gloria and Carissa. "Don't forget to be good, Gloria," he said.

Gloria clapped her hands. "And I get a pwesent."

He nodded. "Indeed you do." Tyler then looked at Carissa, and for a moment she thought she saw something more in his expression. It was like a deep longing—a desire that she thought clearly matched her own. And then just that quickly it was gone.

"Remember not to worry," he said softly. "You're in good hands. I'll be prayin' for you."

"I'll pray for you, too," she said, her voice nearly breaking.

"Time to go, boys! We need to catch up with the others," Will called out. "See you in a few months!"

Carissa hurried into the house with Gloria. She couldn't bear to see the men ride out. She stumbled through the door, blinded by her tears, and nearly ran headlong into Marietta Terry.

"Whoa, now. Don't be takin' a tumble." Marietta noticed the tears and smiled. "It's hard to see them go, I know. But the time will pass before you know it. There's so much to keep our hands busy with."

Swallowing hard, Carissa released Gloria and nodded. "I know. I'm hoping to spend a little more time getting to know God and what He wants for me and my future . . . and hers." She nodded as Gloria scampered off down the hall.

Marietta put her hand on Carissa's arm. "I'd be happy to help you in any way I can. You just let me know. We can read the Bible together if you like."

Carissa bit at her lower lip and nodded. She knew better than to try and speak. As the voices of others sounded just outside, she nodded again and hurried to run after Gloria.

Just when she thought her heart couldn't break any more, she was certain she felt a decided rip right through the middle.

That night with the men gone, the house felt empty and quiet. Once the children were in bed, Hannah pulled out some knitting and settled into a chair in the front room. Berto had stoked the fire for them before leaving to head to his own little house, and Carissa relished the warmth. Holding her hands toward the flame, she pondered the day and all that had happened.

"You're awfully quiet tonight," Laura said. "I don't suppose you'd like to talk about it, would you?"

Carissa turned and found the other women watching her as well as Laura. "I'm just tired. I suppose I ought to go on to bed."

"Oh, don't go just yet," Marietta said. "I thought I'd read a little from the Word." She picked up a large leather-bound Bible and opened it.

"Please do," Hannah said before Carissa could comment. "I think something from the Psalms would help."

Marietta nodded. "I had just that in mind."

She flipped through the pages, and Carissa found herself longing to stay and hear the words. Sinking to the nearby settee, Carissa joined her sister and awaited the reading.

"This comes from the sixty-first chapter of the Psalms," Marietta began. " 'Hear my cry, O God; attend unto my prayer. From the end of the earth will I cry unto thee, when my heart is overwhelmed: lead me to the rock that is higher than I. For thou hast been a shelter for me, and a strong tower from the enemy. I will abide in thy tabernacle for ever: I will trust in the covert of thy wings. For thou, O God, hast heard my vows: thou hast given me the heritage of those that fear thy name. Thou wilt prolong the king's life: and his years as many generations. He shall abide before God for ever: O prepare mercy and truth, which may preserve him. So will I sing praise unto thy name for ever, that I may daily perform my vows.'"

"I love that passage," Hannah said, clicking away with her knitting needles. "I love that God is a strong tower from the enemy."

"And the rock that is higher than I," Marietta said. "I think of how precious it is that He covers me with His protection. I marvel that even a strong man like King David could yield himself to know that."

"Is he the king that the verses talk about?" Carissa asked.

Marietta nodded. "Yes, indeed. King David was said to be a man after God's own heart, yet he was human and sinned mightily. Yet God forgave him, and David turned his heart back to God. See, that's one of the things I really like about seeing David's thoughts in the Scriptures: So often I feel like I could have written those very words myself."

Hannah nodded. "I feel that way, too. The psalms aren't all written by King David, but they are full of moments when the writer feels sad or lonely, happy and filled with praise. They reveal that folks have pretty much always known sorrow and happiness—whether they are poor or rich, slave or king."

Carissa thought about this for a moment. "It's good to know that even kings, who are in charge of everything and can have anything they want, get overwhelmed."

Marietta smiled. "Having everything you want can be the most overwhelming of all. I've seen times when the things I loved overwhelmed me, controlling my thoughts and dealings. I remember getting so angry once when one of our cats broke a favorite dish of mine. I started picking up the pieces, ranting about how that cat was never coming back in the house. Ted reminded me that it was just a possession and that the cat certainly hadn't meant to break it. But then he said that even if the cat had intended to break it on purpose, it was up to me to extend grace and let it go. Otherwise, he said, I might as well pick up all the broken pieces and just carry them around with me instead of throwing them away."

Carissa realized that she was always trying to drag around broken pieces. She wondered in silence if she could ever learn to throw away the chards and start afresh. Somehow she doubted such things were possible on her own. She would definitely need the power of something or someone bigger than herself. No doubt that someone was God . . . not a husband or a father for Gloria.

She thought of Christ's sacrifice on the cross—of being broken. Jesus was broken for the sins of the world . . . broken on purpose. Yet the result wasn't the bits and pieces, but rather the Resurrection. The way that Jesus allowed for those broken bits to re-form and lay a path back to God.

Carissa smiled, and for the first time in a long while she felt herself take a spiritual step forward. Perhaps she could even let go of a broken piece or two.

"You look mighty content, Carissa." Marietta's voice was soothing.

"I must say those verses gave me some peace. I'm glad you chose them and glad I listened."

Marietta nodded. "One does have to be willing to receive God's gifts. I think in time you'll begin to see that God is offering a great deal to us—to you. But you have a choice to accept it or not."

11

Riding drag at the rear of the cattle drive was usually reserved for slackers as a means of punishment, but the men were all performing above and beyond the call of duty, so Tyler volunteered to eat trail dust for the day.

They were finally making good progress and were well on their way into Indian country. More than once they'd been approached or shadowed by small groups of "friendlies." Mostly they wanted to trade, but from time to time an Indian woman or old man would lay claim to a steer and swear it to be their own. Tyler did his best to avoid the encounters. Even if the Indians weren't Comanche, he still didn't want any dealings with them. William understood, and though Tyler knew he didn't approve, neither did he condemn.

Most of the time Tyler rode in silence and thought of Carissa and Gloria. The cattle moved at a slow pace, strung out along a two-mile length, interested mainly in grazing. Ted Terry had assured the men from his sickbed that once the animals were used to the schedule, the days would pass more or less in a routine, bar the occasional mishap, accident, or stampede.

At night the animals were exhausted and if possible, the cattle were camped along or near water in an area with plenty of grass. They were secured by four riders who changed shifts every four hours. It worked well, and most of the time the men got decent sleep. Sometimes a few of the animals would wander off only to be rounded up in the morning, but for the most part things had gone smoothly. The farthest Tyler had needed to ride to recover cattle had been about two miles out of the way. And that hadn't been difficult, since the animals had simply followed the water. The horses, however, were a different story. They were more likely to wander and more likely to be stolen. Each night Brandon secured a rope pen for the animals, and camp was made nearby to help keep an eye out for thieves. So far they'd managed to hang on to all of their mounts.

A slight breeze came up from behind him, clearing a bit of the dust and pushing it forward. Tyler paused his horse, pulled off his kerchief, and took a long drink from his canteen. A few of the steers were ambling toward the brush, but otherwise the herd continued forward in a steady progression.

Tyler shook the dust from the kerchief, then poured a bit of water on it before replacing it around his face. He secured the canteen and urged the horse forward to catch up to the steers that had wandered from the rest of the herd. Tyler maneuvered his horse, rounding up the animals much like a parent seeing to wayward children.

Around noon they rested near a large stream of water.

Andy and Newt took horses to Brandon to be changed out, while Tyler and William consulted their map.

"I had one of the boys scout ahead," William said, pointing to a position on the map. "He says we're just east of Fort Arbuckle—Chickasaw country. Said the fort is full of Buffalo Soldiers."

"Blacks?" Tyler asked, knowing the term.

William nodded. "Phil Sheridan uses the fort for his main supply center. Now that he's heading up the Indian campaigns, he stores a great deal of grain and hay there, as well as other provisions."

"Are we heading to the fort?" Tyler asked.

William shook his head and smiled. "Not on your life. I wouldn't want you former Rebs startin' up the war again. I don't know if the general is in the fort or not, but some of our boys aren't too fond of him. I don't want to see trouble—especially when we've got so many miles ahead of us."

Tyler nodded. "So where are we headed now?"

"Up the Washita for a spell. I figure if we push hard and take advantage of the good weather, we can camp tonight maybe no more than five miles out from Cherokee Town. There's a good trading post there, and if we need to pick up provisions, we can trade a steer."

"Sounds good to me. You gonna let Brandon know?" Tyler asked.

"I will. Best grab some corn fritters and ham for the road. I don't intend for us to stop longer than to feed and change out the horses. I'll be sending Osage on ahead with the wagon as soon as he gets you boys fed."

Tyler nodded and made his way to the chuck wagon while Will rolled up the map. Osage handed out food to a couple of the men who were clearly in a hurry to get back on their way to keep the cattle from roaming too far. Tyler filled his canteen from the water bucket and waited his turn.

Osage grinned at him. "Your pa would be proud of you. You ain't walkin' lopsided or holdin' your backside."

Tyler laughed. "I spent four years in the saddle for the South, if you remember." He took the fritters Osage offered and stuffed them in his coat pocket. Next he took a thick slab of ham and instead of pocketing this, Tyler began to eat it. Driving cattle was hard and tedious work, even when things went well, and Tyler was half starved.

"Hope there's more of this tonight," he said, turning to walk away.

"You bet there will be—along with beans, sourdough biscuits, and a nice hunk of molasses cake in honor of you."

Tyler stopped and threw a gaze back at Osage. "What are you talkin' about?"

"Your birthday." The older man grinned from ear to ear. "Didn't think I'd remember, did ya?"

Shaking his head, Tyler stepped back toward Osage. "We don't need to be celebratin' my birthday. I'd all but forgotten it anyway."

"You gonna be selfish and not let these boys enjoy some of my Dutch oven molasses cake?"

Tyler laughed and shook his head again. "Well, when you put it that way, I can hardly refuse. After all, I'm sure you'd let it be known that I was to blame."

"You bet I would," Osage replied.

"Guess we'll be havin' cake, then," Tyler said, resuming his retreat. He saw Andy coming with his fresh mount. "Thanks for that, Andy. I appreciate the help."

"No problem. Will says I gotta be good at doin' everything." He grinned and pushed back his white-blond hair. Dirt smears could be found on his face and dust on his clothes, but Andy's hair seemed as bright as always.

"You lose your hat?" Tyler asked, taking the reins.

Andy shook his head. "Just lettin' my head breathe—leastwise that's what Newt calls it." He grinned. "You see him slidin' before we left the ranch?"

Tyler nodded. "He seems pretty good at it."

Andy laughed. "Yup. He's just waitin' for that moment when he can slide under his first steer."

Tyler laughed and mounted. "I wouldn't let your head breathe too much, Andy. Not if Newt is any sign of what happens." He maneuvered the fresh horse on toward the back of the herd, gnawing off pieces of ham as he went. He couldn't believe his birthday had come again; leave it to Osage to remember. He was thirty-three.

He thought of Carissa and wondered if she had any idea it was his birthday. It was silly, he supposed. She hardly spoke two words to him when he left and probably wasn't thinking about him at all.

Thirty-three . . . and what did he have to show for it? No wife or child. No home. No business of his own. He'd certainly turned out to be a disappointment. He frowned. A part of him wanted to blame the Comanche, but that really didn't seem right. He could certainly hold them responsible for some of his woes, but the war had robbed him, as well. And of course, there were his own mistakes. . . .

Thirty-three. Wasn't that the age of Jesus when He died for the world and rose again? Jesus had a ministry and purpose that was clearly defined and fulfilled by the time He was Tyler's age. It made Tyler's own situation even more discouraging—even though Jesus was the Son of God, and Tyler was just the son of a man killed by Comanche.

"Well, nothin' gained by mullin' over that," he said, shaking his head. He took another bite of food and encouraged his mount to a trot. Tonight he'd eat his cake and pretend to be happy.

∼

The weeks passed more quickly than Carissa could have imagined, and before she knew it the calendar revealed the first of June. Ted recovered with surprising speed, so he and Marietta returned to their ranch, leaving the Barnett house rather empty without their stories and laughter. Carissa had enjoyed the tales told by both Ted and Marietta and was sorry to see them go.

Marietta promised they would return on Sundays if possible, and that Ted would offer short sermons. She had emphasized *short*, as the man was given to being rather longwinded when speaking on God's Word.

Laura was growing quite large in her pregnancy, and Hannah was finally starting to show just a bit. Carissa found herself almost jealous, as she remembered what it was like to marvel at the knowledge of a child growing within her. She wondered if she'd ever know that feeling again.

Word arrived to the Barnett ranch that the army had driven the Comanche and Kiowa far to the north and west. Everyone seemed to relax and breathe a bit easier with the news. The strain of worrying about an attack had been uppermost on everyone's minds, despite Hannah's belief that the Comanche would leave them alone.

"I'm glad the army feels they have matters under control," Hannah declared. "I think this would be the perfect time for a trip to town. I know the men didn't want us leaving with the threat of attack, but now that things are fairly secure, I believe we could risk it."

"I definitely want to go," Carissa said, desperately needing the diversion. "It's nearly Gloria's birthday, and I want to get her a present."

"I'll just stay here if it's all the same," Laura said, patting her stomach. Daniel came to pat her as well. "Bee-bee," he said and grinned.

"Yes, that's your baby brother or sister," Laura told him. He patted his own stomach and repeated the word before toddling off.

"Oh dear. I hope he doesn't think that *baby* is the word for stomach," Laura said with a frown.

Hannah laughed. "Even if he does, he'll learn soon enough." She got up from the table. "I'm going to go talk to Berto about the trip to town. He might not be as easily convinced to allow us to go, but I'll do what I can to sweeten the deal by taking him some of his favorite strawberry tarts."

Carissa watched her go, then asked her sister, "Would you mind keeping Gloria here with you?"

Laura shook her head. "Not at all. She keeps Daniel distracted. Besides, I'm sure Hannah will want Marty to stay here and so I'll have her help."

"Can I pick up anything in particular for you?"

"Maybe some more white flannel. I'll need to make more diapers."

Carissa got to her feet. "I'll get a piece of paper and a pencil and we can make a list." She felt a bit excited. "It's been so long since we've been anywhere else that I feel like a child at Christmas." She hurried to retrieve the articles and came back to the table.

"Would you like me to bring you some peppermints, too?"

"Oh, that would be nice. But, really, we probably shouldn't spend the money. We don't know when we can count on more."

"I can always wire the bank in Corpus to send me some here," Carissa offered. "Papa put plenty into my account before leaving."

"No, I wouldn't want you to risk it. Could be if someone thinks we're sitting on a pile of money they might very well try to take it from us."

"Well, I think we can spare enough for peppermints," Carissa said, writing the word down on the paper.

By the time Hannah returned, Carissa had added several other items. "Berto finally agreed," Hannah announced. "He knew I'd just figure a way to go without him if he didn't give in." She smiled in a most self-satisfied way. "He'll come along and so will his brother Diego and a couple of the other men. They want to pick up some supplies, so we'll take the wagon and they'll ride. The rest will stay here."

Carissa stood. "I'm going to go trace Gloria's feet. She's about worn out her shoes, and I'd like to at least order her another pair if they don't have any in stock."

"That sounds like a good idea," Hannah said. "I'll measure Robert, too."

Two and a half hours later they were in Cedar Springs, and Carissa couldn't help but marvel at how busy the little town was. "I didn't know it was so big."

Hannah nodded. "They say it's growing right into Dallas—or the other way around. There's still space between the two, but who can say how long that will last?" She brought the horses to a stop in front of the mercantile and pointed to a sign that read *P&L Dry Goods*. "This used to be Pritchard's Mercantile, but he lost it shortly after the war ended. Some sort of gambling thing," Hannah said, stepping down from the wagon with Berto's help.

Carissa allowed the man to assist her, as well. "Who owns it now?" she asked.

"Some businessmen from Dallas. One of the men put his brother in charge. His name is Thomas Parsons. He and his family have done well with the place—doubled the size and offered a lot better selection than we could get during the war." Hannah turned to Berto. "Would you mind picking up the mail for us?"

"Sí. I get it, then I come and load the wagon for you."

"That won't be necessary. I'm sure we can get the clerk to do it for us," Hannah replied.

Glancing down the street, Carissa spied a hotel and café, a bank, several saloons, and a bevy of other shops. It wasn't Corpus, but it would do.

"Come on with me. I'll introduce you to Thomas and his wife, Betty."

Hannah led the way into the store, and Carissa followed behind, glancing quickly at her list. Compared to the bright outdoors, the store was much darker inside, but Carissa's eyes quickly adjusted and she saw that the shelves were well stocked, something rather unusual in the postwar South.

"Carissa, this is Mrs. Betty Parsons," Hannah introduced from across the room.

Crossing to the counter, Carissa smiled. "Pleased to meet you, Mrs. Parsons. I'm Carissa Lowe."

"Have you moved to the area recently? I don't recall seeing you before. Who are your people?"

Betty Parsons was a short, rather round woman who had a pleasant smile and faded blue eyes. "I am rather new," Carissa said. "I came from Corpus Christi to stay for a time with my sister and brother-in-law. Perhaps you know Brandon and Laura Reid?"

"I do. Sold them a pair of shoes for their little one. I heard they had a widowed sister and her child comin' to stay. That must be you. Where's your little one?"

"She stayed back at the ranch with my sister, Laura," Carissa replied.

"They're staying with us while the men are on the drive," Hannah offered.

The bell over the door rang as Ava Lambert entered the store. She was dressed in a bright pink-and-orange-striped gown that was unlike most of the dresses Carissa had seen in Corpus Christi. This gown wasn't nearly as full in the skirt, and it was cut rather low for a day dress. Not only that, but Carissa noted the woman wore quite a bit of face paint.

"Good morning, all," she said, sweeping across the room to join them at the counter. "Goodness, but it seems forever since I saw you ladies last."

Hannah smiled. "I risked a breakout from our little prison."

"Good for you," Ava said, beaming. She turned to Carissa. "And how are you, Mrs. Lowe? I certainly hope well—your daughter, too."

Carissa stiffened. "We're fine, thank you." She looked to Mrs. Parsons. "I have measurements here for my daughter. I need a new pair of shoes for her. And my nephew is already outgrowing that pair you sold them. Here are his measurements, too."

"Oh, come along this way. I'll see what we have in store. Just got some lovely high-top brown leather boots for children. You might like them."

Following Mrs. Parsons, Carissa didn't even excuse herself. She knew she was being rude, but seeing Ava Lambert again rattled her. She tried to forget about the woman as she examined the boots for Gloria. She chose a pair and then went to explore the other areas of the store, hoping Ava had already departed. She wasn't so fortunate, however.

"I wonder if you've heard from Tyler and the others," Ava asked. "Have you picked up your mail yet?"

Carissa turned to face the woman. "No. We came here first, and Hannah sent Berto to get the mail." She tried hard to remain civil, but talking to Ava Lambert was the last thing she wanted to be doing.

"I do miss that man. He and his boys were faithful customers."

Without meaning to reveal her shock, Carissa's eyes widened. "Customers?" Goodness, was this woman a prostitute?

Ava laughed, almost seeming to read Carissa's mind. "Don't look so shocked. I own the supper club on the south side of town. Tyler and his friends were always coming there to see me. Tyler enjoyed himself there a great deal . . . and I enjoyed his being there."

"How nice," Carissa replied, trying to keep a civil tongue.

"I do a show there—singing and such," Ava continued. "Tyler loves to hear me sing. He said he's never heard anything like it."

Carissa wanted to remark that such a comment might not be a compliment, but she held her tongue.

"I think he's the finest man west of the Mississippi," Ava said in a rather coy manner.

If Carissa didn't know better she would have thought the woman was baiting her. Uncomfortable with the entire matter, Carissa moved to one side. "If you'll excuse me, I need to conclude my shopping."

"Personally, I think he'll make a great husband."

Her words felt like a knife in her back. Carissa whirled around to find Hannah approaching, and she hastily swallowed back a retort that had very nearly escaped her lips. Ava Lambert was positively brazen.

"Are you finished here?" Hannah asked. "I thought we might go over to the café to have some lunch before we head back. I promised Berto we wouldn't dally too long."

"I am most definitely ready to leave," Carissa said. "Just let me settle the bill."

Still unable to get Ava's words out of her mind, Carissa mulled over the idea that this woman appealed to Tyler. Ava was so much more worldly and refined than Carissa could ever be. Her very manner radiated knowledge and experience.

"Mrs. Barnett, I heard you were in town and was on my way to find you," a man said, approaching. He tipped his hat briefly.

Carissa saw he wore a badge and for a moment feared some bad news had come about the men. She braced herself for the worst.

"Afternoon, Sheriff," Hannah said. She nodded to Carissa. "This is Mrs. Lowe. She's staying at my place with her sister and their children while the men are on the trail. I believe William mentioned that so you could keep an eye out for their farm."

He tipped his hat again. "Yes, ma'am. Pleased to meet

you." He looked back to Hannah. "I hate to be the bearer of bad news, but you need to know something."

Carissa felt her heart in her throat. She prayed silently, begging God to have mercy on the men—particularly Tyler. She was so engrossed in prayer, in fact, that she very nearly missed the sheriff's announcement.

"Herbert Lockhart escaped from prison. He had help, but they don't know who."

Hannah had paled. "Herbert Lockhart escaped? The man killed my father and threatened to kill my brother and sister, as well as me. And now he's just out there—free?" She looked to Carissa. "I was wrong to come here. We should go home."

That was just fine with Carissa, who was more than ready to leave Cedar Springs in order to avoid encountering Ava Lambert again. But the fear in Hannah's voice revealed the urgency of the news she'd been told. Carissa realized this Lockhart man was a very real threat.

"We will keep an eye out and let you know if we hear anything," the sheriff said. "I seriously doubt he'll come this way. He's too well known. My guess is he'll head west—probably California."

Hannah nodded but said nothing more. She took hold of Carissa's arm and started for the wagon. She spied Berto and waved him over. He came at a trot, the mail tucked under his arm.

"Sí, Miss Hannah?"

"We need to go back to the ranch—now. The sheriff just told me that Herbert Lockhart has escaped prison."

Berto frowned and nodded. He handed her the mail. "I get the men." He hurried off toward a saloon.

"Who is this man—this Herbert Lockhart?" Carissa asked

as Hannah climbed into the wagon. She settled in beside the woman, only to notice that Hannah's hands were trembling. Carissa had never known Hannah to be afraid of anything. She reached out and squeezed Hannah's arm.

"He used to be my father's partner." Her words were matter-of-fact. "Herbert Lockhart killed my father."

"But why?" Carissa asked, as if that mattered.

Hannah fixed her with a frightened look, and Carissa could see that most of the color was gone from her face. "Lockhart wanted my father's fortune. He had my father killed and stole what assets they had in the business together. Then he decided to try to force me to marry him so that he could claim the rest of it." She shook her head and tears came to her eyes. "He very nearly succeeded. He threatened Marty and Andy if I didn't cooperate. William saved us from him . . . and I had hoped he would rot in jail."

Her words were a surprise to Carissa. Hannah never had anything but a kind comment for most everyone. "I think the sheriff surely must be right. Lockhart would be a fool to come here. If he's gone to all the trouble to escape prison, most likely he will flee the area so that they won't recapture him."

Hannah held her gaze for a moment. "I know you are probably right, but it's just so disturbing. I had hoped we'd seen the last of him. Now I just want to get back to the ranch and make sure that Marty and Robert are all right."

Carissa patted Hannah's arm. She wished she could say something to offer more comfort. Berto and the other men were approaching now, and Carissa watched as they hurriedly mounted their horses and gave Hannah a nod.

Once they were well on the road and headed back to the ranch, Carissa thought about Ava again and wondered if

Hannah had any insight. "I know this might seem like poor timing," she began, "but I wonder what you know about that Ava Lambert woman."

Hannah's gaze never left the road. "All I know is that she owns the supper club and came here from California. I don't know where she's from, however. The boys at the ranch don't go there too often. She charges way too much for a meal, according to Tyler."

"She says he likes it there and goes all the time."

Hannah gave a harsh laugh. "Of course she would. She's convinced everyone likes it there. Frankly, I think Miss Lambert is more than a little fond of herself."

"She seems quite fond of Tyler, too."

For the first time since they'd started home, Hannah looked at Carissa. "I don't think she's any real competition for you. Believe me; Tyler doesn't frequent her place all that often. Most of the time he's been right there at the ranch."

"She plans to marry him," Carissa blurted out.

Hannah frowned. "Well, her plans and his aren't necessarily the same thing. Don't go asking for trouble. Tyler cares about you. I'm sure of that."

"I saw him with her . . . when she came that day to the ranch with the doctor. She was very familiar with him—kept touching him and holding his arm."

"I still don't think you should worry. She's been running her supper club for some time now, and the few times I've known Tyler to go there, I've not heard him say much more than how good the cooking is and that she sings well. He certainly doesn't go on and on about Ava Lambert. Not the way he went on and on about you."

"What?"

Hannah smiled. "Ever since he came back from Corpus Christi I've heard about you."

"Me?"

"Indeed. He talked about how silly and funny you were at first. He said you were quite spoiled, but a real beauty." Hannah seemed to forget about her woes and actually slowed the horses a bit. "Then later, after you came to stay with your sister and Tyler found out about it, he was hard-pressed to keep from talking about you at every meal."

"I can't believe that."

Hannah laughed. "Well, believe it. Like I said, I've never heard him speak more than a few words about Ava's suppers, but I've heard great details about you and Gloria—especially of late. I don't think Ava is any serious concern."

Carissa fell silent and tried to absorb all that Hannah had said. Could it really be that Tyler cared for her and not Ava? By the time they reached the ranch, Carissa had just about convinced herself that her reaction to Ava Lambert had been born out of pure jealousy rather than reality. She'd feared Ava was taking Tyler from her, but Hannah was convinced that wasn't possible.

Upon their return, Hannah reined back on the team and set the brake. She looked to Berto. "Would you take care of the horses and unload?" She jumped down before he could help her and nearly fell.

Berto flew off the horse, but by that time Hannah had righted herself. "I'm fine. Please . . . just take care of everything."

The man nodded and Hannah all but ran for the house. Carissa allowed Berto to help her from the carriage. "Berto, one of my packages has presents for Gloria's birthday. Could you maybe just take it to your house for now and have Juanita hide it? Gloria is always into everything, and I'm afraid she'll find it."

"Sí, I do that. You no worry. Juanita will find a good place to keep it."

Carissa smiled. "Thank you." She turned toward the house and looked over to where she'd seen Tyler and Ava together. She tried to remember every moment and realized that Tyler truly hadn't seemed all that interested in the woman. She drew a deep breath and gazed heavenward, whispering, "Please God, don't let him love Ava Lambert."

※

Tyler knew that if things went well, they would have less than a week left on the trail to get to Abilene, but already he was anxious for the drive to be over. The cattle were restless and tired of the road, as well. They seemed to sense the end of the trip was upon them and like thirsty animals running for the watering hole, they were wont to run and stray.

There had been only a few delays and complications here and there, but even with the nearly perfect trip, they'd managed to lose some forty steers. He supposed it wasn't such a big loss, but having nothing else to compare it with, Tyler could only imagine that representing as much as two hundred dollars, and the thought sickened him.

But it really wasn't about the money so much as the hope it represented. Hope to buy back his ranch. He tossed and turned on his bedroll, finding sleep wouldn't come. By the time his watch came, he was exhausted.

In the distance he heard Newt singing a song he often used to calm the cattle. The distant sound of thunder was stirring the herd. Newt's voice acted as a balm to soothe them.

Tyler smiled. *If I tried to sing to them, they'd stampede for sure.*

Newt's voice filled the air.

> "He turned his face unto the wall—as deadly pangs
> he fell in.
> Adieu! Adieu! Adieu to you all! Adieu to Barbara
> Allen!
> As she was walking o'er the fields—she heard the bell
> a-knellin'
> And every stroke did seem to say, unworthy Barbara
> Allen."

The melody was haunting, and the words tragic. Love unrealized because death stole it away. Love unrealized because of pride. Tyler shook his head and turned his horse to pace back the long line of cattle. Most had calmed, probably due to the singing, but occasionally a bellow rose as if to join in. Tyler saw a flash of lightning far off on the horizon. Maybe the storm would go around them as some of the others had. They'd been more fortunate than others; just the night before they'd caught up with another drive and heard horror stories of storm stampedes. It reminded him of stories his father had told Tyler years and years ago.

Tyler looked heavenward and fixed his gaze on a cluster of stars. He remembered his father pointing out various constellations and telling him myths of old. "I miss you, Pa," he whispered. "If you can see me up there, I sure wish you'd put in a good word for me. Times are hard, and I feel close to failin'. They won't let me have your ranch—our ranch. The ranch we were gonna turn into an empire." He shook his head. Looking back at the cattle, Tyler felt such a wave of sorrow wash over him, he thought he might well break down and cry.

He had failed in so many ways. He'd failed to avenge his father's death, and he'd failed to reclaim the land his father had worked so hard for. How could he even think of Carissa and a life with her when there was so much undone that he needed to do?

They'd come through Indian Territory without any difficulty, but Tyler found he'd had to keep away from the Indians who came to beg food and favors. He knew that he couldn't blame an entire race of people for what a few bad men had done. Still, he felt such a sense of raging anger whenever he set his gaze on an Indian. How was he supposed to offer love and pledge his life to a woman and her child when there was such hatred in his heart?

"God, I need your help," he prayed. "I don't know how to lay this anger down. I don't know how to stop hating."

The storm moved in faster than Tyler had anticipated. Thankfully, William's leg sensed the weather changes and the pain woke him in time to rally the entire gang to get on their horses to keep the herd from stampeding. They forced the cattle to mill in a circle in an effort to hinder them from striking out in a straightforward run. But the lightning was unnerving the beeves and the bawling was intense. The horses, too, were frightened, but Brandon had secured the extra mounts before climbing into the saddle to help the trail drivers.

Tyler was more than a little concerned for Newt and Andy. This was their first experience with a truly anxious herd. Osage had commented on how fortunate they'd been on the trip, but now even he had taken to horseback to help with the herding. The sense of danger seemed to engulf the entire camp.

The wind blew up dust, stinging Tyler's eyes. He pulled his kerchief around his nose and mouth.

"If we can keep them circling," William yelled, riding up alongside Tyler, "I think we'll be okay. We pushed them hard today, and they're awfully tired." Lightning flashed, this time much closer.

"They aren't the only ones. I don't think I slept more than ten minutes." Tyler tightened his grip on the reins as his horse did an agitated side step.

"I think we're in for it," William said, rubbing his right thigh. "Keep alert."

"If you think . . . well . . . if you need to pull Andy out, you could have him watch over the horses. He and Newt aren't used to this, after all."

"I think we're gonna need every hand we got," William replied. Rain began to fall, and he pulled his hat down more firmly. "I'd best check on the others."

Tyler could hear the tension in his tone. He knew Will would rather put Andy someplace safe. It wouldn't serve any of them to be worrying about the boys. Longhorn cattle by nature could be more than a little cantankerous when disturbed, and while both Andy and Newt had served well on the drive, Tyler knew this would truly prove their mettle.

The storm hit in full force some minutes later. The wind was intense and the rain pummeled them with huge drops and marble-sized hail. Tyler was grateful for the slicker he'd donned, but he could still feel the sting of the ice pellets.

The cattle weren't willing to be contained in the circle, and it wasn't long before a large number broke off to run wild. Chaos soon erupted. In the predawn, several hundred longhorns stampeded out across the open prairie with several riders close behind them. Tyler decided to stay with the milling herd and see if they couldn't keep the remaining animals circling. They could always round up the strays tomorrow. Tyler whistled and called loudly, uncertain that the cattle could even hear his efforts. He also prayed, knowing that God could hear, even if the beeves couldn't.

The trees along the river seemed to bend in half at one point, and it was during this same time that Tyler very nearly lost control of his horse. The gelding reared when one of the longhorns came too close and the steer's horn ripped across the side of the horse's neck. Tyler saw blood and could only hope the injury wasn't serious. He worked to calm his mount. The force of the rain was making the ground thick with mud. They'd be lucky if they weren't mired down here for days to come at this rate.

"Of course we have to make it through this storm first," Tyler said aloud, knowing that no one could hear him above the din.

An eternity seemed to pass before the wind and the animals calmed. Gradually the storm moved off to the northeast, and the herd slowed its pace. Rumbles of thunder and flashes of lightning could be heard and seen in the distance, but by this time the remaining herd was exhausted from the ordeal and seemed inclined to settle down. Tyler wondered how the others were doing with the stampeding animals. It wasn't until William came in search of Andy that he realized who had gone after the beasts.

"You mean to tell me Andy and Newt both went off with those beeves?" Tyler questioned. "Are you sure they aren't here?"

"I've checked everywhere else. They're gone, and so are Grubbs and Sidley."

"They're good men," Tyler said. "They'll know what to do."

William looked grim in the new dawn light. "But Andy and Newt won't."

Tyler followed William as he headed in the direction the stampeding cattle had fled. He knew better than to try to offer words of comfort. Andy was like a son to Will, and Will would never forgive himself if something happened to the boy.

They rode for at least three and a half miles before catching sight of a few strays. Tyler could make out a couple dozen beeves loitering by the creek bank. William motioned them on, and Tyler knew they'd worry about rounding up the animals on the way back. It was nearly another three miles before they located the bulk of the herd. The animals were still agitated, but Grubbs and Sidley were doing their best to round them up. The only saving grace had been that the animals had headed themselves into the rocky ravines near the river and were slowed by the landscape.

"You boys seen Andy and Newt?" William called out.

Grubbs turned and lowered his kerchief. "Ain't seen nobody else till you came along. These have gotta be the meanest bunch of steaks I ever worked with."

Tyler nodded and rode forward. "The boys came after the stampede or else got caught up in it. We need to find them."

"The herd split again after it got up this far," Sidley said. "We were just getting this bunch together, but I noticed a ways back that a bunch went down toward that canyon area by the river. Could be the boys went thataway."

William nodded and without another word reined his mount hard to the left and headed off in the direction Sidley pointed to. Tyler followed, knowing that if the boys were left to themselves, it could be they'd find one or both of them injured.

He caught up to William but said nothing. They soon found the trail Sidley was talking about, and it looked as if quite a few head had come this way. The trail wound into a hilly area of rocky ledges and boulder-strewn paths. Not far away the river twisted along its course.

Tyler stopped and looked around. He could hear the sound of cattle lowing. "They gotta be just down by the river," he told William.

Nodding, William urged his mount forward, and silence descended between them.

They rode along the rocky path, knowing that the cattle had probably gotten themselves quartered off in one of the small canyons. Perhaps the boys had followed along just as they were doing now and were keeping the cattle under control until someone else came to assist them. But somehow Tyler doubted that.

The walls of rock closed in a bit, narrowing the trail. The cattle couldn't have passed through here more than eight or so abreast, Tyler surmised. They wouldn't have come this way under normal circumstances, but at the height of the storm the animals wouldn't exactly have been doing anything that resembled normal.

The floor of the canyon was covered in about an inch or so of water in the lowest areas. Tyler studied the limestone walls and scrub for any sign of the boys. If they came this way, there would surely be something. It wasn't long before his efforts were rewarded.

"Look there," he called out and pointed. "It's Andy's hat." He jumped from his horse's back and sloshed through the muddy water to retrieve the piece. "They did come this way."

William took the hat and looked it over. "I don't see any blood."

"It probably just blew off. At least we know we're heading the right way," Tyler declared and remounted.

They pressed forward and had gone no more than another fifty yards when they heard the distinct sound of cattle and someone calling out.

"I'll throw you down my rope!" the voice called.

"That's Newt!" William said, giving the horse a touch of spur.

Tyler followed after him, and as they rounded the bend, they came face-to-face with the problem at hand. Newt stood atop the rocky ledge overlooking about a hundred head of longhorn. Andy was nowhere to be seen.

William pushed back his hat and called to the young man. "Newt! Where's Andy?"

Newt didn't seem to hear. "Andy, I'm gonna tie this off and come down for you."

At this, William's face paled a bit. "Newt! Where's Andy?"

But Newt had disappeared behind a rock and still didn't appear to hear. William looked at Tyler and then at the restless herd. A rather large steer came directly at them as if to challenge their approach.

"Yah! Yah!" Tyler called out, positioning himself between the steer and the opening. The animal stopped and sized up this new obstacle. For a moment Tyler thought the beast would charge him, but instead the longhorn turned and acted as though he had no interest whatsoever in the two men.

"I've got to help Newt," William said, climbing off his horse. He handed Tyler the reins. "I'm going up there."

Tyler knew better than to argue. "I'll tie off the horses and join you."

He secured the reins around a couple of rocks, despite

both horses having been trained to stand when the reins were dropped. There was no sense in risking the animals getting spooked by the steers. Tyler grabbed his rope and noticed that despite his bad leg, William was already halfway up the rocky ravine.

The two men climbed about fifteen feet before the ground leveled out again for a short ways. The limestone face gave them easy handholds as the ledge disappeared and they were forced once again to climb. Tyler could hear Newt calling to Andy.

"I'm almost there. Don't move or you'll be trampled to death."

William and Tyler exchanged a look and picked up the pace. They made it to the top and turned to look down on the cattle. Tyler spied the rope before William and followed it to the edge of the rock wall. "There!" he called and William hurried to join him.

Down below, in the middle of the agitated herd, Newt edged off the rock and maneuvered . . . across the tops of the steers. Will's mouth dropped open about the same time Tyler's did. They watched in disbelief as the young man finally jumped from the back of a longhorn and disappeared into the herd.

"Well, I think I've seen just about everything now," Tyler said, shaking his head.

Will went to where the rope was and called down. "Newt? You hear me?"

"I hear you, Mr. Barnett. I've got Andy. He's hurt, but he's okay. I don't think he can climb back up, though."

"I'll come down and get him. Tyler's here, too, and he can help pull us back up. You secure the rope around Andy, and I'll be there as soon as I can."

"You gonna walk on the backs of the steers, Will?" Tyler asked with a cocky smile.

Will shook his head in wonder of the feat. "Not me." He started down the side of the ravine, rope in hand. Tyler watched as William maneuvered through the now calmer steers. They were none too happy to have people around them, but as if divinely appointed, they all but parted as Will made his way along the canyon floor.

Tyler held his breath as he watched William lift Andy. The boy looked unconscious. At least Tyler prayed it was just that and not that the boy was dead. There was no telling what had happened, but what mattered now was that they needed to get Andy and Newt to safety.

William slung Andy over his shoulder, then began climbing. Hand over hand on the rope, he walked up the side while Tyler pulled. Before too long, the top of Will's head was at Tyler's feet.

"Here, give me Andy," Tyler said, flattening out on his belly. He grabbed the back of the boy's shirt and pulled.

Will held fast to the side of the rock while Tyler pried Andy loose and edged him up. The jostling managed to send a shower of rock down on the longhorn, however, and set the animals off once again in agitation.

"Newt!" William called out. "Watch out."

Tyler had no sooner got Andy onto the top of the rock when William began to lose his hold on the crumbling rock. In a flash, Tyler grabbed the rope and pulled William up over the edge.

Neither men paused to draw a breath but turned to see if they could spot Newt in the midst of the cattle. Most of the steers were heading toward the narrow canyon opening rather than waiting around in the closure. This made it easier to spy Newt, who was penned between the rock and several mean-looking animals.

"Newt, get out of there!" Will hollered down.

Tyler didn't know what William expected the boy to do. "I could go down there and fire a shot. It might get them running toward the opening."

"It might not," William said, shaking his head.

Newt glanced around as if to assess his situation. The steer closest to him began to lower his head as if to charge. To the boy's right were a couple of animals about twelve feet away who seemed uninterested in the entire matter and chose instead to butt heads with a couple of other steers. Tyler could see that beyond the first set of animals the edge abruptly cut and angled down into the river. Apparently Newt saw it too, because without warning he took off at a dead run, hit the dirt and slid under not one steer, but two, and disappeared over the ledge.

Tyler didn't wait to see the results. He jumped up and ran across the rock to see where Newt had ended up. There below, Tyler found the young man swimming to the edge of the river, fighting the strong current. Tyler quickly took up the rope he'd brought and threw one end down to Newt.

"Grab the rope, Newt," he called.

Newt seemed far more interested in fighting for his life, but as the current brought the rope closer, he finally grabbed on to it. Tyler strained every muscle he had left to hoist the young man to the edge of the river. Once Newt was back on land, Tyler breathed a sigh of relief.

"Just stay put. I'll be down to help you in a minute," Tyler instructed.

Coughing and sputtering, Newt fell onto his back. "I ain't . . . goin' . . . nowhere."

∽

"It looks like Judge Peevy is here again," Hannah said, glancing out the window. It had been raining off and on all day, so to see a visitor was quite a surprise.

She opened the door and ushered the man into the house. "Goodness, come in, Judge. Let me take that wet coat and get you a towel to dry off with."

"Much obliged, Mrs. Barnett. Much obliged." Judge Peevy slipped out of the coat and hat and handed them quite willingly to Hannah.

Carissa got to her feet. "I'll get you a cup of hot coffee."

"That sounds really good. Might I trouble you to put a couple of spoonfuls of sugar in it?"

Carissa smiled. "Of course." She put aside her sewing and hurried into the kitchen. Juanita had apparently heard the conversation and was already pouring the coffee.

"Thank you," Carissa said, taking the cup and saucer. She added the sugar and hurried back to the room as Hannah handed the towel to the judge.

"Come sit over here," Hannah instructed, leading the judge to William's favorite leather chair. "What in the world brings you out on a day like this?"

The judge settled into his seat and dabbed the towel to his face and shirt. "It wasn't like this when I left Cedar Springs. Just a few odd sprinkles—but certainly nothing like this downpour."

Carissa stepped forward with the coffee and handed him the cup and saucer. The older man smiled. "Thank you. I must say the Southern hospitality here beats anything in the North."

"Have you been north, Judge?" Hannah asked.

"I have. I'm afraid it did me little good. I went to see some people in Washington."

"Oh, goodness," Hannah said, shaking her head. "I had no idea you'd been gone. When did you get back?"

"I've been home only two days. I had to come right away and give Mr. Atherton the news myself."

Carissa felt her stomach flip. "What news?" she asked before Hannah could speak.

The man sipped his coffee and smiled. "Very good brew. Thank you again."

"Judge Peevy," Hannah interjected. "What news did you bring?"

He frowned. "Are the boys back from the trail drive?"

"No. They won't be for another few weeks," Hannah replied. "I presume this is about the Atherton ranch."

The judge nodded. "It is. I'm afraid the news will not be to your liking. The decision has been made to continue the negative example to those who fought against the North. The ranch is lost to Tyler."

"No!" Carissa declared. "They can't do that."

The older man nodded. "I'm afraid they can. In fact, it will become part of several parcels put up for new ownership."

"Then we'll simply buy it," Hannah declared. "William has already offered to do this."

"I'm afraid there are some restrictions that will prohibit William from taking that action. You see, these tracts of land are to be made into homesteads. The plan is to encourage people to move west. The group in charge is trying to cultivate interest from those in the North and East. They want to find Northern families in particular."

"How is any of this legal?" Laura asked.

The judge gave a harsh laugh. "I've seen all manner of wrong called legal since the war ended and those radicals took over, Mrs. Reid. At this point, I'm afraid there's nothing more that can be done."

"Tyler will be heartbroken. This is beyond belief," Hannah said, shaking her head.

Carissa sat down and tried to organize her thoughts. She had long reasoned that she might take up a homestead, so maybe now was the time. "Judge Peevy, can anyone apply for these new homesteads, or must they have residence in the North?"

"I believe that is their hope, but not a solid requirement. Why, do you know someone who might wish to homestead?"

She nodded. "I do." She glanced at Laura before looking back at the judge and smiling. "I would like to homestead. I wasn't a Southern sympathizer, although my husband fought for the South. However, I am a widow with a child and would like to make a new life for myself and my daughter."

"That should work, shouldn't it?" Hannah questioned.

"Our uncle lives in Chicago," Laura interjected. "We could even make the application through him—at least through his address. Might that not help?"

The judge considered this for a moment and drank his coffee. Carissa wanted to scream at the man and demand an answer, but she waited in ladylike patience. Finally he put the cup on the saucer.

"I believe you ladies may have something." He nodded thoughtfully. "In fact, I see no reason this young widow should not be allowed to strike out on her own. She has a child to provide for, after all." He smiled. "Let me see what I can do."

"He walked on the backs of those steers?" Sidley questioned in disbelief.

"More like ran," Tyler interjected.

William nodded. "If I hadn't seen it with my own eyes, I wouldn't have believed it, either. We came up on them to find Newt acting like he was crossing a bridge, only this one was made of cattle."

Osage slapped his leg. "Well, if that don't beat all."

Newt looked up in confusion. "Couldn't get 'em to move out of my way to walk through 'em. I only did what seemed reasonable."

"Just like with the steer slidin'," Tyler said with a grin.

"Saved my life," Newt said, nodding most enthusiastically.

One of the trail drivers pushed back his hat and eyed Tyler. "What's he talkin' about? Ain't he figured out that we was just funning with him?"

"No need to think that your intentions were other than

proper trainin'," Tyler declared. "We saw Newt slide under two steers. Saved him from being gored to death by a particularly mean piece of work that had in mind to charge."

The men gathered round the fire looked at Newt with new respect. Sidley posed the question on everyone's mind. "How'd you do it?"

Newt grinned. "Just like Andy showed me." He looked at the boy who was seated beside William. "I saw that my only way out was under them beasts, so I hit the dirt runnin' and gave a good slide just as I reached the side of the first steer."

"And they just stood there?" Grubbs asked, shaking his head. He looked to Tyler. "He tellin' it true, Lieutenant . . . I mean, boss?"

"He's tellin' the truth, Grubbs. I saw it with my own eyes. Slid right under the two of them and off the ledge into the river below."

"Steer slidin' saved my life," Newt said. He took a long drink of coffee and smiled. "I'm sure glad you fellas taught me."

"But that weren't nothin' but a joke," one of William's men said. "Ain't no such thing as steer slidin'."

Newt's expression turned puzzled. "Whatcha mean?"

Tyler laughed. "Ain't no sense in tellin' him that it was a joke. That joke saved his skin. I figure if anything, this boy needs to be teachin' the rest of you how to run atop the backs of steers."

The men laughed, and Newt relaxed a bit. He looked to Andy. "Sure glad you're gonna be all right. I thought for sure your arm was busted."

Andy nodded. He had a good-sized knot on his forehead and his right eye was turning black, but he was alive. Tyler reached over and barely touched the boy's jaw with his fist.

"You'll have a great story to tell everyone when we get home."

William rolled his eyes to the heavens. "His sister isn't going to think it's so great. I was charged with keeping Andy safe. Hannah thought him too young to be out here, and now—"

"And now she's gonna realize she was wrong," Osage said with a smile. "The boy's just been initiated, that's all. Got his shoulder pulled out of socket and back in, and took a hoof to the head. He'll be just fine."

"Weren't no hoof," Newt announced. "He fell off the ledge. It was something terrible to see."

William put his arm around Andy, careful not to disturb the sling that secured his right arm. "Well, I for one am hoping that the bruises and pains will all be gone by the time we see your sister."

"He can ride in the chuck wagon with me," Osage threw in. "We'll be short a hand, but we're short a few head, as well."

"Speakin' of which, we'd best get some sleep," William announced. "The ground's too wet to move out, but we need to locate the rest of those beeves. I figure we're still missin' about seventy head."

"We'll find 'em, don't you worry," Grubbs spoke up.

Tyler chuckled and tossed the last of his coffee to the ground. "I don't think I'll have any trouble sleepin' tonight. I'm worn out."

"Me too," Newt said, putting his cup aside and yawning. He stood and stretched, only to be surprised when a couple of the men jumped up and lifted him in the air.

"You're the hero of the day," one of them declared. "That deserves special treatment."

They carried Newt off toward his bedroll with the other

men laughing as they went. Tyler feared the men might mean mischief and throw Newt back in the river, but instead they lowered him to his bed and bid him good-night.

Looking at William, Tyler shook his head. "Been a long day, Will."

"Yup, sure has." Will turned to his young brother-in-law and smiled. "I'm proud of you, Andy. You did good."

Andy looked confused. "I fell off the ridge and got hurt. Newt's the one done good."

"You went after the steers," William countered. "You saw to stick to your responsibilities. Yes, it didn't go the way you expected, but you done good all the same. You're gonna make a fine rancher one day."

"If Hannah will let me," Andy said with a grin. "You know she has her heart set on me goin' off to college."

"We'll work on her," Tyler said, laughing. "Will's got a way with her. I'm sure between the lot of us, we can keep her distracted while you grow up. By then you'll be so good at ranchin', she'll know better than to try to send you off."

Yawning, Andy nodded. "I sure hope so. I wanna help Will make a really big spread. Mr. Terry said maybe we could buy out his land one day."

Tyler smiled, but inside he felt the overwhelming pressure of his fears rise. Ranching was his dream, as well, but at this rate he might always be forced to be someone's hand. Or he might very well have to leave Texas. Neither idea appealed.

❧

After days of being mired in the mud, William finally felt it safe to move north again with the cattle. The grass was thinning out considerably due to herds that had already passed ahead of them, and now the cattle were beginning to get restless. They continually wanted to stray to any place that might offer better grazing. Unfortunately, Kansas farmers weren't very happy to share their crops.

"We need to keep them moving. My best guess is we can be in Abilene in a week," William said, looking again at his map.

"Boss, we got riders approaching," Grubbs called.

William straightened up and Tyler got to his feet. There were five men approaching on horseback. When they came close enough, they called out.

"Hello to the camp!"

"Welcome," William said, stepping toward the now stopped riders.

Tyler followed, glad for the gun on his hip when he spied that two of the men were also armed with revolvers. Another quick glance revealed that the other three men had rifles on their saddles.

"What can we do for you?" William asked.

One of the men dismounted. "Name is Bosterman. Hank Bosterman." He extended his hand. "I farm the lands to the north of here. We came to inspect your cattle. We don't want you bringin' in tick fever and infectin' our animals."

"You can look the herd over," William replied, "but you needn't worry. We're not trailing up from southern Texas. We're from up near the Indian Territory. North of Dallas."

"That ain't north of the thirty-sixth parallel," Bosterman said.

William nodded. "True, but we haven't had any tick fever in our area. Our animals are clean."

"You can't prove where you brought these longhorns from." The man narrowed his eyes. "We got laws in this state. We're aiming to have a few more before it's all said and done. You ever seen an animal get sick from tick fever?"

"Can't say I have," William replied.

"Well, it ain't pretty." Bosterman looked across the horizon to where the cattle were feeding. "I've had animals die, and I don't intend to see it happen again."

Tyler wondered if the men on horseback would seriously challenge them or if they were just along for show. He didn't want to risk a problem either way. He and William knew all about the fight of the Northern states for quarantine laws. So far they were few and poorly enforced.

"I understand town's just about three miles to the east," Tyler said. "Is that true?"

"More like five," Bosterman replied. "What of it?"

"I was just thinkin' that if you have telegraph, maybe we could send a wire to Cedar Springs. That's near where we're from. You could ask the sheriff there for verification of who we are and where our animals range. Believe me, mister, we didn't work this hard to raise ticky beeves," Tyler said.

"It'll take a little while to confirm," William said, "but in the meantime you can leave a couple of your men here to look over the herd."

Bosterman looked to the four riders and then back to William. "I suppose if we can verify who you are and where you're from, we could allow you to move on."

William smiled. "Good. I'll ride with you to town and pay for the wire. You can send it so there's no fear that I've somehow tricked you. Good enough?"

Bosterman's stern expression relaxed just a bit. "Guess so."

"Good. Then let's be about it," William replied. "I left a wife who's expecting a baby. Our wrangler did, as well, and we need to get these steers to market." He looked to Tyler. "You let Bosterman's men stay here with you. Feed 'em and see to their comfort."

Tyler nodded. "Sure thing."

Bosterman hesitated for only a moment, then motioned to two men. "Sam. Jake. You stay and look things over."

The two men with pistols nodded and separated from the other two riders. William went for his horse. Tyler extended his hand to Bosterman. "Sure glad we could reach an agreement. Figured to have to fight Indians on the way up, but never figured to fight my own."

The man refused to shake. "You're Southern scum, as far as I'm concerned. Lost a brother in the War Between the States. You ain't my own."

Tyler swallowed hard and pulled back his hand. "Sure sorry you see it that way, mister. I thought the war was over."

"Not for me it ain't." He narrowed his eyes. "Not for a good many of us. You ever lose someone you cared about? Have 'em outright killed?"

Tyler thought of his father and nodded. "I have."

Bosterman considered Tyler for a moment. "Then you know what I'm talkin' about. Ain't easy to let go of a wrong done you—is it?"

The hatred Tyler held against the Comanche threatened to spill over into his anger for this man. He fought back words that would only serve to further aggravate the situation.

"It's not easy," Tyler finally admitted.

By then William had returned. "I'll be back as soon as I can."

Bosterman went to his horse. "We'll both be back."

Tyler and the other men used the time to see to any repairs

they had. The hours passed slowly, and when night came, Tyler felt more than a little concerned that William and the others hadn't returned. Andy, too, was worried.

"You think they'll kill him?" the boy asked Tyler fearfully.

The man Bosterman had called Sam stepped forward and put a hand on the boy's good shoulder. "We ain't killers, boy. We're just lookin' out for our own. Your pa is safe enough."

Andy looked up at the man without fear. In that moment he truly passed from being a boy to a man. "Well, if he ain't, mister, you'll answer to me."

Tyler hoped the man wouldn't laugh or disregard the boy, and to the man's credit he didn't. In fact, he didn't even walk away. He looked Andy in the eye and nodded. "I give you my word, son. Your pa will be safe."

"He's married to my sister," Andy replied. "But I reckon he's the closest thing I got to a pa."

"He seems a good man," Sam said. "You all seem like right good men."

Tyler gave the man a nod. Just then Osage announced supper and the other men who weren't on watch began to gather. Jake came up to join Sam, and both men looked to Tyler as if for an invitation.

"Well, come on then, boys. Osage makes a mighty fine meal." Tyler turned to the gathering of men and let the tension ease away. "Let's pray."

✑

It was nearly noon the next day when William and Bosterman returned. Tyler could see that the two men were talking and even laughing by the time they reached the camp.

Sam and Jake soon rode up from the herd and awaited

instructions. Bosterman motioned them to join him. "Wire came through. These men seem to be who they say they are. We're gonna take a chance and let 'em pass."

"Didn't see any sign of trouble," Jake said. "'Course, them longhorn don't usually seem bothered by the tick fever themselves."

"True enough," Bosterman replied. He looked at Tyler. "I think I owe you an apology. William here tells me he fought for the Union. I never figured to see any Texas boys what fought for the North. I guess I'm a mite touchy on the subject."

Tyler wanted to tell the man that just because Will fought for the Union didn't mean the rest of them hadn't supported the South. He could see the look in William's eyes, however, and held his tongue.

"No hard feelin's," Tyler said. "No hard feelin's."

14

Carissa awoke to the sound of someone crying. At first she thought it was Gloria, but the child slept soundly at her side. It was then she realized someone sounded to be in utter misery. Grabbing her wrap, Carissa hurried to find the source. The moans came louder as Carissa approached Laura's room.

Without knocking, Carissa threw open the door to find Laura writhing in pain. A single lamp burned beside the bed, and Daniel slept restlessly in a small boxed bed on the opposite side of the room.

"What's wrong?" Carissa asked, coming to Laura's side.

"It's . . . the . . . baby," Laura said from behind clenched teeth. Laura's pale, pain-lined face left Carissa little doubt that the situation was serious.

"How long have you been hurting?"

"For a few hours now."

"Why didn't you let someone know?"

165

Laura's forehead beaded with perspiration as she cried out. "It's too early for the baby to come. I was praying it would stop."

Wringing her hands, Carissa shook her head. "What can I do?"

"The baby . . . is coming," Laura said, falling back against her pillow. "You have . . . to . . . help me deliver."

Carissa knew the infant wasn't due for several more weeks. It was way too early, but apparently there was little they could do to stop it. Laura pushed back the covers, and Carissa gave a quick examination of the situation. The baby's head was already visible. Soon the delivery would be complete.

"What's going on?" Hannah asked, coming into the room.

"Laura's having the baby," Carissa said. Just then Laura bore down and the baby slid onto the bed. "Correction. Laura just had a little boy."

"I'll get Juanita to help us. Clear the baby's mouth," Hannah said, now fully awake. She left the room before Carissa could say anything.

The tiny infant didn't move or cry and Carissa feared he'd been stillborn. She took up a towel from the nightstand and gently wrapped the baby as Laura cried.

"He's dead, isn't he?" Laura sobbed.

"I don't know," Carissa said. "He's so small." She didn't want to rub the baby too much for fear she might well rub off his thin skin. She put her finger in the infant's mouth to make sure the throat was clear. The tiny infant drew a shallow breath.

It seemed like forever, but finally Juanita and Hannah returned. Hannah quickly took charge and cut the cord. "Juanita, please fetch some water from the stove. It may still have some warmth."

"Sí, I get it."

The weather had been hot for several weeks, much too hot for a fire in the bedroom fireplace. But Carissa knew that keeping the baby warm would be of the utmost importance. "I'll get a fire going."

"Yes, build it up," Hannah said, continuing to minister care to the infant.

Carissa had just managed to lay the wood when she heard a tiny squeaking sound from the baby. It was like music.

"He's alive?" Laura asked.

"Yes," Hannah said, smiling. Just as quickly she grew serious. "He is small, but I think you may have been farther along than you realized. He seems quite healthy."

Laura nodded. "Let me see him. Please."

Hannah moved closer with the baby. "We must keep him warm. Put him against your skin, and I will go get water. You must lie still and keep warm. Do you understand?"

"I understand."

Carissa hurried to get the fire going. She kept casting a glance over her shoulder to Laura. Her sister seemed to be completely unaware of anyone else in the room. Finally the kindling caught, and Carissa breathed a sigh of relief. She took great care to stoke and build the fire as quickly as possible, all the while praying for her new nephew.

Juanita and Hannah reappeared and over the course of the next hour worked together to clean up Laura and the baby and see to their well-being. It was then Carissa learned Juanita had sent Berto for the doctor.

"He should be here in a few hours," Juanita said. "Until then we do our best. We need to keep this room very warm."

Carissa nodded. "I can keep the fire going. I need to go

for more wood, and I'll have to check on Gloria." By now Daniel was awake and crying for his mother.

Hannah motioned to the door. "I've roused Marty. She'll see to the children, and Pepita is fixing breakfast." Within a matter of moments, Marty appeared to scoop up Daniel.

"Why do babies have to get born so early?"

Hannah laughed. "Because they have to make sure everyone knows they're in charge. Now, Carissa, if you'll sit here with your sister, I'll go get a few things we need."

At first Carissa thought her sister was sleeping, she was lying so still, but Laura quickly opened her eyes at the shift of the mattress.

The two sisters locked gazes, and Carissa could see the fear in Laura's eyes. She reached out and touched Laura's cheek with the back of her fingers. "It will be all right. You'll see."

"He's so small and the delivery is early—even if I was farther along," Laura said, tears filling her eyes. "I want to call him Lucas Brandon. If anything happens to me or to him, you will see to it, won't you?"

"Nothing is going to happen to either of you," Carissa said, still unwilling to believe the worst could happen. "Now focus on keeping your son warm and let us do what we can to make you comfortable."

The hours seemed to stretch for an eternity. Carissa was just dozing in the bedside chair when she heard the unmistakable sound of male voices. For just a moment she dared to hope that the men had returned from the drive, but when the doctor bounded into the room, she knew it was otherwise.

"Seems we have a little fella mighty eager to make his appearance," the doctor said, taking the infant from Laura. "I'll have him back to you as soon as possible." He took the baby to the small table Hannah had put by the fire. On it she placed a small quilt folded and draped to add padding and warmth.

Carissa watched the doctor as he examined the baby. He made several comments to Hannah and Juanita, but didn't seem all that alarmed. He left the baby to the women and came back to examine Laura.

"You both look to be in stable condition, given the experience," the doctor said upon completing his examination.

Carissa let go of her breath, not even realizing that she'd been holding it. She patted Laura's hand. "See there, I told you all would be well."

Laura's voice sounded quite weak. "Will he live?"

The doctor gave her a hint of a smile as he offered her a soothing nod. "I don't see any reason why he shouldn't. He's breathing well and his color is quite good. The important thing will be to get him to eat and to keep him warm. You're fortunate to have him born in the heat of summer. That and keeping him near the fire will both be to his benefit."

"But you can't be sure," Laura said.

"No one can be sure," Carissa interjected. "Remember what you told me about loving? It's a risk, especially since people are bound to die one day."

Laura looked at Carissa and smiled for the first time. "You are right, of course. It seems harder now that I'm on the other side of the issue."

The doctor patted Laura in a fatherly manner. "There, now. You need to rest. You're gonna need your strength to see this little one through. I'll be back tomorrow."

"Why don't you stay with us, Dr. Sutton?" Hannah questioned, coming into the room with a small wooden box.

"I can't. I have another couple of patients to visit. I'll get back out here first thing in the morning if all goes well. If you need me before then, just send Berto again, and I'll come as soon as I can. But, frankly, there isn't a great deal I can do at this point." He looked at Laura and then back to Hannah and Carissa. "These things are out of our hands."

"What we can do is place the babe safely in God's hands," Hannah said. "Carissa, come help me. We're going to make something for the baby."

"His name is Lucas," Carissa said. "Laura named him Lucas."

Hannah smiled. "I like that name, Laura. It's strong."

Laura gave a brief nod. "Lucas Brandon Reid."

The doctor took his leave, and Juanita went to tend Laura while Carissa held her new nephew. He couldn't have weighed more than five pounds. He was so very small and looked rather like a wizened old man. Fuzzy hair like that of a peach covered his body, and on his head were fine wisps of brown hair.

"I'm going to create a warming bed for him," Hannah said, taking the quilt from the table and replacing it with the box. "I'll be right back," she told Carissa.

It was hard to figure what Hannah was up to, but when she returned with a tray of stones, Carissa was even more confused. "I heated these in the oven," Hannah said. "I'm going to put them around the sides of the box and then we'll put the quilt over that. We'll fix it so that the warmth heats the baby . . . Lucas . . . but doesn't burn him."

"That's brilliant," Carissa said, nodding her approval.

Within a moment, Hannah had it all arranged. She put her hand into the box and felt all around. "Perfect. Now we have a nice warm bed for Lucas."

Carissa gently placed the baby in the box, and Hannah

quickly tucked the quilt around him. Glancing at the fire, Carissa went to add another couple of logs. She would sit and keep the fire all day and night for as long as it took. She would do whatever was required, if it meant helping keep Lucas alive for Laura.

"Let's check him frequently to make sure he's not too warm," Hannah said, her brows knitting together. "I don't know how warm would be too warm, but hopefully we'll be able to tell."

The next twenty-four hours proved to be good ones for the baby. He managed to suckle, and though Laura's milk seemed slow in coming, Lucas continued to fight. By the third day, however, it was obvious that Laura wasn't doing well. She seemed to weaken by the hour and a fever started that had Juanita and Hannah quite worried.

"We need to bind her breasts and dry up her milk," Juanita told Hannah and Carissa. "It is taking her strength. We must do this to help her be stronger."

"But what about Lucas?"

"We feed him canned milk," Juanita replied.

"Juanita is right," Hannah replied. "I've seen this before . . . when Marty was born. . . ." She fell silent.

Carissa looked at the two women in grave worry. "She can't die. Daniel and Lucas need her. Brandon needs her." She glanced at her sister's pale, lifeless body. "I need her."

Dr. Sutton finally arrived on the fourth day, and the prognosis wasn't good. Carissa could scarcely believe him as he shook his head and closed his bag. "It's childbed fever. Happens all the time, and we can't really say why. There's little I can do."

"There has to be something!" Carissa said, refusing to give up.

The doctor gave her a sympathetic glance. "You can work to get her fever down. Get fluids in her."

"What about willow-bark tea?" Hannah asked.

"No, it will increase her bleeding. The risk is too great," Dr. Sutton replied.

The baby began to cry, and Carissa hurried to pick him up. "He's hungry—probably starving."

The doctor frowned. "If the mother dies, he will most likely die, too. Frankly, that's often a blessing. Awfully hard for others to take care of a baby without a mother to feed it."

"But it can be done," Hannah said firmly. "I've done it before with Marty."

"They aren't going to die," Carissa said, clutching Lucas closer. "I won't let them." A sob broke from her throat, and Hannah came to put her arm around her.

"We'll do everything we can," Hannah whispered in her ear.

"Dilute some canned milk and warm it," the doctor suggested as he headed to the door. "Try giving him some of that every hour. If that doesn't work—at least give him some sugar water. You will have to pursue it vigilantly, or he will grow weak from lack of fluids and starve."

The doctor glanced back at Laura's lifeless body. Carissa had never been more frightened. "I can't lose her," Carissa told them. "And she won't live if this baby doesn't, so I will do whatever I can to see this through."

Dr. Sutton nodded. "I know you will, Mrs. Lowe. I know you will."

⸎

"It's not the news you want to hear," Ted Terry said, "but that's the truth of it."

Hannah sat at the head of the table, and Carissa had joined them for the meal while Juanita cared for Lucas and Laura. The Terrys had come with news of another Indian attack.

"The Cheyenne are working with the Comanche and Kiowa. It's been quite bad up and down the plains. The sheriff told me they just learned that there was a massacre of several families in the panhandle area."

"Are you going to stay at your ranch or will you join us here?" Hannah asked.

"For now we'll go back and do our best to defend the place."

"But why? You needn't risk your lives. Just come here and stay with us," Hannah insisted. "We'll be stronger together, and you know that the Comanche have long respected our ranch."

"I'll take it under advisement," Ted promised. He glanced at Marietta, who looked none too happy. "For now, however, I have to go back and do what I can to secure what's mine."

"Well, at least eat your fill before you go. I wouldn't want to send you off on an empty stomach."

Ted laughed. "No chance of that. I know my way to the trough."

Carissa felt Marietta's hand on her arm and startled. "I'm sorry. Did you say something?"

Marietta nodded. "I wondered how your sister was doing. Hannah said she's been quite ill."

"She is and I must say I'm so frightened. She's desperately weak, and it's hard to get any kind of fluids into her, but the doctor says that's critical." She felt such a sense of dread. "I don't know if I could bear it should Laura . . ."

"Hush, now," Marietta told her. "You gain nothing by fretting over the matter. Give it to the Lord and let Him work."

Carissa felt so hopeless. "I'm trying. I'm really trying."

"That's all the Lord asks of us. Now, you need to eat more than that to keep up your strength. And where is that little gal of yours? I understand she's had a birthday and turned two."

"She seems more like four or five," Hannah interjected. "I've never seen anyone so smart and active. That child is everywhere at once and talks a blue streak."

"It's true," Carissa replied. "But as for where the children are—they ate earlier and now Marty is putting them down for naps. She has been an absolute godsend. I know we would never have managed without her."

Marietta bobbed her head. "My mother always said that there was never anyone too young to learn how to help. She had me shelling peas when I was just a little one. Life sometimes necessitates we grow up fast and out here—it's a rule."

"I hate seeing them grow up too fast," Hannah said with a sigh. "I've been so worried about Andy. I never wanted him to go on the cattle drive, as you know. I received a message from William once the cattle were safely delivered to Abilene. Apparently everyone is fine, but I won't really rest until they're all back home."

"I'm sure the boys feel the same way," Ted said.

A knock was heard coming from the front door. Being closest to the hall, Carissa jumped to her feet. "I'll get it." She hurried, hoping the doctor had made another return visit. Instead she found Judge Peevy on the other side of the door.

"Well, well. Just the woman I wanted to see."

She smiled. "Is this about the ranch, then?"

He nodded. "It is. Everything has gone quite well. The Atherton ranch will be yours, but not only that—our idea to purchase the piece outright was well received. I gave them your draft and the sale went through. The county will pocket the money, and that seemed to make everyone happy."

She clapped her hands much like Gloria might have. "I'm so happy. This is wonderful news."

"I agree. You do need to know, however, that you are under obligation to live there for five years."

"But I thought . . . I mean we aren't homesteading."

"True, but that was a provision I had to agree to. They also made it clear that you could not sell the land back to Tyler."

"Then what good does it do for me to have it? I've saved the place for nothing."

The judge grinned. "Not exactly. To my way of thinking, you could still manage to get it back into his hands, if say . . . you were to marry him."

Carissa felt her cheeks grow hot. "There's no plan for that."

"Well, I understood that you two were mutually interested in a future together. I'm just saying that there's nothing in the contract that would keep Tyler from taking ownership if he's married to you. After all, there wouldn't be a sale involved."

Instead of feeling pleased about the news, Carissa suddenly felt sick. What if Tyler had no interest in marrying her? What if his feelings for her . . . feelings he had never spoken of but that Hannah and Laura assured her existed . . . had changed?

"I suppose we will just have to wait and see," she said in a barely audible voice.

"Judge, how nice to see you. Won't you join us for dinner?" Hannah asked, coming to join them. She looked at Carissa. "You were gone so long, I feared something was wrong."

"A bite to eat sounds just right to me," Judge Peevy declared. "Is that fried chicken I smell?"

Hannah laughed. "It is indeed. I fried it myself. Now, come along. The Terrys are here, and you men can discuss the affairs of the world. Ted has been telling us about the Indian troubles."

The two continued to talk as they walked away, leaving Carissa to close the door. She paused and leaned against the frame, wondering if she'd made a serious mistake. She wished she could have told Tyler about her plans prior to taking action. But that was the whole reason she had rushed to action—all the men who could have advised her were gone.

She closed her eyes and tried to imagine telling Tyler the news that she'd just bought the ranch. Worse still, she had spent every cent in her bank account to do so. If Tyler asked her to marry him, there would be no problem. But if he didn't . . .

Carissa tried to push the thought from her mind, but it wouldn't go. Tyler might hate her for what she'd done. The long months away could have given him a new direction for his life. What if he didn't even return to Texas?

She shook her head. "I'm borrowing trouble, and I already have plenty." She opened her eyes and pushed off the doorframe. "There's no sense in fretting about this now." But even speaking the words aloud didn't help her to let the matter go.

Looks like they're setting up for quite the Fourth of July celebration," William said after he and Tyler concluded business at the bank. All around Abilene streamers and banners were being hung in red, white, and blue.

"You won't see them celebrating as much in Texas," Tyler countered. He pointed to a mercantile. "I'm going over there to pick up some presents for Gloria and Carissa. You ought to come and get Hannah and Robert something."

William glanced toward the store and then back to the building just ahead. "I'll probably do that, but first I'm going to send a wire. With all the newspaper stories about Indian attacks and such, I'd like to hear from the sheriff in Cedar Springs."

"That would be wise," Tyler said, bothered that he'd not thought of it himself. "How fast do you reckon we can start back?"

"Hard to tell," William replied. "The horses are in decent

shape, but the new stock Brandon's picking up might not be as cooperative. I'd like to think we could push hard and be back in two weeks or less. Now you go ahead to the mercantile, and I'll get this wire sent, then join you."

Tyler nodded and headed out across the busy street. They'd been in Abilene for two days and finally business had been concluded. They'd received top dollar for their steers and had managed to make it to market with 2,442 head. The loss was far less than they'd anticipated, especially with the storm, and the profit was a good one. Tonight they would pay the men, and tomorrow they would head home. At least Tyler hoped that's what they'd do.

He entered the brightly decorated store and grinned at a display of red, white, and blue hair ribbons with a sign that read, *Show your patriotic spirit with the colors of Old Glory!*

An older man stepped forward from behind the counter. "Morning, mister. Can I help you?"

"I hope so," Tyler replied. "I'm here to get a couple of presents. One for my sweetheart and one for a two-year-old girl."

The man led the way. "Over here we have a nice selection of toys and doodads to please the children. I think you will find our selection the best west of the Mississippi."

Tyler didn't bother to say that he had no way to compare. Instead he studied a stack of books, marionettes, puzzles, blocks, and stick horses. Nothing seemed quite right. He continued glancing through the merchandise until his gaze fell upon a beautiful china doll. He supposed that Gloria was really too small for such a present, but the doll was enchanting.

"I see you've spied our finest doll," the store clerk said, reaching out to pick up the elegant doll. "The dress is a replica of one worn by President Lincoln's wife. Note the care given to the doll's hair. That's real human hair. I like the gold color, don't you?"

Tyler didn't give the details much attention. "I'll take it." It didn't even matter what the price was; he knew it would impress Gloria, and if she were too little for it, Carissa could save it until she was older.

"And for your sweetheart . . . did you have anything in mind?"

"Well, I had thought maybe a new gown, but now I'm inclined to consider a ring."

The man grinned. "Ah, so it's quite serious?"

"I suppose it is," Tyler said, knowing that his heart was doing all his thinking.

"I have a selection of rings that I keep in the safe. Let me take you back to my private office." The man went to where a woman and another man were working to serve additional customers. He whispered something to the woman, who nodded with a glance Tyler's way. She smiled and said something to the man.

"Right this way," the man announced, returning to Tyler. He took them down several aisles until they reached the back of the store.

Tyler felt awkward and a bit out of place as the man led him to the office and pulled a tray of rings from the safe.

"Now, some of these I have bought off widowers and widows. Some are brand-new. All are of the finest quality."

Looking over the selection of rings, Tyler picked up first one and then another. There were several gold bands, simple yet purposeful. A silver ring with a small blue stone seemed particularly pretty, but not exactly right. He held each ring up to the light and imagined it on Carissa's finger. Finally, in the corner of the tray, Tyler spied a small, wide gold band. He'd almost overlooked it. Picking the piece up, he noticed beautiful etching on the band. Someone had gone to a great deal of trouble to create a beautiful piece of art in a wedding band.

"This ring is new, never worn before," the store clerk explained. "We had a young man in town who was to be wed. He was a jeweler and created this ring himself."

"What happened?" Tyler asked.

"His young lady ran off. He was heartbroken, but said this ring deserved to fit the finger of a woman in love." The man smiled. "Might it work for you?"

Tyler nodded. "I believe it would." He thought the small ring would be a perfect fit for Carissa. "I'll take it."

The man took the ring. "I have a lovely little box we can put it in." He went to his desk and rummaged in a drawer, then produced a small velvet-lined leather box. The piece itself was a work of art.

Though Tyler left the store considerably poorer than when he'd entered, he felt a great sense of satisfaction. He patted the box in his pocket and clutched the paper-wrapped doll. Now he had a purpose and a direction to his life. Now his future was about more than fighting to get his ranch back. It was about a family.

The weeks on the trail had changed him. There'd been a shift, where God worked within his heart to show him what truly mattered. He thought of his father for a moment. Tyler's anger over his death seemed lessened by the love he felt for Carissa and Gloria. He couldn't bring his father back by acting on his rage, but he could bring new life for Carissa and her daughter by allowing love to grow.

William was heading toward him. "I got the wire sent," he announced. Two very dirty cattlemen pushed past him as they headed toward the nearest saloon. William ignored their rudeness and looked to Tyler. "We probably won't hear anything for a day or so. I hate to delay the return, but I'd really like to know what we're heading into."

Tyler nodded. "Knowin' the sheriff, he'll get right back to us. Maybe even today."

"Either way, the earliest we can leave is in the morning, at this rate. Osage is securing the wagon with the provisions we'll need and anything else we want to take back. I see you have a package under your arm, so your shopping must have gone well."

Tyler smiled and reached into his pocket. "I found a pretty doll for Gloria and this for Carissa." He dug into his pocket and pulled out the leather box.

William looked at it for a moment and frowned. "What is it?"

"Open it and see."

He took the box and carefully unhooked the tiny latch. William's eyebrows rose considerably at the sight of the ring. "This mean what I think it does?"

Tyler drew a deep breath. "I'm gonna marry her."

William grinned. "I hope you know what you're gettin' yourself into." He handed the box back to Tyler and nodded his approval. "Seems like we ought to celebrate. How about I buy you the best steak in town?"

"I think I'd like that. I've worked up quite an appetite shoppin'."

Tyler woke early the next morning and found William had already left the room. For a moment he stretched in the bed, relishing the feel of the clean sheets. It sure beat sleeping on the ground. He smiled and thought again of the gifts he had purchased for Carissa and Gloria. Would they like them? Would Carissa say yes to his proposal of marriage?

When they had first met, Tyler had been more interested in her sister Laura, and prior to that it had been Hannah. But he came to realize that Hannah and Laura reminded him of his mother in certain ways. They were sensible, matter-of-fact women who saw a need and took care of it. Carissa, on the other hand, needed someone to take care of her, and Tyler liked that idea. Of course, when they'd first met, Carissa was already married to Malcolm Lowe, and though Tyler thought her quite pretty, he respected the sanctity of marriage and went no further in his thoughts.

Now Lowe was dead, leaving Carissa a widow with a child, and Tyler was certain he was in love. He knew there would be obstacles to overcome. Carissa was reluctant to trust anyone. He knew that she feared men and preferred to keep to her own company or that of her sister. But he hoped that the time she spent at the Barnett ranch would help her to come out of her shell a bit.

Getting up, Tyler stretched again and thought of the long ride home. How he wished there were a railroad that ran the full length of Kansas to Texas. How pleasant it would be to just board a train and be home in a matter of days instead of weeks.

Tyler dressed and gathered his things and made his way downstairs. If he knew William, they would leave as soon as he had a reply to the telegram he'd sent yesterday. Brandon, too, was chomping at the bit to head back. He was uneasy about Laura and had been restless for days.

"If you're lookin' for your friend," the hotel clerk said, "he's in having breakfast. Said to tell you to join him if I saw you."

Tyler nodded. "Thanks, mister." He made his way across the hotel lobby to the adjoining dining area. Spotting William across the room, Tyler made his way through the crowd of other diners and pulled out a chair.

"Guess you're savin' this for me," he said, grinning. Tyler sat down and nodded to William's uneaten plate of food. "Not hungry? I feel like I could eat a buffalo."

A young woman came to see what Tyler would have. "Coffee, to start," he replied. "Then bring me a plate like his." The thick beefsteak, fried eggs, and potatoes seemed to beckon to Tyler.

The woman nodded and quickly returned with a cup of coffee. The entire time William had said nothing, and Tyler chalked it off to his wanting to be on the road. "So how soon you reckon we can leave?"

William looked up just as Tyler took a long drink of the strong, black coffee. Tyler got a strange feeling that something wasn't right. He put the cup down and looked hard at his friend. "What's going on? Is there a problem?"

"I had a telegram."

Tyler frowned and immediately the skin on the back of his neck tingled. "Guess the Indian troubles are worse than we expected?"

William slumped back in his chair. "They aren't good, but that's just a part of it."

Tyler leaned forward. "So tell me what's going on." He eyed William's plate with growing hunger. "I guess it's bad enough you've lost your appetite."

"You will, too," William replied. "I've sent Osage to rally

the men—at least those who are going back with us. I'm expecting Brandon to join me here anytime now. I sent the clerk to wake him."

"William, you've never been one for beatin' around the bush, so how about you just tell me what's going on before I lose my mind tryin' to guess."

His friend nodded. "Brandon's wife had the baby early. They're both in a bad way, it sounds."

Tyler shook his head. He'd never anticipated something so grave. "I am sorry. What happened?"

William shook his head. "I don't know. The telegram was brief."

"And now you have to tell Brandon." Tyler sat back and crossed his arms. This was not going to be easy. Brandon would be anxious to get back to Laura, and there were nearly five hundred miles between them.

"Maybe you shouldn't tell him, Will. Maybe we should get on our way first. I mean, if the worst happens there isn't anything that he can do about it."

"Would you want me to keep bad news from you?" William asked.

"Well, no. I guess I would want the truth, no matter how hard it was to hear."

William leaned forward. "I'm glad to know it, because I have to tell you something as well."

Tyler shook his head. He couldn't imagine anything as bad as having a wife and baby sick. "Me?" Then he felt his chest tighten. "Has something happened to Carissa?"

"No. It's nothing like that," William replied, his voice tight. "I'm sorry, Tyler. There's just no easy way to say this. You've lost the ranch. The county sold it out from under you."

For just a moment the words didn't register. Tyler looked at William, trying to make sense of it all. "Sold it to whom?" It was the only question he could think to ask.

"I don't know. The sheriff didn't say. He just put in that the county had sold it and wanted you to know in case . . . well . . . in case you preferred Kansas, I guess."

Tyler felt like his legs had been kicked out from under him. Just then the waitress brought his breakfast. She set two plates down in front of him, one for the steak and one with everything else. She smiled and promised more coffee before leaving the two men.

"I'm a Texan," Tyler said, staring at the food. "At least I used to be."

"Look, I don't know who bought the place, but maybe I can buy it from them. I know Judge Peevy has been doing everything he could to get the land back for you, but apparently it was out of his hands."

Brandon joined them at that moment and the young woman brought more coffee. Tyler was just as glad for the diversion. He couldn't think. Couldn't breathe. *What is this all about, God? Why have you forsaken me?*

He looked across the table and saw William speaking to Brandon. The man's face went white, and Tyler knew Will had just delivered the blow. He shook his head, unable to say anything. The look of shock on Brandon's face and the worry on William's was enough to finish off any thoughts of eating. Tyler pushed back from the table.

"I gotta get out of here," he said, knocking the chair over backward as he pushed his way through the room.

"Well, we certainly weren't expecting to see you folks today," Hannah declared as Ted Terry helped his wife down from the wagon.

"Kiowa are on the warpath," he said in a matter-of-fact manner that still managed to shock Carissa to the bone.

She looked at the riders about him and noted they were well armed. "Are they headed this way?" she asked.

"Who can say?" Ted replied.

Marietta came to where Carissa and Hannah stood. "Now, we're not gonna borrow trouble, girls. We're just takin' some precautions."

"That's why we're here," Ted told Hannah. "I was hopin' Marietta could stay with you until this trouble blows over. I can keep my mind on other things if she's here with you."

"Of course she can stay," Hannah declared. "You know that. All of you can stay. I think it would be safer than returning to the ranch."

Ted shook his head. "I have to protect what's mine. Won't be the first time and probably won't be the last. I just wanted to get Marietta to safety. I left some men on alert at the ranch, and now we're headin' into town to let the sheriff know what's happening. I'm hopeful he'll get the army notified and they can deal with the matter."

"Do you think they will?" Hannah questioned.

"I do. There's a strong push to round up the Indians. All of them, no matter the tribe. Phil Sheridan is in charge now, and he's determined."

"What's got the Indians so stirred up?" Carissa asked.

"Mostly Sheridan's demands they all head to reservations." Ted shook his head. "Doesn't seem to be any peaceable way to live side by side. The Indians hate us for being on their land and killing their game. The whites hate them for making war on 'em and stealing their livestock. It's a vicious cycle that doesn't look to stop anytime soon. Just when the army thinks they have a good hold on things, something happens and the war flares up again. I don't know what it'll take to put an end to it."

"I read in the paper that Sheridan believes if they eliminate the buffalo, they will eliminate the Indians," Hannah said.

"He did say that, and he has even encouraged buffalo hunters to come west," Marietta added. "His plan is to wipe out the herds and leave the Indians hungry enough that they'll have no choice but to return to the reservations."

Hannah shook her head. "I don't see this war ending anytime soon. I'm afraid we are just seeing the beginning of hard times."

Carissa bit her lip to keep from saying anything. She thought of the children and how vulnerable they were here, so far from town. Not only that, but Laura remained gravely ill and tiny Lucas still fought to live. How could they ever get those two to safety if they needed to leave the ranch?

"I'd take precautions if I were you," Ted instructed. "I'll speak to Berto myself, but if I were you gals, I'd store up plenty of water and food in the house. And get the windows covered just in case."

Carissa saw Hannah nod but didn't hear her response. Her thoughts went to Tyler and his hatred of the entire Indian population. If she or the others were hurt in a raid, he would never get over it. His anger over the Indians' murder of his father had eaten holes in his heart. What would this do?

She drew a deep breath and tried to force herself to be calm. Tyler had no way of knowing the peril they were in, but even so, Carissa couldn't help but pray he and the other men would return soon. They were due back most anytime. William had sent a wire earlier when they'd reached Abilene. Surely it wouldn't be all that long now.

"I just hope the men don't run into any war parties on the way home," Hannah said, immediately catching Carissa's attention.

Looking at her hostess, Carissa felt all pretense of calm escape her. Ted's serious expression told Carissa she'd find no comfort from him. He, too, was worried for the men.

Later that day as Carissa wiped Laura's body with cool compresses, Marietta joined her to offer a hand.

"It's a good sign she's come this far," Marietta said, taking up a pan of water and a cloth rag. "I think she'll pull through this if we just keep getting fluids down her."

Carissa glanced at her sister's pale face. She seemed so small and childlike in the large bed. "I'm so afraid." She glanced over at Marietta. "For her, for us. I know it might sound foolish to stew and fret over things for which I have no control, but I can't seem to help myself."

"I understand. Our men are in danger. We're in danger. It's just a part of life here on the Texas frontier," Marietta said. She offered Carissa a bit of a smile. "But you know, it's the life we've chosen. Maybe not you so much, but the rest of us."

"I've chosen it, as well. I just bought Tyler's ranch." Carissa continued ministering to her sister. "I signed an obligation to live there for five years."

"Whatever caused you to do that?"

"He would have lost it otherwise. The decision had been made to sell it. Judge Peevy told me it was to be sold off right away. I couldn't just let it go." She looked at Marietta. "Do you think I was wrong to do it?"

Marietta shrugged. "Who can say? Frankly, I'm glad you did it. Keeps a chance for Tyler to get it back. Still, I'm not so sure he'll see it that way."

Carissa shook her head and stopped wiping her sister's arm. "What do you mean?"

"Well, a man likes to do things for himself," Marietta began. "Tyler might resent you taking charge of the matter."

"But if I hadn't, the property would have gone to strangers. Surely he would prefer I buy it. At least this way he can run the place."

Marietta smiled in a motherly fashion. "Carissa, if all these years of marriage have taught me anything, it's that you can never tell how a man is going to see a matter. Tyler might be grateful for what you did, but he also might feel grouchy that a woman had to pull his bacon from the fire. That's hard for a man. Believe me. I've had to do similar things for

Ted from time to time, and it's always been a subject of irritation between us."

"That's silly," Carissa said, dipping her cloth in the cool water. She put the rag to her sister's head and was surprised when Laura opened her eyes.

"How do you feel?" Carissa asked.

Laura tried to lick her lips. "Water, please."

Carissa quickly complied. She had worked tirelessly to get fluids into her sister, and for Laura to request them herself was nigh onto a miracle. She helped Laura drink from a small tin cup.

"The doctor says that the more you drink, the quicker you'll rally."

Laura shook her head. "I'm so tired."

"Do you think you could eat a little soup?" Marietta questioned. "It will help you regain your strength."

"I'll try." Laura's voice was weak and barely audible. "Where are my . . . boys? I want to see them."

Carissa went to the bed box and retrieved the sleeping infant. "Lucas is right here," she said placing the baby beside Laura on the bed. "I'll get Daniel."

"No, I'll get him," Marietta said, getting to her feet. "And the soup."

Laura tried to reach up and touch her son's face, but she appeared too weak. Carissa took hold of her sister's hand and helped her. "He's a fighter, Laura. Just like you."

"Will he live?"

"I determined a long time ago that both of you would," Carissa replied. "Laura, you've come through the worst of it, and now it's time to put all of your energy into getting well. Your sons need you . . . Brandon needs you."

"Is he here?" Laura asked, her voice a little stronger.

"Not yet, but they are on their way. The men should be home any day now." She knew there was no way of telling whether this was the truth of the matter, but it was what they all anticipated. Hopefully they would see it come true in a short time.

Just then Daniel came into the room with Hannah. "So she's awake," Hannah said, lifting Daniel to the bed.

"Mama." He fell upon her breast and clutched her tight. "Mama."

"I'm here, Daniel," Laura whispered. She looked to Carissa. "If I don't make it, please . . . promise me you'll help Brandon and the boys."

"You're going to make it." Carissa refused to think otherwise.

"She's right, you know," Hannah interjected. "The worst is over. Your fever is down and now you can start building your strength. Your boys need you, Laura."

Laura looked briefly to Hannah and then back to her sons. She closed her eyes. "I know."

Hannah scooped Daniel up, but he started to cry. This caused Laura to open her eyes again. She whispered his name and to Carissa's surprise the boy heard it and calmed.

"Be a good boy," Laura told him. "Watch for Papa."

Marietta came with the soup and took a seat beside the bed. She looked at Carissa. "Why don't you tend to Lucas, and I'll get your sister to eat some of this rich beef broth. Smelled so good I was tempted to eat some myself." She smiled down at Laura as if she, too, were a small child. "Now, if you eat all of this, I'll see to it that you get some applesauce for dessert."

Carissa took Lucas in her arms and stared back at her

sister. Already Marietta was getting her to take a spoonful of the aromatic liquid. Maybe Marietta's mothering skills would cause Laura to fight harder. Looking down at the still sleeping babe in her arms, Carissa could only pray that it would be so.

⌒

That evening as she put Gloria to bed, Carissa couldn't help but worry about Tyler. She wondered if he and the other men were safe or if Indians had somehow managed to attack them. She tried not to think morbid thoughts of the men being killed, but those fears kept creeping in to haunt her.

"I want Papa," Gloria said, startling Carissa.

"You need to sleep." Carissa reached out to stroke her daughter's hair. "It's getting very late."

"I want my papa Tyer."

Carissa felt her breath catch. Gloria had decided that Tyler was her father. At least that was how Carissa interpreted her words. Should she correct her? After all, Tyler might return and decide to part company forever. There was no sense in getting the little girl's hopes up. Carissa shook her head.

"Darlin', Tyler took the cows . . . the steers away to Kansas. Remember?" Her mind raced to think of how she could get Gloria's thoughts going in another direction. "Do you remember all those steers we saw?"

"Big ones," Gloria said, nodding.

"Yes, they were very big, and there were a lot of them. Tyler and Uncle Brandon took them away to sell. They are working hard and can't come home just yet."

"Maybe when I get up?"

Carissa smiled, feeling a bit relieved. "Yes. Maybe. We'll just have to keep watching for them. One of these days they'll be home. Now you be a good girl and go to sleep. I need to help Hannah and Juanita in the kitchen."

Gloria didn't say anything more about Tyler, so Carissa took the opportunity to direct her in prayers before leaving to join the women. She wondered if she should say something to Hannah or Marietta. Perhaps they might have some idea of what she should say to Gloria regarding Tyler. Clearly the child had attached herself to him.

"Marietta is staying with Laura and the baby," Carissa announced, pulling on an apron. "I thought I'd help you here."

"We're getting beans snapped for cooking and canning tomorrow. Tomatoes and carrots and beets need cleaning for the same," Hannah said. "Take your pick."

Carissa took up a bowl of green beans. "I'll see to these."

She glanced to the window and relished the breeze that trickled in. They did most of the preparation work inside these days, due to the possibility of Indian attack. The summer kitchen outside would still serve as the place to cook and can so as not to overheat the house, but simple work like this could be handled inside.

"The men haven't been able to get over to your sister's place," Hannah said as they worked. "I am sorry about that. I know you're probably anxious about it."

"Not so much as wondering where the men are," Carissa answered honestly. She and Hannah had grown quite close since Laura fell ill.

"Me too," Hannah admitted. She looked at Juanita. "You can bring me another basket of beets when you have time.

I'm nearly done with these." The Mexican woman nodded and went to retrieve the vegetables.

Carissa snapped the ends off the green beans and then broke them in two-inch-long pieces and put them in a clean bowl. "Something happened with Gloria tonight. Something that I'm not sure how to deal with."

"What was it?"

She looked up to find Hannah's gaze still fixed on her work. "She asked for her papa."

"Well, that seems normal," Hannah replied. "After all, she hears the other children asking for theirs. She's probably just imitating them."

"She wanted her 'papa Tyer.'"

This time Hannah stopped cutting beet tops and looked up. She didn't try to hide her smile. "I guess Gloria knows full well what's good for her."

"I didn't know what to say. I don't want to give her false hopes."

Hannah nodded. "I can understand that."

"She told him she loved him before he left on the cattle drive."

"But you didn't."

Carissa felt a lump in her throat. "No. I didn't."

"But you wish you had?"

She shook her head. "I don't know. I don't know that it would have made a difference, what with Ava there, laying her claim."

"Ava has no claim on Tyler, silly. She's just a lonely woman who thinks she can have whatever she wants. Tyler is a sensible man, however. He will listen to his heart, and I've no doubt his heart is telling him that you're the one."

"But what if he comes back and hates me for buying the ranch?"

Hannah put down her knife and placed the last of her beets in a box. "You did the right thing, Carissa. I would have done it myself if I could have. If Tyler is angry at first, it will be because he feels his country has turned against him."

"They have," Carissa countered.

"Be that as it may, Tyler is a smart man. In the long run he will see the sense in what you did. When he proposes marriage, it will all come together in a neat package."

"If he proposes marriage," Carissa muttered.

Hannah laughed. "You know, sometimes I think being in love makes us a little dim-witted. Of course he'll propose. You'll see. He loves you—of that I'm certain. Now it's just a matter of his returning with the proper funds to support a family. This will be a new start for the both of you."

A knock at the back door drew their attention. Hannah started to get up, but caught her foot in the box of beets.

"I'll get it. It's probably Juanita needing help with the beets."

Carissa jumped to her feet and hurried to help. Opening the back door, Carissa started to say something about the beets and instead screamed. There, standing in the doorway, was a large Indian warrior.

Tyler knew he should try to sleep, but he didn't think it'd do any good. All day long as they rode he'd tried to occupy his mind with thoughts other than the ranch and how it was lost to him. Sitting here at the campfire while the others snored around him, Tyler could think of nothing else.

What do I do now? I have no home for Carissa and Gloria. I have no place to go. He shook his head and stared into the flames.

"Sleep comin' hard?" Osage asked, sitting up.

"I thought you were asleep."

The older man chuckled. "I couldn't sleep for all that loud thinkin' you were doin'."

Tyler shook his head. "I'm trying to figure out what to do with my life now that the ranch is gone."

"Weren't the only ranch in the world," Osage countered. "You need to strike out for yourself. Maybe Mr. Terry and William would sell you a chunk of their land. You could put together a decent spread—maybe even buy Mr. Terry out when he's ready to sell." Osage checked his watch by the fire's light. "Nearly ten. If we're getting up at four, you'd best get some sleep."

"I know," Tyler said, feeling no sense of peace. "Sleep doesn't seem to want to come. I keep asking God what the answer is, and I feel like He's not speakin' to me. I feel like maybe He's forsaken me altogether." He eased down on his bedroll and yawned.

"Don't reckon I know the mind of God one way or the other, exceptin' that He's always showin' himself faithful in the Bible. Don't recall a time when a man of God called out to Him and was ignored."

Tyler nodded. "I know what you're saying makes sense, I just don't know how to apply it to my situation."

"Maybe you worry too much. Bible does say we ain't suppose to be worryin' about tomorrow 'cause it has enough worry of its own. Maybe God wants you to stop frettin' and start trustin'."

Closing his eyes, Tyler said nothing for a moment. Finally he let go a heavy breath. "Maybe so, Osage."

"No maybe about it, Tyler. You know it, and I do, too."

"Guess I do." Tyler had just begun to relax when several bloodcurdling screams cut through the silence. Every man in the camp jumped to his feet—all reaching for their rifles at the same time.

"G oodness, you put a scare into us for sure," Hannah said, moving past Carissa. "Night Bear! Come in. You are very welcome here."

She embraced the warrior and cocked her head to one side. "You must have known I'd baked sweet rolls this morning."

He smiled. "You make me glad with such talk. I am hungry."

"Come on in, and I'll get you some." Hannah looked to Carissa. "This is my friend Night Bear."

Carissa felt like her feet were nailed to the floor. She looked at the man and gave a brief nod. "Sorry I screamed."

He smiled. "Hannah never screams."

Hannah laughed. "Oh, I do if the occasion calls for it." She led the way back to the kitchen, and Carissa reluctantly followed after the warrior.

Juanita came back about that time, as well. "I heard someone scream." She dropped a box of beets beside the table and noticed Night Bear. "I see why now."

"He startled Carissa."

"Nearly scared me to death," Carissa admitted and settled back down to snap beans. Her back ached and she was more than ready to go to bed, but they'd already agreed a nap could be had during the warmer parts of the day so that work could be done in the cool of the night.

"Would you like to stay with us tonight?" Hannah asked Night Bear as casually as if he were her long-lost brother. She put two large rolls on a plate.

His expression grew serious. "I cannot. I came here at great risk. My people have joined with other tribes to attack and burn out the settlers in this area. I feared for you and wanted to warn you."

"But why should they attack us? We've done them no harm," Hannah said, putting the plate and glass of milk in front of the man.

"Times are hard for my people. They hate the whites for what they are doing—killing the buffalo and killing the people. We have nowhere to go but those places the whites tell us to go. The people are angry. Why should the white man tell the Numunuu where to live?"

Hannah didn't even attempt to answer his question. "But the Numunuu have always shown us kindness. You have told them of my helping your people. You have made peace between us."

"I cannot make it any longer," he replied. "There will be war."

"What should we do?" Carissa asked, putting aside her fears.

He looked at her for a moment. "You should go." He got to his feet after wolfing down one roll and most of another. "I go, too. I shouldn't be here."

"Wait, I'll send some more rolls with you," Hannah told him.

Night Bear seemed as though he might refuse, but then he beamed her a smile and nodded.

"I can tell the warriors that I took them." He laughed and looked at Carissa. "I can tell them that I gave much fear to a white woman. It will all be truth."

Hannah went quickly to work stuffing an old flour sack with several rolls and some cookies. While she did this, Night Bear tossed down the rest of his roll and drank the milk Hannah had brought.

"I'll let William know as soon as he gets back," she told Night Bear.

He frowned. "Your man, he is not here?"

"They drove cattle to the North," Hannah explained. "We have a few men here, but not many."

"Then you should go to the town. It is not safe here for you and the little ones." His eyes narrowed. "I cannot save you, Hannah, even though you saved me."

"I understand." She handed him the sack. "Please be careful. I hate to think of harm coming to you." She reached out to hug him, and Carissa could see it made the young man quite uncomfortable. Nevertheless, he allowed her affection.

"I will do what I must," he said, finally pulling away. With a nod, he took the flour sack and left by way of the back door.

For several moments no one said or did anything. Carissa held a string bean in her hand but couldn't quite bring herself to snap it.

"Are we being foolish by staying?" Hannah asked to no one in particular.

"How can we possibly leave?" Carissa asked. "Laura and

the baby can't travel." She thought of her meager skills with a rifle. "I suppose I could stay here with them. I can shoot if need be."

"No," Hannah said. "We either all go, or we all stay. There's no compromise on this. It would be foolishness to leave you here alone without at least some semblance of protection." She looked around the room. "We can continue to make arrangements for our safety." She was silent then, deep in thought for several minutes.

Carissa couldn't suppress a yawn, yet the thought of trying to sleep with the threat of Indian attack at any given moment kept her from seeking the comfort of her bed.

They gradually went back to their work, and when the clock struck midnight, Hannah called a halt to it. "We should get some sleep. Marietta said she would get up with Pepita in the morning and see to everything. Marty said she'd check on the children and see to them so we don't need to get up until seven."

"The men will see to the chores," Juanita offered. "I will speak to Berto and make sure. It will be better if we do not have to go far from the house."

Hannah nodded her approval. "Then I'll see you in the morning."

Carissa made her way to her room, lamp in hand. She turned the flame low before entering. Gloria slept soundly, thumb in her mouth. Carissa put the lamp on the nightstand and sat down beside her daughter. She thought of the savages who waited to attack. Would they kill them outright or sell them into slavery? She shook her head in horror at the thoughts running through her head.

"What have I done in bringing you here?"

⤜∾

"It looks to be about fifty or so braves," Osage said.

Tyler and William were flat on their stomachs looking over the ridge. Mounted soldiers had surprised a renegade band of warriors and now had them in custody. The screams had been the war cries of the Indians as they attempted to fight, but now they were silent.

"Glad to see the army out here," one of Will's men said, crawling over to where William observed the affair.

"They must be bringing Indians to Fort Arbuckle," Osage declared. "We ain't that far off. Maybe they caught 'em causin' trouble."

"Could be," William said, easing back from the ridge. "I don't suppose any of us will sleep all that well tonight."

But they did sleep. It was restless and troubled as Tyler recalled the next morning, but when he went to the ridge to once again observe the army camp, he felt a sense of relief to find them gone.

"They must have moved out before first light," he told William.

Pouring himself a cup of coffee, William nodded. "They did. I was on watch. They bound 'em and tied 'em together in a line." He paused a moment. "I reckon it won't hurt us time-wise to make a stop at the fort. You have a problem with that?"

Tyler knew he was mainly speaking to him. William would be concerned about Tyler having to deal with the captive warriors or even the friendlies who hung around the fort.

"I say we go and figure out what the ruckus was all about," Tyler said with a shrug. "Better to know what we're up against, and it isn't that far out of the way."

William met his gaze and nodded. "That's my way of thinking."

"I say we go to the fort," Osage agreed. The other men murmured their approval. Only Brandon seemed reluctant.

"We won't stay long," William told him. "We've pushed hard and fast to get home, and we will continue to do so. Believe me, I know how you feel about wanting to get back to your family."

Brandon's jaw tightened, but he gave the slightest nod. Tyler could see he wasn't at all satisfied with such a comment.

"Good. Let's break camp then and head on down. Shouldn't take us too long." The men dispersed to gather their things, but William reached out to stop Tyler. "You sure you're gonna be all right with this?"

"I reckon I'll survive," Tyler said, forcing a smile. "We're just a few days from . . ." He fell silent. He'd started to say home, but the truth was, he didn't have a home.

"You'll always have a place with us," William said, seeming to understand. "You're like a brother to me."

Tyler drew a deep breath. "I know, and I appreciate that more than you'll know. I just wish I knew what it was I'm supposed to do now. I have money from the sale, but no land to buy. I have a ring in my pocket, but no woman to wed."

"You have Carissa waiting at the ranch. I doubt she's gone anywhere."

"I can't take a wife without a home to keep her in." Tyler shook his head and walked away. "Even if you're giving me a place to stay—it isn't the same."

Tyler kept thinking about Carissa as they rode into the fort. Was she safe? All along the way they'd heard tales of tragedy from other drovers. Indians all over the prairie seemed to be uprising. The army was pursuing any and all renegade bands, and it didn't sound as if much mercy was being shown.

With each report, Tyler felt a growing uneasiness. Why were they making this stop? It really wasn't necessary. Sure, it would be nice to know what was going on in the area and whether there was news about the raids, but it'd be better to get back to the ranch and see that everyone was safe.

How can we keep them safe in the middle of this war? We're just a handful of men. My father and his men were just a handful, and they died fighting the Comanche.

He thought of Carissa and her desire to learn to shoot in case she had to defend her family. She wasn't at all proficient with the rifle or revolver. Hannah was a good shot, but knowing her, she'd probably just walk out to meet the Comanche as she had done so long ago when Night Bear was injured. This actually brought a smile to Tyler's face, as he imagined her offering them cinnamon sweet rolls and coffee.

"You look happier than I'd figured," William commented.

"Not for the right reasons," Tyler countered, sobering quickly. "I keep thinkin' this might not be our best plan—that gettin' home and seein' if they're safe is more important."

"And that made you smile?"

"No, it was the thought of a Comanche standoff with Hannah meetin' 'em all with sweet rolls and coffee."

William grunted. "And she would. Believe me, the thought has crossed my mind more than once."

Tyler noted a group of black soldiers drilling on the far side of the grounds. He wondered if these men had faced the Indians in battle. Did they know there were women and children—men too—dependent upon them to keep the peace? Did they care?

Lord, I don't have a good feelin' about this, he prayed, following William across the fort grounds. The hewn log buildings were arranged with barracks on opposing sides. There were numerous other buildings, as well as a sutler's store about a hundred yards north of the commissary. Some of the men headed into the store, but Tyler accompanied William to the stockade to hear what was going on with the captured Indians.

"Sergeant," William said, climbing down from his horse.

The man in blue glanced up and eyed William suspiciously. "What do you want, mister?"

"I'm here seeking information. I'd like to see your commanding officer."

The sergeant eyed him a moment longer, then nodded. "Come inside."

Tyler looked at William and nodded. "I'll just wait for you here."

William said nothing but followed the soldier into the small building. Tyler leaned up against the wall and tried to ignore the foul smells around the stockade. The prisoners were treated little better than the cattle he and William had penned in Abilene. There were a great many men inside the fenced area, and all were Indians. No doubt this space served as their living quarters, latrine, and infirmary.

Tyler tried not to think for long on the matter. He heard Osage pass by, talking with Andy and Newt. The boys were commenting on their fascination with the buffalo soldiers. Tyler watched them cross the grounds with Osage, and he suddenly felt very old. Had he ever been that young and carefree? He thought again of Carissa and how much she had changed in the short time he'd known her. She used to be just as happy as Gloria, enjoying life and living for the moment. But Malcolm Lowe had changed all of that for her. She had lost her girlish innocence in the face of his treacherous dealings.

Pa's death took the last of my innocence, Tyler thought. For many a man it might have been the war that did such a thing, but for him the death of his father served that purpose.

Try as he might, Tyler couldn't put aside the conflict in his heart. He felt the presence of the Indians, and with that his anger grew. He tried to pray, but the words wouldn't come. Closing his eyes, he longed for peace.

God, I don't want to be this hate-filled man. I want to let this anger go. I want to start a new life and take Carissa as my wife. I want to be a father to little Gloria.

But could he be either of those things when he had no home? No land? No place in which to bring a family? Maybe it was God's way of telling him to leave Texas. But why? Would a different place be any better?

"They've got 'em, Tyler."

Tyler opened his eyes and found a stunned-faced Osage standing in front of him. "What're you talkin' about?"

"The army caught the warrior that killed your pa. He's here. Here at Fort Arbuckle. They brought him in this morning just afore we got here. He was in that bunch we saw rounded up last night."

A tightness formed in Tyler's chest and spread throughout his body. "Are you sure?"

"I saw him myself. He ain't that much older. He's in there, all right."

Tyler kicked off the wall. "Show me."

Osage nodded and walked toward the stockade fence. Tyler noted that Andy and Newt were nowhere in sight. He supposed he should have asked about them, but right now his mind was fixed on the man he'd hated for so many years.

"Right there," Osage said, pointing to a fierce-looking warrior standing at the stockade gate. He stared hard at Tyler and Osage, unflinching, unconcerned with the hatred they bore him.

Tyler walked right up to the fence. "Who are you?"

The proud man sneered. He jutted his chin forward and muttered something to his companions. Tyler narrowed his eyes. "I asked you your name. Are you deaf?"

The man only stared. Another of the Indians came up alongside him just as William came to stand beside Tyler. "He hears the white man's talk," the Comanche replied, "but he will not speak your words."

Tyler let his gaze travel to the man who answered. "Then you tell me. Who is he?"

The man nodded. "He is Runs With Buffalo, great war chief."

Runs With Buffalo's chest puffed out. He pounded his fist against his breast as if in greeting. He spoke in Comanche, but Tyler had never bothered to learn more than a few words.

"He says he has killed many white men and will kill again. The white man is his enemy, and he has a great hatred for them. He will not be caged as an animal. He will avenge his people."

It was William who interpreted, much to Tyler's surprise. He looked to his friend, then turned back to point a finger at Runs With Buffalo. "You tell him, I will avenge my people, too. Tell him he killed my father, and I will kill him in return."

The chief smiled; clearly he already understood the words Tyler spoke. William didn't bother to translate as Runs With Buffalo was already muttering to his companions.

"What's he sayin'?" Tyler asked William.

"You don't want to know." William took hold of Tyler and pulled him away. "Come on. Let's get out of here."

"No. I want to know," Tyler said, yanking away from Will's hold. He held his ground, waiting for William to speak.

By now Runs With Buffalo was speaking to them again. He was calling out in a loud, harsh manner as if taunting them for turning away.

"He said he was glad he killed your father—that it gives him great pleasure to meet the son of such a coward so that he might kill you, as well. He says we are both cowards because we stand so brave as long as there is a wall between us."

Tyler balled his fist and headed back to the stockade. Coming within an inch or so of the fence and the chief, he let years of rage guide his thoughts.

"We'll see who's the coward. When I get my chance, you won't even know death is coming, although I'd like to make you suffer. I'd like to see you tormented and tortured like you've done to so many. When the time comes—when I get my chance—I will kill you."

By now the sergeant had joined them. "He's an animal, but he'll hang soon enough. He's heading to trial for killing settlers up Kansas way. He was chased all the way down here and the men caught 'em last night."

William tapped Tyler's shoulder. "Come on. Let's go see where Andy got off to and then get on our way."

Tyler nodded and drew a deep breath. He started after William, but the sergeant called him back. William paused, but Tyler motioned him on. "I'll be right there. Go on."

William didn't seem too happy with this comment, but he nodded and headed toward the sutler's without Tyler. Turning back to the sergeant, Tyler eyed him questioningly.

The man grinned and came forward to speak in a hushed voice. "I heard what you said about that savage. You know, for a price I could see to it that he gets shot tryin' to escape."

Tyler felt a chill run down his spine. "A price? What kind of price?"

The man's grin broadened. "Ten dollars a head. You tell me which ones you want dead, and I'll see to it that it's done."

The very proposition fed Tyler's anger. In that moment he held life and death in his hands. He had the power to finally end the life of the man who had killed his father. And why not? The government would no doubt end it soon enough. What did it matter if Tyler had a hand in seeing the deed done sooner? The man was a killer. He would go on killing, if allowed to.

Just then the sergeant stiffened. "Come back later and tell me your decision, but don't say anything about it to anyone."

Tyler noted that other soldiers were headed their way and nodded. The sergeant turned to address the other men, and Tyler glanced back at the stockade where Runs With Buffalo watched him with great intensity.

I could finally end it here and now. I could avenge Pa— avenge all the people that animal has killed. His rage grew to an inferno that threatened to burn away every peaceful, loving thought of Carissa and Gloria—of his family and friends—even of God.

⁓

Before they were able to leave the fort, word came that there was a major uprising of Indians in the vicinity. The commanding officer rallied his men and ordered William and the others to remain at the fort while the army dispersed to deal with the matter. Tyler could tell William was uneasy with the order, clearly wanting to continue heading for Texas but hesitant to put Andy and his crew in jeopardy.

"Let's just sit tight," Tyler said. "We won't gain a thing if we get out there and get in the army's way."

William seemed relieved to hear Tyler's words. He nodded. "Guess one night here is no different than one night on the range." Of course, he said nothing about the loss of time and miles.

Brandon sat nearby, his posture radiating tension and frustration. But it was evident he had no desire to talk, and this suited Tyler just fine. Tyler was mulling over the idea of paying to have Runs With Buffalo killed, and he didn't want to discuss much of anything. William left to inform the crew of the delay, and Tyler and Brandon sat in silence, each nursing a cup of coffee while the rest of the world seemed oblivious to their pain. After nearly an hour of this, Brandon finally spoke.

"I heard one of the Comanche here is the one that killed your father."

Tyler met Brandon's stern face. "Yes."

"That must be hard."

Tyler nodded. A part of him wanted to rant and rave about the hideous things done to his father and friends. He wanted to remember each and every detail of what he'd seen when he returned to the ranch with his grandfather. The Comanche had been cruel—not only killing but mutilating the men.

For several long minutes the silence held them. It was Tyler who broke it. He couldn't bear the ugly images alone. He had to talk. "That man was responsible for killing my father and the men who worked alongside him. They were good men, just like my father."

"I am sorry."

Looking at Brandon, Tyler could see the sincerity in his eyes. "The Comanche slaughtered them. They tortured them. It wasn't enough to just kill them—they wanted to see them suffer."

"And now you want to see them suffer?"

Tyler didn't bother to deny it. "I do. God help me, but I do." He studied the man next to him. Brandon had seen war up close. He knew the anger and frustration of being held here rather than allowed to get back to the wife he loved—a wife who might already be dead. Tyler decided he had to tell it all.

"One of the sergeants offered to kill him for me. Said it would cost me just ten dollars a head." He returned his gaze to Brandon's face, certain he would find condemnation. Instead, the man held an expression of understanding.

"What did you decide?"

"I want Runs With Buffalo dead. I want him to suffer like he made my family suffer."

"And can you live with the guilt of ordering a man's death?" Brandon asked, and still there was no disapproval in his voice. It was a simple question, nothing more.

"I killed a lot of men during the war. This is just a war of a different kind."

"But those men were trying to kill you," Brandon countered.

"Runs With Buffalo wants to kill me, too. He would kill all of us if given the chance."

Brandon leaned back and rubbed his stubbled jaw. "I don't doubt that. What I doubt is that you could live with hiring a man's death. For the time I've known you, I've never seen you as a cold-blooded killer."

"There's nothing cold-blooded about killing an animal. Runs With Buffalo is here because he and his men murdered families in Kansas. The government plans to hang him and the others."

"So why not let that be enough?"

Tyler felt some of his rage fade in that simple question. Why couldn't that be enough? It should be. Dead was dead, after all. Did it really matter that he have a hand in the killing of Runs With Buffalo? It wouldn't bring his father and friends back. It wouldn't give him back the ranch or ensure that Carissa and the others were safe from harm.

Shaking his head, Tyler tried to sort through his thoughts.

"I don't know if anything will ever be enough. I have so much hate inside me."

"I can imagine. It seems justified to feel the way you do. You and your family were definitely wronged."

"We wanted to live in peace with the Indians," Tyler said, remembering his father's plan. "Pa always said we would be a friend to those who befriended us. We would live at peace with all folks, just like the Bible encouraged."

"But the Comanche weren't following the same rules."

The statement was matter-of-fact, and Tyler felt as if it were a knife to the heart. "As far as I can tell, they don't have any rules but to kill."

Brandon nodded. "And now you're taking up their ways?"

Tyler felt his anger return. "I didn't say that." He glowered at his friend. "I'm not sayin' that at all." But the words sounded false even to his own ears.

Tyler spent the day trying his best not to think about his surroundings and the Comanche warrior just yards away. He had tried to sleep at one point that afternoon, hoping that he might be able to find peace for even a few hours, but it wasn't to be.

"God, what do I do? I need some direction here," Tyler murmured.

You have to forgive him, Tyler heard deep in his heart. Whether it was God's voice or his own conscience, he didn't know.

Forgive? Forgive that savage and his men for what they took from me? How can forgiving solve anything here, Lord? Tyler's silent prayer continued. *That man killed innocent people and he laughs about it. He's glad to be a killer. Glad to cause pain. He's neither asking for forgiveness, nor would he respect it.*

The heat of the humid evening caused perspiration to run

down the sides of Tyler's face. With very little trouble he could have mingled it with tears.

I want you to forgive him.

The voice was nearly audible, and Tyler found himself looking around the room to see who had spoken. There was no one. Despite the heat, he felt a chill run through his body. Was God actually speaking to him?

Tyler looked toward the ceiling. "Lord, if you're talkin' to me, I'm listenin'. But I don't pretend to understand any of this. This man killed my father and his friends—my friends. This man is heartless and cares nothing about the pain he's caused. He would willingly kill again and said as much. How can I forgive him such a sin?"

The silence was nearly deafening. Tyler longed for God's voice, yet there was nothing but the stillness of the room and the beating of Tyler's own heart. He shook his head. "I don't know how to forgive this, Lord. I don't."

What he did know beyond any doubt was that if he couldn't forgive Runs With Buffalo and let go of the past, he couldn't have a future with Carissa or anyone else. He feared the hatred and rage that filled him would destroy any relationship he might otherwise attempt to have. Unless he could put this aside, he was destined to spend his life alone. That would be the simple price.

The room felt as if it were closing in on him, so Tyler got up and went outside. The sun was sinking toward the west, but there was still plenty of light. He walked to the stockade and found that Runs With Buffalo was still standing at the gate. The man looked as though he'd not moved from that position all day. He still wore the same fierce scowl, and his eyes burned with bitter hate.

Tyler stood in front of the man and just stared at him for several minutes. He couldn't help but wonder at the life this man had known, and for the first time, Tyler actually felt something akin to guilt. Had the whites taken this man's home from him? Had they killed his father and friends? Was he no more than a victim of this vicious circle of hate—just as Tyler was?

Tyler turned away and stalked off across the parade grounds. He walked from one end of the grounds to the other, his heart in turmoil over what he needed to do. Could he forgive Runs With Buffalo? Could he let go of the pain and bitterness that had held him captive for so many years?

He glanced toward the skies and shook his head. "Pa, if you can hear me, tell me what I need to do."

A slight breeze blew and the sounds of fort life carried on the air, but he heard nothing more. No words of wisdom or directions. No comfort. For so long Tyler had imagined the moment when he would come face-to-face with the man who'd murdered his father. He'd imagined putting an end to that man's life and seeing his father's untimely death avenged. But then what? What would come after that?

Nearly two hours later with only a hint of light left in the sky, Tyler made his way back to the stockade. Runs With Buffalo remained at his post, as if he expected Tyler to return.

"I know you understand English, even if you won't speak it," Tyler finally said. "Fact is, I don't much care if you ever say another word. I came here to do the talkin'."

The chief narrowed his eyes but said nothing. Tyler folded his arms against his chest and prayed for a moment. For the first time in a long, long while he felt his prayers finally ascend to heaven.

God, I don't want to let this hate dictate to me anymore. I don't want to give this man another day of my life or another thought. Help me. I can't let this go on my own. I can't be free if you don't set me free.

Peace didn't come instantly, but rather Tyler felt a tiny corner of his heart soften. He wanted to forgive Runs With Buffalo. He wanted to forgive all of the Comanche and Kiowa. He wanted to forgive the men who brought on the War Between the States. He even wanted to forgive Malcolm Lowe. But wanting was only the first step, and Tyler knew it would be a journey—a deliberate walk in God's grace—that would allow for true forgiveness and healing.

"You killed my father and friends. For a long time I've carried that with me. For a long, long time your actions were like a burden I bore, but no more. I'm not going to be in bondage to you any longer. You may have killed my father, but you will not kill me."

Tyler squared his shoulders and shoved his hands into the pockets of his pants. He still didn't trust himself not to lunge at the smug-faced Comanche warrior. "I had the opportunity to have you killed. I could probably even put a bullet in you here and now, and no one would say another thing about it."

For the first time the chief glanced at the gun belt on Tyler's hip. It was just a brief glance, but Tyler could see for a fleeting moment that the truth of what he'd said really hit the chief. But just as quickly the moment was gone, and the hardness returned to the man's eyes.

"I could kill you," Tyler said, feeling a certain amount of power. "I could end your life and the lives of your men, just as you ended the lives of my father and friends." He paused. "But it wouldn't prove a thing, and I'd still be in bondage.

It's better to give this whole thing over to God and let Him deal with it. I figure I can let God have it, and I can just forget about you altogether."

Runs With Buffalo's eyes narrowed, and his nostrils flared in obvious anger. He rattled off something in his native tongue, and Tyler just shrugged.

"What you've got to say means nothing to me. Because from now on—as far as I'm concerned—you don't exist. I've just eliminated you in my own way." He smiled at this thought, realizing just how liberating the moment was.

"In the flesh, you'll be dead soon enough," Tyler continued. "And without Jesus, you'll be spiritually dead, as well. But from this moment on, I forgive you for what you did." Tyler couldn't help but smile. "And that's something you have no say over—something you can't refuse or stop from being."

"You are a foolish white man," Runs With Buffalo called after him in English. "I will live to see you dead. I will kill you myself. I will kill all the white men and their children."

Tyler didn't acknowledge the man. He continued walking away, knowing that there was nothing left to say to the Indian chief. He drew a deep breath and let it out slowly, even as Runs With Buffalo continue to yell at him.

William came alongside him from seemingly out of nowhere. "You all right?"

Tyler looked at his friend. "Better than I've been in a long while."

"You sure riled him. I didn't think he was willing to speak the white man's words." William's tone was laced with sarcasm.

Nodding, Tyler continued to walk away from the stockade. "I could stand somethin' to eat. How about you?" He looked to William for an answer.

His friend seemed to understand. "I think that'd suit me real well."

~~~

Carissa sat in the early morning light relishing the quiet and reading in the Bible of God's faithfulness. The months spent growing closer to God through reading His Word had helped her to put aside the pain in her past.

Turning the page, her gaze fell on Psalm 5.

Give ear to my words, O Lord, consider my meditation. Hearken unto the voice of my cry, my King, and my God: for unto thee will I pray. My voice shalt thou hear in the morning, O Lord; in the morning will I direct my prayer unto thee, and will look up. For thou art not a God that hath pleasure in wickedness: neither shall evil dwell with thee. The foolish shall not stand in thy sight: thou hatest all workers of iniquity.

She let the words wash over her. She read them again, focusing in on the third verse. *My voice shalt thou hear in the morning, O Lord; in the morning will I direct my prayer unto thee, and will look up.*

Glancing to the porch roof, Carissa prayed. "I am directing my prayer unto thee. O God, please keep us in your care. Please put an end to the Indian wars. Please let there be peace. The times are so dangerous—so full of fear. Let me rest in you, Lord."

She drew a deep breath and returned her gaze to the Bible. Picking up again in the fifth psalm, Carissa continued to read.

Thou shalt destroy them that speak leasing: the Lord will abhor the bloody and deceitful man. But as for me, I will come into thy house in the multitude of thy mercy: and in thy fear will I worship toward thy holy temple. Lead me, O Lord, in thy righteousness because of mine enemies; make thy way straight before my face. For there is no faithfulness in their mouth; their inward part is very wickedness; their throat is an open sepulchre; they flatter with their tongue. Destroy thou them, O God; let them fall by their own counsels; cast them out in the multitude of their transgressions; for they have rebelled against thee.

She thought of Malcolm and the evil he'd done. There had been no faithfulness in anything he'd said or done. He flattered with his tongue, but he was wicked through and through. The only good thing Malcolm had ever done was in fathering Gloria.

"And he fell by his own counsel," she murmured. "As I nearly did."

Her thoughts went to Tyler and the ranch she'd purchased. "Please let him understand, Lord. I'm so afraid that he'll hate me for it, but I did it . . . I did it . . . out of love."

It was hard to admit the truth even to herself. She had fought so hard to avoid entangling her heart. She wanted to be reasonable and sensible—words that were always associated with her sister's choices, not hers.

Thinking of Laura, Carissa looked upward again. "Thank you for saving her, Lord. And thank you for helping Lucas to thrive." The doctor had come only the day before to declare that both mother and baby were moving well past the point of danger.

Of course with little ones, danger seemed to follow them always. She thought of Gloria and knew how frightened she was every time her child ran a fever. Sickness was so hard on children. "Keep her in your care, Lord. I thank you for giving her to me. She is so precious, and my life is better because of her. Gloria brings me such joy. Tyler . . . oh, Tyler brings me joy, as well." She couldn't imagine a more perfect union than with Tyler Atherton. Not for her, and definitely not for Gloria. The child adored him.

"There you are," Hannah said, stepping onto the porch. "I wasn't sure where you'd gone off to. I saw that the biscuits were already baking and knew you had to be somewhere nearby."

Carissa nodded. "I came here for my morning prayer time."

"I can leave, if you'd like."

"No, please stay. I was just coming to the end of my Bible reading and prayers."

Hannah took a seat beside her. "Why don't you read it aloud."

Carissa held up the Bible. " 'But let all those that put their trust in thee rejoice: let them ever shout for joy, because thou defendest them: let them also that love thy name be joyful in thee. For thou, Lord, wilt bless the righteous; with favour wilt thou compass him as with a shield.' "

She lowered the book and met Hannah's smiling face. "God will defend us. I really believe that. I know there are those who thought as much and still endured attack and death. But no matter what happens, I know God will defend us." Carissa closed the Bible and reached her hand over to Hannah's. Taking hold, she smiled. "I have such a joy that I have never known until these past few weeks. It seems so strange that in the middle of the Indian threat, I am finally at peace."

"Nothing strange at all, Carissa. God wants you not dependent upon the circumstances around you, but rather on Him.

These things are just light and momentary troubles." She gazed off across the landscape and sighed. "I love it here. I cannot imagine ever leaving it, yet I know my home in glory will be even better. It seems to me that God's blessings here are just a foretaste of those to come. And His peace is just one of those blessings. Relish it and don't think it strange. We serve a mighty God."

Carissa released Hannah's hand and hugged her Bible close. "I love him. I love him so."

Hannah studied her for a moment and smiled. "You aren't talking about God, are you?"

"I love Him, too," she said, shaking her head. "But no, I was talking about Tyler."

"I know."

Hannah's matter-of-fact reply caused Carissa to continue. "Oh, how I want him to be pleased that I purchased the ranch. I don't want him to feel pressured in any way, but I very much want us to be married. To be a family. Gloria needs him so."

"As do you."

Carissa met Hannah's eyes. "Yes. Yes, I need him. I never thought I could love another. I never thought I would trust enough to need anyone. Tyler . . . well . . . he worked through my defenses and now I am overwhelmed by my feelings. I suppose my only fear . . ." She fell silent.

Hannah finished Carissa's sentence. "Your only fear is that he won't feel the same way."

"Yes," Carissa whispered.

"Then you really have nothing to fear. I know Tyler. I believe with all my heart that he loves you. If he comes back here and fails to understand the love and sacrifice you showed in saving the ranch for him—I personally will hit him with a frying pan."

The seriousness of the moment was broken, and Carissa giggled. "You'd do that for me?"

Hannah nodded and got to her feet. "That and more. You've become a dear friend, Carissa Lowe. I look forward to the day when you are Carissa Atherton. For now, however, I think I'd best go pull out those biscuits before they burn."

"Oh goodness, I forgot all about them," Carissa declared, getting to her feet. She moved for the door, but Hannah took hold of her.

"You are like a sister to me. I hope you know that you will always be a special part of our lives. This time together—with the men away—well, it's been so precious to spend it with you and Laura. I hope we'll always stay close."

Carissa nodded and gave Hannah a hug. "I know we will."

Tyler looked to where Brandon Reid sat atop his horse. "Thanks for talkin' to me back at the fort." Tyler mounted and settled into the saddle. "I don't think I would have been able to put things aside if you hadn't said what you did."

Brandon pushed his hat back a bit. "Sometimes it's hard to see a matter clearly when it's staring you in the eye. I'm glad I could help."

"Maybe you can help me with something else," Tyler said. It was Tyler's turn to aid Brandon with his new horses. The four mares and one stallion had to be kept separated to ease tensions on the trail. Today Tyler would lead the mares. He took the rope Brandon offered and tied it around his saddle horn.

"I'm happy to help with whatever I can."

"You boys gonna jaw all day?" Osage asked, riding up alongside them. "Will done moved out and said you need to get caught up. We gotta stick close together."

They were still a good three-day ride from the ranch, and with each passing mile the tension seemed to grow. Twice they had passed burned-out ranch houses and seen signs left by the warriors who'd done the deed. To their relief, so far there hadn't been any bodies to bury or wounded to contend with.

They followed Osage and soon caught up with William and the others. William gave Tyler a brief nod before turning his attention back to the landscape before them. Each of the riders, including Andy, nervously scanned their surroundings for any sign of Indians.

"So what do you need my help with?" Brandon asked Tyler.

Smiling, Tyler felt rather sheepish now that the words actually needed to be said. "I'd like to . . . well . . . I plan to propose to Carissa. I guess I'd like your help, or maybe your blessin'. I know her folks are abroad, and we don't know what we'll find when we reach the ranch, but I'm prayin' for the very best."

Brandon frowned. "Me too. Nothing feels quite so bad as not knowing what's going on." He said nothing for a few minutes, then added, "I'm glad, though, that you want to marry Carissa. I think you two fit together. She's gonna need a strong man who loves the Lord. One who knows her past and can be patient with her."

"Well, I've thought about it for a long time now. Had nothin' but time to think for months now." He continued to watch the horizon for any sign of trouble. "The fact is, I love her. Love little Gloria, too. I don't have a home to give them, but you can be certain I will provide for them. I've got the cattle sale money, and I've got additional cattle back home if the Comanche haven't killed 'em off. I'll give Carissa and Gloria a good home. I want you to know that."

"I do, and I wasn't worried in the least. Living on the trail with a fella for months on end lets you get to know their character pretty well. I already had a high opinion of you, but these months out here have proven that opinion is well-founded. I'm proud to call you friend."

Tyler straightened a bit and nodded. "I feel the same. I have since we met in Corpus, and then when we had to go after the girls when Lowe meant to kill them . . . well . . . there isn't much I wouldn't do to help you."

"So how soon you figure to marry?" Brandon asked.

"I guess that's gonna depend on how quickly I can convince Carissa. She's been hurt pretty bad. I reckon it's not fair to push her too hard. I'll ask when we get back, and if she says no, then we'll just have to put our heads together and figure out another plan. If she says yes, then the sooner the better."

"I know Laura will help us." Then Brandon grew quiet and shook his head. "I cannot imagine my life without her, Tyler. She just has to be all right."

"I've been prayin' to be sure. I wish we could have found a faster way to get you back home. If the Indian troubles hadn't destroyed the telegraph lines into Cedar Springs, we might have been able to send a wire."

"At least then I'd know if . . ." He didn't finish the thought. "We did as good as anyone could," Brandon stated instead. "The trip to Kansas went well over all, and we've just had a few delays comin' home. I know there's absolutely nothing more I could have done."

"Probably nothing you could have done if you'd stayed behind either," Tyler added.

Brandon seemed to consider this for a moment. "I know you're probably right, but still, I'd feel better had I done just that. Maybe my leavin' caused her to worry more, and that brought the baby on early. Maybe she's had to work too hard. Whatever caused the trouble, I know she must be afraid. I know that it can't be easy."

"But she's in good hands." Tyler met Brandon's fretful expression. "Hannah is good at doctorin', and so's Juanita. I'm sure Laura has had the best of care. If those two couldn't give her the help she needed, then there sure as shootin' wouldn't have been anything for you to do."

"Still, I would have felt better just bein' there."

Tyler nodded. "I know you would've."

❦

"Just thought I'd ride out to let you know the latest," the sheriff announced to Hannah, Carissa, and Juanita. The day was hot, and the sheriff took off his hat and wiped his forehead with the back of his sleeve.

"I appreciate that, Sheriff. It's good to know that the army has driven the Indians back toward the reservations," Hannah said, shifting baby Lucas in her arms. "Has there been any word on Herbert Lockhart?"

"No, I'm afraid there's nothing to report where he's concerned. The telegraph lines are down. Last I heard, though, the trackers figured him to be headed toward Mexico."

Hannah's expression seemed to relax. "I hope that's the truth and that he's soon caught."

"Like I said before, it ain't likely he'd be fool enough to come this way. Too many folks know him, and quite a few hold him a grudge." He glanced around. "I heard tell the Terrys were stayin' here with you. They still here?"

"Marietta was with us for a time, but Ted came to get

her the day before yesterday." Hannah motioned to the front door. "Would you like to come in or sit here on the porch?"

"Don't really have time for either, though I wouldn't mind a cool drink," he said, smiling.

"I get it," Juanita declared and disappeared into the house.

"Much obliged." He nodded to the baby. "And how's Mrs. Reid doing? Doc said she was takin' a turn for the better."

"That she has," Hannah confirmed. "She's still quite weak, but recovering."

"In fact, I was just about to go to her," Carissa said, reaching out to take the baby from Hannah. "I'll tell her you asked about her."

"Do," the sheriff said with a smile. "I hope, too, that your men will be home soon."

"We expect them most any day," Hannah replied.

Carissa passed Juanita as she entered the house. The woman carried a small tray with not only some lemonade, but cookies, as well. No doubt the sheriff would appreciate the extra treat.

She quickly checked to see that Marty was still playing with Gloria, Daniel, and Robert in the backyard before heading to the bedroom to see Laura.

"So you're awake," she said, noting that Laura was sitting up in bed.

"Just," Laura admitted. "I'm glad you came to visit me."

"Would you like to hold your son? Juanita started him on some goat's milk, and it seems to agree with him better than the canned or cow's milk. He's fattening up quite nicely."

Laura held out her arms for the baby. Lucas knew his mother despite the conflicts and troubles that had surrounded them since his birth. He nestled against her breast and settled almost immediately into sleep.

"He's still so very small. I know neither one of us would be here if not for you, Rissa." The sisters locked gazes. "Thank you for what you've done," Laura added.

"We all had a hand in fighting for you." Carissa settled beside Laura on the bed. "I've never been more frightened."

"Me either." Laura glanced down at her son's sleeping form. "I can't remember much about those days right after Lucas was born, but I knew it was desperate."

"It was. All I could think about during that time was what you'd said to me about if I wasn't willing to risk loving someone because they might die, then I'd have to include you. I kept wondering if your words were some kind of a forewarning of your . . . death. It was more than I could bear. I begged God for your life and for Lucas's, too. I knew I had to keep him alive for you or you'd give up fighting despite having Brandon and Daniel to live for."

"I suppose I might have," Laura admitted. "I certainly didn't have a lot of strength to fight." She seemed to grow weak. "Why don't you put him in the cradle? I'm feeling tired again."

"That's to be expected." Carissa reached out to take the baby. "Remember what the doctor said: You will need a good long time to regain your strength."

"I'm so glad you came to stay the summer with us."

"Well, if I have anything to say about it, I'll be staying in the area permanently." Carissa put the baby in his bed and returned to Laura's side. "I bought Tyler's ranch."

"What?"

"You heard me right. I took the money in that account Father left me and bought Tyler's ranch. The county was about to auction it off or let it go for homestead. I couldn't let that happen. I couldn't let Tyler lose his home."

"So will you sell it back to him?"

"No, I can't," Carissa admitted. "Terms of the sale forbid it. So my plan is to get him to marry me instead."

"Marry?" Laura looked at Carissa as if she'd suddenly grown a second head. "For land?"

"No, silly, because I love him." Carissa smiled. "I love him more than I thought possible, and Gloria loves him, too. She already has been calling him her papa Tyer."

"Oh dear. What if Tyler isn't of a mind to marry?"

Carissa shrugged. "I can't let myself think that way. I have to stay positive for Gloria's sake as well as my own. I believe Tyler cares a great deal for her. He said he loved her. Maybe that's enough for now. I mean . . . well . . . if he doesn't love me."

Laura smiled. "I think we know he cares quite deeply for you."

"He's been gone a long while and things could have changed. I'm trying my best to leave it in God's hands and not be that silly girl with stars in her eyes who married Malcolm Lowe."

"You'll never be that girl again," Laura said, "and frankly, I'm glad. That Carissa was self-centered and had no purpose to serve but her own. I loved her, but I love and admire the woman you've become."

"Thank you." Carissa got to her feet and leaned down to kiss Laura's cheek. "I love and admire you, as well. But then, I always have. I suppose I will always look up to you. That's why it's important to me that you approve of my marrying Tyler."

"Of course I approve," Laura said, sounding even more tired.

"Good," Carissa replied. "You get some rest and when you wake up, we'll talk about planning the wedding."

Carissa left her sister and made her way back to the kitchen. Hannah and Juanita were busy preparing food, so Carissa presumed the sheriff had headed back to town.

"Lunch is nearly ready," Hannah said. "Would you mind fetching the children?"

"Happily," Carissa said, patting her own waist. "I feel like I could eat a bear."

Hannah laughed. "Well, it's just stew and biscuits. Hopefully that will satisfy you."

Carissa had no sooner stepped out the back door when Gloria began pulling her toward the other children. "Mama, come see the kitties." She let go of her hold on Carissa and reached into a basket of kittens.

The mewing animal protested the loss of its mother's nearness, and Marty chided Gloria. "Put him back. He's too little to be away from his mama." Gloria frowned, but did as she was instructed. Marty rubbed her curly blond head. "Good girl."

Carissa peered in the laundry basket at the swirling mass of fur. "How many are there?"

"Eight," Marty said as proudly as if she'd borne them herself.

"That's a quite a few mouths to feed." Carissa saw Gloria reach again for the babies. "No, no, Gloria. You must leave them to be with their mama."

"Besides," Marty said, getting to her feet, "it's almost lunchtime. Remember I told you that when we finished eating we'd make some toys?" She glanced up at Carissa. "We're gonna make some new playthings for Lucas."

"That sounds like a fine idea." She straightened and nodded to Gloria. "You go wash up with Marty and the boys. I need to visit the necessary and then I'll join you."

Carissa quickly saw to her needs and was about to head to the house to wash up when she heard a noise coming from behind the pen where the goats were kept. She listened and thought it sounded like one of the goats was in distress. Seeing none of the men who might help, Carissa went to investigate on her own. When she arrived at the pen she spotted the problem immediately. One of the young kids had managed to get tangled in the lines where the older goats were often tied to be milked.

"Poor baby," she said, pulling the kid's legs from the mess. Once she'd freed the animal, Carissa had to laugh at the way he jumped and kicked his way across the pen. "I'd probably do the same," she called after him.

Making sure that the ropes were hung over the top of the fence, Carissa secured the gate. The latch wanted to stick, and so she leaned closer to inspect the problem. As she straightened, rough hands clamped over her mouth.

"You'd do well not to scream. I've got orders to bring you back alive, but I won't be shot in the process. So if you wanna live, keep your mouth shut."

Carissa's knees nearly buckled in fear, and she thought she might well faint. She couldn't have spoken if she'd had to. Shaking from head to toe, she didn't even fight until after the man had gagged her and tied her hands. As he placed a bag over her head, Carissa seemed to wake up to the reality of what was happening. Giving the man a swift kick, she tried to run, only to have him grab her and throw her over his shoulder.

"You ain't goin' nowhere but with me."

She couldn't reply, nor could she see anything. The man didn't seem to care about being gentle. He tossed her across his saddle without any concern for the pain he caused. Carissa moaned as the horn dug into her ribs. The impact nearly knocked the wind from her. She tried to move her arms, but the bag came down too far and much too tight.

The man hit her hard across the backside. "Settle down now or I'll make you sorry."

Carissa did as he told her, not knowing what else to do. She was helpless to move, and without the ability to speak, she couldn't even attempt to reason with the man.

They rode for what seemed like hours. Twice Carissa had felt the contents of her stomach rise into her throat only to swallow it back down. She didn't know if it was from the ride itself or the stench of the man, but the nausea refused to leave. Pain ripped through her body. She cried out, but the muffled sound didn't even merit the attention of her captor.

Carissa tried her best to rationalize what was happening. The man who'd taken her wasn't an Indian, but rather a white man. He seemed intent on taking her specifically, saying that she was to be brought back alive. But why? Dread settled over her. Was this man one of Malcolm's cohorts? Had he come believing she had some treasure of Malcolm's?

Her mind whirled with questions and images. She could only hope and pray that there weren't others—that her being taken was an isolated incident and not just one of many other plots against the women on the Barnett ranch. Tears poured from her eyes, dampening the sack around her face.

Oh, Father in heaven, where are you? Help me! Help me, please!

"Where's Carissa?" Hannah asked her sister.

"She went to the outhouse," Marty replied, helping Gloria onto a chair. "She said she'd be right here."

But ten minutes later there was still no sign of Carissa. Hannah shook her head. "This isn't right. Juanita, you all go ahead and pray so that the children can eat. I'm going to see what's going on. Maybe Carissa is sick."

She moved quickly to the back door. "Or maybe something is very wrong," she muttered. A sense of dark trepidation came over her. "Carissa! Carissa!" she called as she made her way across the yard.

She checked the outhouse but no one was there. Glancing around the yard, she saw nothing that indicated Carissa had been there at all. The hairs on the back of her neck prickled. Carissa was gone. Hannah quickly searched through the outbuildings. Some of the men were working to break a horse in the far pen, but Berto wasn't among them. Continuing her search, Hannah found Berto sharpening an axe.

"Have you seen Carissa?" she asked the man.

"No. Why do you ask?"

"She was supposed to join us in the house for lunch. She went to the outhouse, but never came back."

Berto put down the axe and got up. "I will help you look."

Hannah nodded, but already she felt certain that Carissa was gone. She didn't know how or where, but something in her mind warned her it wasn't going to be to anyone's liking.

I just don't understand," Laura said. "Why would anyone take Carissa?"

Hannah shook her head and patted Laura's hand. She hadn't wanted to give bad news to Laura, fearing it would cause a setback in her weakened condition.

"I don't know. I don't even know if it was Indians." Hannah forced back tears. "She went to the outhouse and that was the last anyone saw of her. Apparently someone grabbed her while she was out there, but no one saw or heard anything."

Thunder rumbled. A summer storm moved ever closer and Hannah knew this would only cause them more problems. Berto had found boot prints leading to a single horse. The horse had been led out in a southwesterly direction, but now the rain would obliterate the tracks. She didn't bother to tell Laura this. It would surely only cause more panic.

Laura looked at Hannah, her eyes wide with fear. "Will they kill her? I mean . . ." She fell silent.

"I don't know. We have no way of knowing. If it were Comanche or Kiowa, I think they would have raided the entire ranch and burned us out. They had ample opportunity to take the children or any one of us earlier in the day. Berto said he found indications of boot prints, so I don't think it was Indians. Some wear boots like ours, but not that many. Most prefer their own style of moccasin or nothing at all." Hannah still held tight to Laura's hand.

"I've sent for the sheriff," Hannah continued to explain. "I expect him most any time." At least she hoped he'd be there soon. There was a fair chance that he wasn't even in Cedar Springs. Pablo had been the one sent to fetch him, and he hadn't returned yet.

"I feel so helpless," Laura said. "I'm still so weak and tired, but I want to do something to help."

Hannah nodded. "I know, but you must rest. Taking care of Lucas is more than enough help. It leaves the rest of us free to do what we can." She didn't have the heart to explain that there really wasn't anything to be done. "And your prayers . . . your prayers are priceless."

A flash of lightning filled the room with a boom of thunder following seconds later. "That storm is right on top of us," Hannah said, getting to her feet. "I need to go check on the children. We've had the house closed up tight ever since Carissa went missing. Just in case."

Laura frowned. "In case there's another attack."

She said it so matter-of-factly that Hannah knew it wasn't a question. "We're doing all we can. Like I said, I honestly don't know what to think about the situation."

But she did. In the back of Hannah's mind she was already wondering if Herbert Lockhart had something to do with

Carissa's disappearance. Maybe he had come and, not being able to get to Hannah, had taken Carissa. Maybe he thought to trade one for the other. A bevy of scenarios played out in her head.

"I'll keep you informed," Hannah said, moving toward the door.

"I want to see the sheriff when he comes. Please."

Hannah nodded. "Of course. I'll bring him in to see you when he arrives."

"And, Hannah," Laura said, fixing her with a stern expression, "no matter what the truth is, I want to know everything. Don't lie to me about this. It's much too important."

"I promise I will tell you everything."

But even as she left, Hannah felt guilty for not sharing her concerns about Herbert Lockhart. She knew that Carissa had had a rough life in Corpus Christi and that Laura likely presumed some enemies of Carissa's late husband had followed her to the area. But Hannah seriously doubted this was the case.

She checked on Marty, who was playing with the children in the loft. Gloria came to Hannah, demanding to see her mother.

"I want my mama."

Hannah lifted the girl in her arms. "I know you do, darlin', but she had to go away for a little while. You play and be good and when she comes home . . ." Hannah choked on the words and found she couldn't continue.

Marty came and took Gloria from her older sister. "I wish you'd let me help look for her."

Hannah shook her head at Marty with a look that demanded her silence. "You are serving a much greater purpose in helping with the children. Pepita will come and relieve you in about an hour, but until then, just keep them busy."

"Hold me, Mama," Robert said, hugging his arms around Hannah's legs. "Pease, Mama." Then thunder boomed overhead, and Daniel began to cry.

"You need to be brave," she told her son. His expression indicated that he, too, was close to tears.

Marty deposited Gloria on the rug in front of the building blocks and picked up Daniel. "He doesn't like storms."

"None of us do," Hannah replied. She could only hope that this storm wouldn't bring any threat of tornadoes. "You children be very good, and I'll have Pepita bring you cookies and milk in a little bit. Would you like that?"

Gloria clapped, now unconcerned with her missing mother or the storm. "I like cookies."

Robert nodded. "Me too. I want cookies."

"Then be a good boy for Marty."

With that, Hannah returned to the first floor and went to the kitchen. She was instructing Pepita when she realized someone was knocking at the back door. She hoped it was Pablo returning with the sheriff. Hurrying to see, Hannah was glad to see the law official standing there.

"Mrs. Barnett," he said, tipping his hat. Water dripped onto the floor and it was then that Hannah noticed the rain had begun to fall.

"Please come in." She stepped aside and motioned him to follow. "I hope that Pablo has filled you in on our situation."

"He did." The sheriff took his hat off and brushed water from the felt.

Juanita was busy making tortillas, but she glanced up long enough to offer the sheriff a cup of coffee. He declined, and

Hannah led him into the dining room, where she hoped they wouldn't be overheard by the children.

"Berto and some of the others have tried to track whoever took Carissa, but now with the storm, I'm sure that will be of no use to us."

"Do they have any idea of who might have done this? Pablo said there weren't any signs of Indians."

"No, there weren't. Not that the Comanche always leave their calling cards," Hannah replied, taking a seat at the table. She motioned the sheriff to do likewise. "But I believe if it were the Comanche, they wouldn't have stopped with taking just one woman. They would have burned us out—killed us. It makes no sense for them to take one woman."

The sheriff took a chair and considered her words for a moment. He didn't get a chance to speak, however, as Hannah continued in a hushed voice.

"What about Herbert Lockhart?"

"What about him?"

Hannah squared her shoulders. "The man wants to see me dead. He isn't the kind to leave business undone."

"But Mrs. Lowe had nothing to do with Lockhart."

"I know, but it's possible he took Carissa in order to hurt me in some way," Hannah replied. "I mean, I know what he's capable of. He could have taken her thinking that it would force us to do whatever he wanted."

"I suppose that is a possibility, but honestly, no one has seen anything of Lockhart in this area. Like I told you, my last report before the lines went down was that word came of him headin' for Mexico."

"I know."

"Did Mrs. Lowe have any personal problems . . . someone

who might have come here with the sole purpose of harming her?"

"Mrs. Lowe had a very bad marriage in Corpus Christi. She was married to a Confederate who plotted against the government. He tried to kill her and her sister." Hannah's voice was just a whisper. "He was killed, but I suppose it's always possible that some of his men might mean her harm. Still, I don't know why they would."

"But it is a possibility that we must consider."

Hannah nodded. "I suppose it is. We could ask her sister, although Mrs. Reid is still quite weak."

"I think we must talk to her," the sheriff agreed. "She might have an idea of something that we've not yet thought of."

❧

Carissa didn't know if she'd passed out or fallen asleep out of pure exhaustion, but when she awoke she found herself stretched out beside a campfire, hands tied in front of her and the dreaded sack gone. Struggling to sit up, she found three men watching her while they ate.

"What's going on?" she asked groggily. "What do you want with me?"

One of the men got to his feet and came to where she sat. He crouched down and Carissa could see in the firelight that he was at least part Indian. "Do you want to eat?" he asked in perfect English.

"I want to go home." She all but spat the words.

He smiled. "You aren't going anywhere but with us."

"Why?" She fixed her gaze on his eyes, searching for the truth.

"Because I said so."

The other men laughed, and the Indian got to his feet. "If you want to eat, there's food and I will give you some. If not—it's your loss."

Carissa ignored the rumble in her stomach and looked instead at the other two men. "Why are you doing this?" They were white men, and it was clear that this was in no way a part of an Indian attack. Apparently the Indian cohort was simply a part of their gang.

"We got our reasons, and none of them are your business," one of the men replied. He continued eating from a metal plate, uninterested in Carissa's concerns.

"My family will never stand for this," she told the men. "They will come after me."

"Most likely they will try," the third man said. "But they won't accomplish much. Long Knife knows how to cover his tracks."

Carissa looked at the man but said nothing. Except for Night Bear, she'd never had any encounters with Indians. Long Knife ladled beans onto a tin plate. Next he added a piece of jerked meat. He looked at Carissa for a moment, then retrieved a spoon from what appeared to be his own plate.

Bristling silently at his approach, Carissa tried to keep a brave front. She didn't want these men to think they had bested her. Long Knife crouched beside her once again. He put the plate on the ground at Carissa's right and pulled a blade from his belt.

The long gleaming knife seemed a poignant reminder of the man's name. He motioned to her hands. Carissa hoped he only meant to cut her bonds loose. She raised her bound wrists. With a quick flick of his knife, the Indian freed her.

"If you try to run; I'll cut the backs of your heels."

She shivered at the thought and rubbed her wrists. "Where are you taking me?"

The Indian stood. "Eat."

She frowned. Why wouldn't they just tell her what their plans were? She was just one small woman and could hardly thwart their efforts. After a moment of contemplation, Carissa picked up the plate and sampled the beans. She felt famished and downed the food without even considering what it was she ate. Her only thought was to keep up her strength and figure a way out of her situation.

When the men finished eating, Carissa waited to see what they might say or do. One of the men stretched out by the fire and pulled his hat down over his eyes. Long Knife came to where Carissa sat and took her plate and spoon.

"You can relieve yourself over there," he said, pointing to a stand of trees. "Just remember, if you try to run away, I will cut you."

Carissa nodded and got to her feet. She felt sore from head to toe and for a moment wasn't even sure she could walk. She took a hesitant step and then another. The trees didn't look to offer much coverage, but she took advantage of the moment nevertheless. When she returned to the camp, Long Knife motioned to the fire. "We will sleep for a time. I will tie you up again."

She said nothing. What could she say, after all? She could tell him that she thought his actions were barbaric. Tell him she wanted to go home. But they didn't care. They were clearly following someone's orders.

"Where are we going?" she finally asked.

Long Knife bound her wrists and this time her feet, as well. With the rawhide straps he used to tie her ankles, he connected the other end to his wrist. "I am a very light sleeper. I will know if you move." Last of all, he took up a blanket and tossed it over her.

Carissa looked him in the eye. "Tell me where we're going. Tell me why you've taken me."

He stretched out at her feet. "Go to sleep."

She wanted to scream in protest. She wanted to kick him in the head. Instead, she forced her feelings to wane. Thinking of Gloria and her longing to be home, Carissa decided she would be far wiser to at least pretend cooperation.

For a long while she considered the situation. When Long Knife had taken her, he said something about someone wanting her alive. So obviously Long Knife and the other men didn't plan to kill her. That gave her some comfort. But who had sent them?

Staring up at the stars overhead, Carissa tried her best not to move. *God, are you there? Do you see me here? Do you care?* She had spent so much time reading the Bible and praying, and she had thought that she was actually starting to understand God. Now this had happened, and she wasn't sure she understood anything at all.

Carissa thought of her loved ones. By now they knew she was truly gone, but would they guess who had taken her or what direction they'd gone? The men said Long Knife would have covered their tracks. She let go a heavy sigh. What about Tyler? Was he home by now? Did he know she'd been taken? No doubt the tired men would jump to action when they heard. At least she hoped they would.

Forgetting about the leash Long Knife had put her on, Carissa rolled to her side. The Indian didn't so much as move. She didn't know if that was because he slept or because he knew she wasn't going anywhere. Either way, she was his prisoner.

Carissa felt that she'd barely fallen asleep when Long Knife was shaking her awake. "Get up. We're gonna ride. You need to eat."

She sat up and looked around her, remembering the night before. She wondered where the other two men had gone. The camp looked deserted. Long Knife untied her ankles but left her hands secured.

"Where are your friends?" she asked.

Long Knife looked at her for a moment. Finally he gave a grunt and replied, "They're readying the horses. You need to go?" He motioned to the trees.

Carissa shook her head. "No, I'm fine."

Long Knife brought her some jerked beef and a canteen. "Eat. We have a long ride."

She ate the beef and took a long drink from the canteen. It was awkward at best with her hands tied, but not impossible. The men approached with the horses, and Long Knife came to pull her to her feet. He took the canteen and motioned to the horses. "Can you ride?"

"Not well, but I certainly don't want to go in the same manner as yesterday." She eyed the large buckskin gelding and then looked back at the Indian. "I'll do my best."

"You'll ride in front of me," Long Knife said. He didn't give her a chance to protest, but lifted Carissa as if she weighed nothing and hoisted them both up to the saddle in one motion. Carissa gasped, fearing he might drop her, but Long Knife's strong arms held her fast.

He rested her in his lap and the forced nearness was enough to make Carissa rebel. "I cannot ride like this."

"You'll ride like this or like you did yesterday," he told her.

The men laughed, and one of them couldn't help but comment, "You'd best get used to it, missus. Ain't nobody here concerned about your comfort."

Carissa narrowed her eyes at the man. She wanted nothing more than to tell him exactly what she thought, but she held her tongue. If she was going to get away, she would have to convince them that she wasn't a threat. Bowing her head, she nodded ever so slightly.

Long Knife kicked the buckskin into motion and the trio made their way across the vast expanse of land. Carissa looked for landmarks—anything that she might recognize—but there was very little to go on. She didn't know where they'd brought her.

The horizon stretched out before them in grassy prairie and rocky hills. Occasionally they crossed a muddy creek or river and enjoyed the shade of the trees that lined the water's edge. They followed small trails from time to time, but mostly they cut across the land and headed ever farther from her loved ones.

If she could have been with Tyler, the ride might have been enjoyable. The views were definitely pretty and she was quite amazed at how this part of Texas differed from that of the coastal south. Herds of longhorn cattle grazed openly, and occasionally a mule-eared dear or a rabbit could be spotted. At one point one of the men riding ahead took off after a rabbit. Carissa heard the shot and in a short time he rejoined them with the rabbit hanging off the side of his saddle.

"We'll have rabbit stew this evening," he said, grinning.

The idea actually sounded rather appealing to Carissa. She wondered if they would expect her to clean and cook the animal or if they'd leave her tied up. Perhaps she could volunteer to be useful and they'd leave off her bonds. It was worth asking about.

"I can cook quite well," she told Long Knife. "Perhaps you'd like for me to prepare the rabbit."

He paused for the briefest moment. "Maybe." That was all he said, however, and Carissa didn't feel she should press the issue.

She noted the sun moving across the sky as the day dragged on, and determined they were headed southwest. At least that was what it looked like to her. Maybe they'd get overconfident that she was far enough away from all that she knew, and they'd leave her unbound if they allowed her to cook. If so, Carissa could take a chance and run tonight.

But what good will it do me? I have no idea where I am or where they are taking me. If I managed to get away, there would be nowhere for me to go. With miles of open land, they would easily find me. She frowned, fearing the entire situation was rather hopeless.

Toward late afternoon they rested the horses, shared some more jerky, and then resumed the ride. Carissa was so stiff and sore she could hardly bear to be put back on the horse. She said nothing, however, afraid that if she did, Long Knife would threaten to return her to her former position.

The heat had grown steadily throughout the day and Carissa found herself quite miserable. Perspiration trickled down her face, and she didn't even have a sunbonnet to ease her discomfort.

"When will we stop?" she asked Long Knife.

"Soon." His brief reply irritated her, but again Carissa held her temper.

The long ride took its toll, and she found herself dozing off and on. She first tried to fight her exhaustion, but soon found sleep a welcome relief from the pain. She thought again of Tyler and how he had plans to teach her to ride. If this trip was any indication, Carissa knew she'd want nothing more to do with any time on the back of a horse. Then she dreamed of Gloria and Tyler together. They seemed so happy, and she couldn't help but wonder if Tyler would remain in Gloria's life—should something happen.

"There's the shack," one of the men called out.

The sound of men's voices slowly awakened Carissa. She was drenched in sweat and now smelled as bad as the man who held her. She longed for a bath but doubted anyone would offer her such a treat.

She tried to get her bearings and noted that the landscape had changed to scrub and rocky ledges. They seemed to be making their way along a dry wash or something of the sort. Just ahead was a small cabin—a shack, just as the man had called it. The unpainted wood made it look ancient and fragile. Carissa couldn't help but think of the seaside shack Malcolm had kept her in just before his demise.

They pulled up to the place and dismounted. Carissa's legs buckled beneath her and without a word, Long Knife lifted her in his arms. She was too tired and sore to protest. Once inside, Carissa couldn't suppress a moan when Long Knife put her upon a straight-backed chair. He looked at her with something akin to sympathy.

"Are you thirsty?"

"Thirsty. Hot. Tired. Hurting. You name it," she replied.

He nodded and brought her a canteen. "Drink."

She did as he instructed. "So what now?"

"Now we wait."

She looked at the men who were busying themselves with lighting a lantern and laying a fire. "Wait? For what?"

"For the man who paid us to bring you here," Long Knife replied.

They didn't have long to wait. The sound of horse hooves coming toward the cabin sent all three men into position. Long Knife put out the lamp and went to the window. The other two men took up their places on the other side of the door. Carissa remained where she was, knowing that if bullets started to fly, she'd most likely be struck.

"It's Jesse!" a voice called out. "Don't shoot."

Carissa could barely see in the faint glow of firelight from the hearth. One of the men went to open the door while the other lit the lamp. She racked her memories for a man named Jesse. Was he one of Malcolm's friends? Perhaps an enemy?

The door burst open and a tall, grizzled-looking man bounded in with an older, shorter man behind him. The older man took one look at Carissa and screwed up his face.

"Who in the blue blazes is she?"

"The woman you sent us to get," Long Knife replied.

Jesse shook his head. "You got it wrong, brother. This ain't Hannah Barnett."

Carissa looked at the men and shook her head. "No, I'm Carissa Lowe. I was just staying at the Barnett ranch."

Jesse spit on the floor and scowled. "Should've gone myself."

"She fits the description you gave us," Long Knife countered.

"Well, she might have Hannah's coloring," the older man said, "but it's not her. You have to go back and get the right woman."

"Go back? Now?" one of the other men questioned. "They'll have the law called on us by now."

The older man moved forward and took a seat across from Carissa. It was then that it dawned on her that this man was the one who'd broken out of jail. The one Hannah was afraid would come to seek her out.

"You're Mr. Lockhart, aren't you?" she asked.

He seemed surprised, but smiled. "I am. I suppose Hannah has talked about me."

She shook her head. "Not much. But the sheriff has. He warned us that you were on the run."

Lockhart sneered. "Well, he might know that much, but he don't know much else."

"So you had these men come to take Hannah, but they got me instead," Carissa said, trying to put all the pieces together. "You were planning to kill her, weren't you?"

"She has it coming," he said without feeling. He looked at Jesse. "You're right, you should have gone yourself. Long Knife and you best go back now and do what you can."

"You're a fool if you think Hannah hasn't already prepared for that," Carissa declared. "She has that place well defended. It was only my own foolishness that allowed me to get taken by your men. Besides, our men are due back anytime. Once they're in place, you won't stand a chance to cause any more trouble."

Long Knife shook his head. "She's right. They had that place pretty well under guard. They even had night riders keeping watch. It won't be easy to get within a mile of it."

Carissa smiled and nodded. "Exactly. You won't ever get your hands on Hannah or anyone else."

Lockhart considered her words. His expression was almost a leer as he turned back to her. "Well, we still have you."

His words caused a chill to go down Carissa's spine, and she could see the cold indifference in the man's eyes. He truly didn't care what happened to her and would use her to suit his purpose. That much was clear.

I can't believe you're finally here," Hannah said, falling
into William's arms.

"Me either." He pulled her to his lips and kissed her, then
stepped back to eye her rounded stomach. "Just look at you."

"I'm a sight to be sure." She sniffed back tears.

"A beautiful sight," he said with a grin.

Tyler looked around for some glimpse of Carissa, but saw
no one else. He pounded the dust off his pants and shirt and
went to the well for water. He gave the handle a couple of
good pumps and was soon rewarded with fairly cool water. It
felt good on his face and with another pump he had enough
water flowing to pour over his head.

"It's good to have you home, too, Tyler."

Snapping up at the sound of his name, Tyler grinned behind the streams of water. "Feels mighty good to be back,
Hannah." He crossed back to where she stood with William
and Brandon. "Although I guess I'm without a ranch now."

His smile faded. "You never know what life is going to throw your way." He tried his best not to sound too discouraged, but in truth, this homecoming was something of a mixed barrel of emotions for him.

Hannah started to say something, but Brandon took hold of her arm. He looked grim and his voice sounded strained "Laura?"

"She's doing very well, and so is your son Lucas."

A look of relief filled Brandon's face. Tyler thought he might actually fall to his knees. "Praise God." Tears trickled down Brandon's cheek. "I've been praying since we got the telegram from the sheriff. I have to say I feared the worst."

"He said something about having sent the news, but I wish he wouldn't have done that. I knew there was nothing you could do, and I knew it would only cause you greater worry to wait."

"I must go see my wife." Brandon wiped his eyes and bounded for the front door of the house.

Hannah said nothing until he'd gone. She looked into the eyes of her husband and then turned to Tyler. "We have an entirely new problem—a very grave matter. Carissa has been taken."

"What? Taken where?" Tyler demanded. "By whom?" He pulled off his kerchief and wiped his face and hair. With his fingers he slicked back the wet strands and waited for her answer.

Hannah shook her head. "We don't know. I know this sounds ludicrous, but someone took her two days ago. She went to the outhouse, and that was the last anyone saw of her. We found some tracks, but whoever took her worked to cover them. Then the rain obliterated any further signs before

Berto could get very far. You can speak with him about it, but he said that once the tracks made a wide circle around the ranch, the rider headed southwest."

Tyler thought surely she was joking. Who would have any reason to take Carissa? "Indians?" he asked aloud.

"Berto doesn't think so. The horse was shod, the man wore boots, and there wasn't any other indication of Indians. The person did try to cover their tracks."

"Then who would want to take her?"

She looked at William. "I think I might have an idea. Herbert Lockhart escaped jail some months back. The sheriff told me he'd be crazy to come here, but I know the man is crazy—and it wouldn't surprise me at all for him to have been the one to take Carissa."

"He wouldn't have done it himself," William said. "He'd probably hire it done. But why take Carissa? Why not wait it out and nab you?"

"If he sent someone to do it," Tyler said, "could be they didn't know what Hannah looked like. The two aren't that different in build. Might be, too, they weren't expectin' any other white women on the ranch. After all, Lockhart would have no way of knowin' that Carissa and her sister were here. He probably told his men to grab the only white woman on the place."

"That would make sense." William looked back at his wife. "Two days ago, you say?"

She nodded. "Yes. It was about lunchtime."

"Did the sheriff have anything more to say about it?" Tyler asked. He moved toward his horse. "Never mind. I'll ride into town and talk to him myself."

William gave Hannah's arm a squeeze. "I'll go with him."

Tyler shook his head. "You don't need to."

"Neither of you need to go. The sheriff is with his men looking for Carissa right now. He promised he'd stop in on his way back to town if he had any news at all. So it would be better if you'd come inside and wait rather than head out aimlessly. Juanita and Pepita are getting supper on."

Everything in him protested doing nothing, but Tyler knew the futility of just heading off on his own without any real understanding of the situation. Especially since they were losing the light. He would talk to Berto and see if he could get the man's fix on what happened, and then perhaps he would head out to search for Carissa after he had a good night's sleep.

"Like I could sleep now," he muttered.

Just then the children came running out the front door with Marty close behind. Robert made his way to William, squealing with delight as his father hoisted him up and tossed him high in the air.

Gloria made a beeline for Tyler and clapped her hands. "Papa Tyer! Papa Tyer!"

He looked at the child in wonder and lifted her in his arms. He hugged her close, and she nestled her head against his neck. "I think you've grown a foot," he murmured.

"I got a foot," she said, her head popping back up. She stuck out her leg. "See."

He smiled. "You sure do. And I got you a present." He tried not to think of the ring in his pocket and the woman who was so evidently absent.

"Mama goed away," Gloria said matter-of-factly. She didn't even seem to care that he'd brought her a gift. "Did you see Mama?" Her expression grew quite serious.

He shook his head. "No, but I will find her for us."

Gloria smiled and nodded. "I come with you."

Tyler shook his head again. "No, you'll have to stay here. But when I find her, I'll bring her right back."

The little girl gave a pout, and Tyler wasn't sure if it was the prelude to tears. So he again brought up the fact that he had a gift for her. "Don't you want your present, Miss Gloria?"

"A pwesent for me." It wasn't a question, but rather a statement of fact.

"Yes, a present for you. Come on. I think I put it in the wagon. Let's go see if we can find it." Despite his desire to talk to Berto, he knew Gloria needed the distraction at the moment.

They retrieved the doll, and Gloria hugged it close. She said very little but studied the doll long and hard. She kept touching the golden hair and china face.

"So what will you name her?" Tyler asked.

"Mama," Gloria replied.

He felt his throat tighten. He hadn't thought of the doll looking similar to Carissa, but apparently it touched that chord in Gloria. He put her on the ground and watched her continue to assess the toy.

"Come on. Let's head back to the house."

As they walked, Gloria chattered to the doll and occasionally stumbled over her own feet. Tyler was poised to right her, knowing she couldn't be bothered with the ground and her feet when such a toy awaited her inspection.

She was such a precious child, and the fact that she was now calling him Papa had touched him in a way he hadn't expected. He wondered if Carissa had encouraged the title, or if Gloria had come up with it herself. It wouldn't have been likely that Carissa would promote such a thing. After all, when they parted company, Carissa had seemed almost indifferent to him. Almost. But not quite.

Now she was gone, and Tyler couldn't help but wonder what they would do if Carissa didn't return.

Don't be borrowin' trouble, he chided himself silently. *Won't do any good to think that way. I need all my focus to be on finding her. Not on what to do if I don't.* He continued to berate himself about how to handle the matter until Hannah interrupted his thoughts.

"Tyler?"

He looked up and met her concerned expression. "Yeah?"

"I'm so sorry. I feel like there's something more I could have done, but I honestly thought we were taking all the necessary precautions."

"Don't go blamin' yourself, Hannah. This is the fault of an evildoer, not some lackin' on your part."

Gloria held out her doll. "See Mama?"

Hannah's look of confusion caused Tyler to speak. "Gloria says she's callin' the doll *Mama.*"

"Oh, I see. For a moment I thought she was calling me that. I couldn't . . . well . . . never mind. I understand now." She smiled and leaned down. "She's a beautiful doll."

"Papa Tyer got her for me." Gloria beamed.

"She's quite lovely. Now why don't you go inside and get washed up for supper. Ask Marty to help you put the dolly up until after you eat."

"No, Mama's gonna eat with me."

Hannah bit her lip and nodded. "All right. Go get washed up."

Tyler watched Gloria head into the house. He turned back

to find tears running down Hannah's face. He shook his head and handed her a handkerchief from his pocket. "Don't be cryin', Hannah. It won't help a thing, and you'll just upset yourself. No sense causin' that baby any grief."

"Oh, Tyler. I wish it had been me."

"No. Don't be sayin' such things," he said, putting his arm around her. "God's got a plan in all of this. I don't begin to understand what it is, but I know He's got a plan. We gotta trust Him with Carissa."

She nodded and wiped her eyes. "I do. It's all that's gotten me through."

⸺

"Oh, Brandon," Laura sobbed. She clung to him, refusing to let go. "I prayed so hard for your return. I've been so afraid."

"I was afraid myself. When I learned you were so sick . . . well . . . all I wanted was to be home," he said, smoothing back damp hair from her face. "I'm so glad you're on the mend."

"I am, but Carissa is gone." She pulled back just a bit. "She's been missing for two days."

"What are you talking about—missing?" He shook his head. "Surely she didn't just take off."

Laura grasped his hand as he sat beside her. "Someone took her. We don't know who did it or where they've taken her." Her voice broke. "I just feel like the entire world has turned upside down. What are we to do?"

"I can tell you what we're not going to do: We're not going to let you get yourself all worked up over this. This is bad, but not so bad that we can't find hope in God. Right?"

She lifted her tear-filled eyes to meet his gaze. "I know you're right, but Carissa is so fragile. She doesn't know how to do much for herself. Even if she managed to escape her captor, how would she ever find her way home?"

"A body usually does what they have to when put to the task. Your sister is stronger than you give her credit for. We'll find her, but you have to calm down. Or is this problem too big for God?"

She looked rather shocked at his question. "Of course not."

"Good." He nodded to the sleeping baby in the cradle beside the bed. "He needs for you to get strong and be back on your feet. Daniel needs you to be there for him. And I need you, Laura. I need you more than I could ever imagine needing anyone." He caressed her cheek, then leaned forward to place a gentle kiss upon her lips. "We will see this through together, and God will oversee it all."

She nodded. "I know you're right. I want to be strong and have faith. Hannah and Juanita have been so good to pray with me. They saved my life, you know."

"I figured as much." He smiled. "William told me Hannah is quite handy with sick folk. I'll admit, I wanted for you to have a doctor and a good hospital for all the best of care, but then I got to thinking about how competent Hannah is—and I figured you had the best."

"I did. The doctor did come, but he said I was beyond his ability. At least that's what Juanita told me. She said the doctor did what he could, but said it wasn't likely for either Lucas or me to make it."

"I'm glad you proved him wrong." William caressed her arm. "I don't honestly know what I would have done if you hadn't made it. I couldn't imagine living my life without you here. I don't care if we never have another baby—but I can't lose you, Laura."

It was her turn to reach out to him. She put her hand against his cheek. "I love you, Brandon Reid. I promise you, I'll do my best not to cause you any more worry."

He grinned and covered her hand with his own. "You'd better not—if you know what's good for you." The baby stirred, drawing Brandon's attention. "He's so little."

"Yes, but he's got a good appetite, and he's eating quite well on a goat milk mix that Juanita came up with. I couldn't provide for him because of the sickness." She frowned. "It's my deepest regret."

"Don't let it be, Laura. God has provided another way, and the most important thing is that you are getting well. That is all I want."

"And all I want, now that you're back, is for Carissa to be found unharmed. Oh, Brandon, what will we do if they have . . . if they . . ." Laura couldn't finish. She lowered her face and shook her head.

"I thought we agreed to trust God." She looked up, and Brandon continued. "We will do whatever needs to be done, Laura."

"But what about Gloria?"

"Listen to you. You're already thinking the worst. Now stop it. You need to have faith that God will get us through this. It might not turn out the way we expect or want, but we will trust in Him."

⌒

"She did what?" Tyler said as the supper discussion turned to his ranch.

Hannah looked momentarily upset. "I suppose I shouldn't

have said anything. I know Carissa wanted to surprise you herself."

"She bought the ranch?" Tyler asked. "How in the world did she do that? Why did she do that?" He didn't know whether to be relieved or angry. Right now what he mostly felt was confused.

"Because the county was going to sell it out from under you," Hannah answered, seeming to put aside all of her doubts regarding the secret. "Judge Peevy came and told us what was happening."

"And she just up and bought it?" Tyler shook his head. "But why?"

"Carissa said she had to try to save it for you."

Tyler tried to imagine Carissa's logic in the matter. "For me?"

Hannah smiled. "Yes. She knew what the ranch meant to you. She had some money her father had left for her and Gloria to live on. She pooled all of her resources, and Judge Peevy secured the property for her."

Tyler was stunned by her generosity. "Then she can just sell it back to me."

"No." Hannah shook her head. "She signed a contract saying she wouldn't."

Tyler frowned and looked at William. "Why would she do that?"

Hannah continued. "It was the only way. They wouldn't allow purchase for those who fought for the Confederacy. The contract required that she never sell it to anyone who'd done so."

"Maybe she figured she could sell it to me and then I could sell it to you," William offered. "After all, I didn't sign any such contract. When we find her, we'll figure it all out. I'll get Judge Peevy on it."

"The contract also said she couldn't sell it for five years," Hannah interjected. "It states that Carissa has to live there for that time."

"Five years?" Tyler asked. "What in the world was she thinking?"

Hannah looked at him with a smile. "Well, personally, I think she had it in mind to save it for the both of you. The contract didn't say anything about marrying a Confederate. If you two marry, the place will automatically return to your ownership. At least in part."

Tyler warmed at this thought, but it still seemed impossible to believe that the ranch hadn't been put out of his reach. "We heard it had sold. I despaired of even returning to Texas."

"I know. Bless the sheriff and his good intentions, but again . . . I wish he would never have sent that telegram."

Tyler's mind whirled about the idea that Carissa had purchased his family's ranch. What was she planning? Did she want the ranch to be their home?

"When I left, she was hardly speakin' to me," Tyler said aloud. Then he looked around to see if anyone had heard him. Of course they had.

"She was upset about Ava, that's all," Hannah replied. She helped Daniel with some green beans, then turned back to Tyler. "She thought Ava was a rival, but I set her straight. She's completely gone over you, Tyler. She and Gloria both."

He couldn't help but grin. "Truly?"

William rolled his eyes. "And he's gone over her. Show them what you bought Mrs. Lowe when you were in Abilene."

Tyler felt his face grow hot, but he did as William instructed and pulled the ring from his pocket. He opened the leather box and revealed the contents. Hannah and Juanita gasped.

"A wedding ring! Oh, she'll be so happy," Hannah declared, then just as quickly fell silent. She looked at her plate and Tyler could see that she was thinking of Carissa's circumstances.

"I will get her back," Tyler said, replacing the leather box in his pocket. "If Herbert Lockhart arranged to take her, he's got no reason to keep her. He's after you and, well . . . we ain't gonna let him have you or Carissa."

"That's right." William cut into a piece of ham and avoided Hannah's gaze. "If the sheriff hasn't sent word in the next two days—we're heading out on our own. I'll need for you to pack us some supplies."

To Tyler's surprise, Hannah didn't protest. "I'll have it ready."

"Tyler and I will go alone. The rest of the men will stay on here at the ranch to offer protection. I'll see to it that they're paid, and I know Ted Terry will spare his fellas. We'll see Ted tomorrow and let him know what's going on."

Tyler cut into his own ham steak and tried not to think about what Carissa might be having for supper that evening. Perhaps her captors weren't even feeding her. He frowned and tore at the steak with a little more effort than was needed. If they hurt her, he'd see to it that they paid the price.

⌇

Lockhart wouldn't allow Carissa to prepare supper. Instead, he instructed Long Knife to tie her to the chair and free her hands. At least this way her sore wrists were relieved of the tight leather straps.

The man called Jesse was a puzzle to her. He looked as if

he might be part Indian, but he wasn't as dark as Long Knife, so he certainly wasn't full-blooded. Jesse called Long Knife "brother" more than once, however, so Carissa was confident they were related at least by one parent.

The real puzzlement was Lockhart himself. Carissa couldn't quite figure him out. He seemed amiable enough with his men, but there was a meanness and a hatred that he held toward her that she couldn't understand. Perhaps he hated all women. Or maybe he just hated her because she was a constant reminder of his failure to capture Hannah. Either way, Lockhart made her skin crawl.

She remembered Hannah's comments about Lockhart arranging for the death of her father. Then he had threatened to kill her brother and sister if she didn't marry him. Apparently it all had to do with his desire for money. She studied Lockhart as best she could without him noticing. He didn't seem suited for this rough kind of life. He wasn't in the best of shape; he looked like he could stand to lose a few pounds. His hair had thinned and was balding on top, making him look quite a few years the senior of any other man in the room. It seemed so strange that he would risk being recaptured by sticking around the area, and yet here he was.

Supper passed with the men rambling on about one thing or another related to their mistake in taking her. Carissa tried her best to focus on every word while appearing completely uninterested. She was pleasantly surprised by the rabbit stew. The men had proved to be well skilled in the kitchen. One had managed some very edible biscuits to go along with the stew, and all in all the meal was filling and flavorful. Carissa ate, even though she wasn't hungry, determined to keep her strength up. She didn't intend for these cowards to get the better of her. In fact, with every passing hour she was getting angrier.

"You don't say much for a woman," Lockhart said, eyeing her over the table. "That's a nice surprise."

She fixed him with a stare but refused to reply. Lockhart smiled. "I figure if looks could kill, they'd be digging my grave."

"You got that right," one of the men said with a laugh. Carissa now knew one man was called Roy and the other one Sage. They seemed to be either related to one another or the best of buddies.

Sage had to join in. "She sure enough did that same thing to us. She asked Long Knife a lot of questions, though. I think maybe she's sweet on him." The man elbowed Roy and both men laughed. Long Knife said nothing.

Lockhart wasn't amused. "I can't rightly blame her for her hatred. This isn't . . . or rather wasn't . . . her fight. I suppose now it is."

Carissa continued to look at him and narrowed her eyes. "You haven't seen half the fight yet."

Tilting his head, Lockhart studied her for a moment. "You know, I have an idea. Long Knife, pull her hair down and cut it. We'll have Sage ride it back to the ranch . . . better yet he can take it to Cedar Springs. That way no one needs to know who brought it. I'll write a letter demanding ransom for her return. We might not have Hannah, but we needn't go empty-handed. The way I see it, we can ransom her for a good sum of money and then lay low until they think we've given up on getting our hands on Hannah."

"You can't cut my hair off!" Carissa said in protest.

But already Long Knife was on his feet moving toward

her. Lockhart just laughed. "You women are a fussy bunch about your hair. It will grow back . . . where as fingers or hands don't."

She took his meaning and settled down. Even when Long Knife pulled her braid loose, Carissa said nothing. She felt the pull on her braid as he cut it from her head. He held it up and showed her that he'd only taken about half the length.

"Good," Lockhart said, nodding. "Now I'll prepare the financial demands. Sage, you'll need to ride this back immediately. Keep to the untraveled ways and deliver it to the sheriff's office at night. We'll address it to the Barnetts—after all, he just made himself a nice profit on cattle as I understand it. If he's not yet back to the ranch, he soon will be, according to Miss Lowe."

"Mrs. Lowe," Carissa corrected. "I have a young daughter waiting for me back at the ranch." She didn't know why, but she thought perhaps it would influence Lockhart's actions.

He merely gave a hint of a nod. "My pardon, Mrs. Lowe." He went to his saddlebag and produced a pencil and piece of paper. "So how many head of cattle did William take to market?"

Carissa couldn't understand why that was of any interest to Lockhart. "I don't know. Something like two thousand."

Lockhart grew thoughtful and for a moment said nothing. "So if they got at least thirty a head, he should have come home with sixty thousand dollars."

Carissa remembered the men talking about a great deal more money, but said nothing. She watched as Lockhart began to write. She couldn't help but wonder what he had planned.

"I think asking for the entire sixty thousand is only fair. Barnett took a good number of years from me."

"But it wasn't just his cattle," Carissa said. "He had Tyler's . . . Tyler Atherton's cattle and Ted Terry's, as well. You can't expect him to give you their money." She hoped that her feelings for Tyler weren't apparent.

Lockhart didn't seem to notice or care. He merely shrugged and kept writing. "That's really Barnett's problem. He caused me as much grief as Hannah did, and it's only right that he suffer. Let him work out the dealings with his Union friends. If they want you back, they're going to have to bring me that money in a week's time. Or next time we'll cut something more permanent from your body." He met her gaze and his expression turned cold. "Like your head."

Carissa stared at the closed door of the shack and wondered when the men would return. Earlier that day
Lockhart had assigned the men various duties and each had
ridden out without another word. Finally, Lockhart ordered
Jesse to get their two horses and they departed, as well. She
had no idea what was happening, with exception to Sage
making the delivery of her hair to Cedar Springs—and he'd
left two days prior.

"If you know what's good for you," Lockhart had told her,
"you'll not try to escape. First of all, you are in an area far
from civilization, as you already know. You wouldn't make
it even a mile before succumbing to complete disorientation.
Not only that, but Long Knife and Roy are riding watch.
They would catch you quicker than lightning could strike.
And then I'm afraid I would have to punish you."

Carissa had no doubt he meant every word and that the
punishment would be cruel. Not that she could even truly

attempt escape. Lockhart had taken her shoes and stockings and had handcuffed her to the iron-framed bed. She had a chamber pot and a pitcher of water, but little else. At least the bed offered a place to rest.

The hours ticked by in excruciating slowness. Carissa watched the shadows play on the wall as the sun crossed the room. The heat was soon unbearable, and she found herself longing once again for a cool bath. She leaned back on the bed and tried her best to imagine swimming in the waters off the coast of Corpus Christi. When she'd been much younger—before the war—there had even been Sunday school outings and picnics near the water. What carefree days those had been.

The light was beginning to fade when she heard the sound of an approaching rider. She wasn't sure if it would be one of the men who held her captive or someone else. She feared being found by Indians, but she was uneasy about her captors, too. Jesse had eyed her in a rather leering manner the day before, but surprisingly, Lockhart had put a stop to it, warning each of the men that they were not to touch her.

The door opened and Long Knife strode in with a small sack. Carissa shot up from the bed and stood to face him as he drew near. "What in the world is going on with you people?" she asked.

He looked at her oddly for a moment, then smiled. "You have a lot of fire. It's hidden down deep, but it burns hot."

"Tell me what's happening. Where has everyone gone?"

"We're seein' to business. We're watching for anyone who might have been able to track us here. Lockhart has other business that he doesn't see fit to tell us about."

"Is Jesse really your brother?" she asked without thinking. Long Knife laughed and opened the gunnysack he'd brought. "Yes, but just barely. We had the same mother, but different fathers. Why do you ask?"

She shrugged. "I just wondered. You two don't look that much alike."

He pulled some jerked meat from the bag and handed it to her. "My father was Mexican and Comanche. Our mother was Kiowa and Cheyenne. Jesse's father was white."

"Well, that would account for why you are so much darker."

She sat down on the bed and began to eat the jerky. Long Knife considered her for a moment, then pulled another piece of meat from the bag. He placed it on the small table beside the pitcher of water.

"It might be late before Lockhart gets back."

And then he was gone just as quickly as he'd come. Carissa couldn't help but wonder just how far from the shack he would go. Was there really no hope of escape? She tugged at the irons but knew there was no way to disengage from the rails of the bed frame. A part of her wanted to break down and cry, but another part was just mad enough that she wouldn't. Instead, she'd keep her thoughts on Gloria and Tyler. Those two gave her a will to go on—to fight against despair. She had no idea if she would ever see them again, but that was the hope she clung to.

Without tracks to follow or word from the sheriff, William had forced them to wait a good four days after returning to the ranch before he'd agree to head out. Tyler had threatened to leave on his own more than once, but each time William had convinced him to sit tight. On the fifth day, Tyler decided he'd had enough and that no matter what William said, he was going after Carissa. While William understood his friend's frustration, there was no real way to know where they should look for her. Leaving without some idea of where to go would simply waste more time. Plus, the sheriff would have no way to get in touch with them if they were wandering aimlessly around the countryside, looking for clues.

"I'm leavin' now," Tyler told William and the others at breakfast. "I'm going to search for Carissa, and this time you aren't going to talk me out of it."

William eyed him momentarily, then nodded. "I wasn't going to try. I think it *is* time we take matters into our own hands. I figure we'll head southwest like they traveled, and we'll just ask everyone along the way if they saw a man traveling with a woman."

He paused with a biscuit halfway to his mouth and added, "We'll offer to bribe folks if necessary."

"Good." Tyler returned his attention to the cup of coffee he'd been nursing. He had no idea how to go about finding Carissa, but just sitting here was driving him insane.

"I wish the sheriff would come and tell us what's happening," Hannah said, helping Robert with his eggs. "It seems like it's been more than enough time. He could have at least sent a telegram."

"Maybe they couldn't get anyone in town to ride out here and bring it," William replied. "Then again, maybe the lines are still down."

"I suppose it's possible." She picked up a piece of cinnamon roll and handed it to Robert.

Marty yawned and poured syrup on her grits while Andy helped himself to a hefty slab of ham and a roll. He popped a large piece of the latter in his mouth and smiled as he chewed.

"Sure good sweet rolls, Hannah," Andy said, shoving another piece in his mouth.

She smiled. "Glad you like them. I'm also very glad you're back unharmed."

Andy flashed a glance at William and then nodded. Tyler knew they had no intention of telling Hannah about his injury during the stampede. The men had all agreed that what happened on the trail was best kept among themselves. The women would only fret, and there would be other cattle drives to contend with next year. No sense in setting the stage for future battles.

Brandon entered the room at that point, carrying Laura in his arms. "Sorry we're late. I was coaxing Mrs. Reid to join us."

"I'm glad you did," Hannah said, jumping up to pull out an empty chair. "Sit here by me. That way I can get you anything you need."

Laura shook her head. "No one needs to make a fuss. I'm doing much better. I feel a great deal stronger."

"And we want to keep it that way," Brandon told her. "So you will allow us to help you, or you will be banished to your room once again."

Hannah grinned. "I think he's serious."

"I know he is," Laura admitted. Brandon placed her on the chair and took the seat on the other side of her.

At the far end of the table, Pepita managed an animated Gloria. Tyler couldn't help but notice that the child was once again refusing to sit at the table without her doll. He supposed she was being indulged because of Carissa's absence, but the toy only served to remind him of the tangible loss for Gloria . . . and for him.

"So when will you two leave?" Hannah asked.

Tyler turned from watching Gloria and motioned to the table. "As soon as I'm done eatin', I figure to get on the trail."

"I've had Juanita put some supplies together for you." Hannah seemed to approach the matter almost casually, but Tyler knew better. "There should be enough there for a couple of weeks."

Juanita came into the dining room just then. "Mister Will, riders come here."

Tyler was on his feet so fast that his chair went crashing over backward. He raced through the house and was out the front door just as the sheriff and several other mounted riders approached the house. Unfortunately, Carissa wasn't among their numbers.

"Sheriff, we'd just about given up hope of hearin' from you. Have you found Cari . . . Mrs. Lowe?" he asked.

The sheriff shook his head. "No, we gave up the trail a few days ago. I got back last night and found this waiting at my office. It's addressed to William. I figure it might be related to Mrs. Lowe's disappearance, seein's how her name is listed as the sender."

By now William and Hannah had followed Tyler outside to hear what the sheriff had to say. William stepped forward and took the brown-paper-wrapped parcel. He cut the string that bound it and opened the paper. Inside was a hunk of honey blond hair and a letter.

"That's Carissa's hair," Tyler said, taking it from the package. He felt the silky strands, thinking of how many times he'd longed to do that when he'd been near Carissa. William picked up the letter and let the brown paper fall to the ground.

"What's the letter say?" the sheriff asked.

"It's a ransom note. The gist of it is that we're to bring sixty thousand dollars in gold to the Whiskey Springs cutoff. We're supposed to leave it there, and they will pick it up. If the gold is all there, they will send instructions as to when and where we can retrieve Carissa." He looked to Tyler and then to the sheriff. "We're supposed to have it in one week's time." Hannah whispered something in Will's ear and he nodded.

"We can't get that kind of gold. There ain't that kind of gold in the South," Tyler protested.

"He's right," the sheriff said, shaking his head. "The man who wrote this seems to be educated enough to explain instructions. Surely he would know that, as well."

Tyler looked at the bearded sheriff and then to William. "We'll have to pretend to do as he says. But how?"

"We've got some gold here, and the bank in Dallas will have some. We could collect what we can and fill a chest. We'll put rocks on the bottom and the gold on top. Then we could make the drop, hide out, and watch them."

"Won't they check the gold right there and then?" the sheriff asked.

"We could put it in a lockbox," William replied. "With any luck at all, Lockhart will send his lackeys for it and they won't bother to open it."

"So you're convinced it's Lockhart?"

"Hannah recognizes the handwriting. She says there's no doubt that it's Lockhart. He was a partner to her father for years. Not only that, but he wrote Hannah letters. I trust that she knows what she's talking about. Besides, there really isn't anyone else who would have a reason to take a woman from this ranch and then ask for ransom. Like we mentioned before, if it had been Indians, they would have burned the place out and killed everyone. Even if they planned to take hostages, they would have killed the men and taken the women and children."

"He's right," Tyler said. He still held fast to the hunk of Carissa's hair.

"Lockhart is a crafty individual," the sheriff said. "I think he's gonna know that you can't possibly get that kind of gold right away. Maybe he expects you to bring what you can and then arrange for the rest of it. Maybe he just figures to get what he can and escape."

"Well, whatever his plans, I intend to interfere with them," Tyler said, his eyes narrowing. "I intend to do what I can to get Carissa back here safe and sound."

"I do, too," William said with a sigh, "but the sheriff is right. Lockhart can't imagine that we would have sixty thousand in gold. I know he believed Hannah's father left a huge treasure of the stuff, but what he left we found long ago. I think maybe we do what we can to set up an ambush in the area of this drop. If we move out and work at night, we ought to be able to use the darkness to conceal our actions. It'll be just like some of the stuff we did in the war."

"Well, we're goin' with you," the sheriff said.

"Give us five minutes," Tyler answered before William could respond. He met his friend's gaze and felt assured by his nod of affirmation.

The sound of other riders drew their attention to the west. William put a hand to his eyes. "Looks like Ted and Marietta are comin' to lend a hand."

Tyler caught sight of the wagon and half a dozen mounted riders. "Good. We can use all the help we can get."

❧

To Carissa's surprise, Lockhart returned to the shack, but Jesse and the others were nowhere to be seen. She felt uneasy being left alone with the known killer.

Watching her closely, Lockhart smiled. "I suppose you've been planning your escape."

She said nothing. Instead, Carissa watched his every move. He removed a revolver from his holster and placed it on the table. Her eyes narrowed and he laughed.

"I guess, too, that you'd shoot me with this if you could lay your hands on it." He leaned back in the chair. "Really, I'm not as awful a man as Hannah Dandridge—excuse me, *Barnett*—would lead you to believe. I only did what was necessary to survive. I had never planned any real harm for Hannah."

"Then why would you order her kidnapped?"

"Because I intend to take her with me to Mexico. Barnett robbed me of what was most important to me . . . my freedom. So I'll take what's most important to him."

"She's expecting a baby," Carissa said matter-of-factly. "Dragging her off on a trip like that would cause her to miscarry or deliver early. She would probably bleed to death." She thought perhaps her frankness would cause him to reconsider.

"Then she would die and I wouldn't have to kill her."

"But you said you didn't plan to harm Hannah."

"No, I said I had never planned any real harm. That was in the past. Hannah is as much to blame for my imprisonment as her husband. I mean to see them both pay for what they've done."

"And what about me?"

"You? Well, I'll simply get the money and leave. I'll send them word where they can find you, but by then I'll be long gone to Mexico."

"Without Hannah?"

"For now," he said, smiling.

She shook her head. "But how can you let me go? I know who you are."

"Unless I've missed my guess, Mrs. Lowe, so do they." He sat down at the table and fixed her with a rather amused expression. "But that really isn't important. I want them to know. I want them afraid. I want you to go back and let them know that I will constantly be a threat in their lives. They will never have a moment's peace. With sixty thousand dollars, I'll have enough to buy all the help I need. And one day, when they expect it the least, my people will strike."

Carissa shuddered at the thought. Lockhart would hold them hostage in a way they couldn't even fight. They would constantly have to watch over their shoulders. Their children would never be safe, and Hannah could never be allowed out of the protection of the family's trusted men.

"So you'll just let this vendetta of yours go on for a lifetime?" Carissa shook her head. "Sounds like you'll be back in prison."

He laughed. "You are such a naïve little thing. I'll have all the freedom I want. That's the glory of hiring the dirty work done by others. You needn't fret, Mrs. Lowe. I'll be quite content."

"I doubt William Barnett will sit by idly," she said. "I doubt any of the men there will tolerate your plans. Not only will they see to her safety, but William will hunt you down."

For the first time since he started talking, Lockhart looked momentarily rattled. He toyed with the revolver and shook his head. "It will do him no good."

"I think you underestimate him," Carissa said, recognizing the need to instill doubt in Lockhart's mind. "You must remember: William was a soldier. He knows about ambushing and waiting out the enemy."

"He also took a bullet in the leg that nearly crippled him. Tell me, does he still walk with a limp?"

"Some," Carissa replied, "but I've yet to see it stop him. While you were sitting in prison, William was making friends and securing his future. And did I mention that my father has been working closely with the Mexican government? I would venture to guess that William could work with him—and authorities in Mexico—to hunt you down." She smiled and leaned back against the iron rail.

"For someone in your position, you run your mouth very freely," Lockhart said between clenched teeth.

Carissa shrugged. "I'm quite confident of my protectors, Mr. Lockhart. You have the power to hurt me—to kill me. I know that. But should you do that . . . well . . . let's just say, it won't bode well for you. And that gives me great comfort."

Lockhart frowned. It was clear she'd unnerved him. He picked up the revolver and got to his feet. For a moment he looked at her, and Carissa wondered if she'd pushed him too far. But without another word, he holstered the piece and headed toward the kitchen area of the shack. Only then did Carissa realize that her hands were shaking. She felt her pulse racing, and she thought she might faint at any given moment.

Lord, give me strength, she prayed silently. Closing her eyes, Carissa forced her breathing to even. She could feel clarity return, and the darkness that had threatened her only moments earlier faded. It felt as if God were speaking to her in this quiet way, to assure her that He had heard her cries . . . and that gave Carissa a great sense of comfort.

That area southwest of here is diverse," Ted Terry told William and Tyler. They had spread out a hand-drawn map on the dining room table and were studying it.

"See this area here?" Ted pointed to the map. "Lots of ravines and rock. I'd say it's about a day's ride, maybe less, from where you're supposed to drop the money. If I were up to no good, that's where I'd go to hide out. And from what I hear, they wouldn't be the first set of thieves to do so."

Tyler looked at the two points and nodded. "Makes sense to me. Too much to the east, and they'd run into Fort Worth. Too much in any other direction and they'd hit ranches or forts."

"Exactly. If they're asking you to leave the money here," Ted said, moving his finger to the area the ransom note indicated, "my guess is that they're hiding out here." He used another finger to mark the second location.

"If we move under the cover of darkness," William said,

"I figure we can get the drop on them. If we head out right away and get ourselves in position, then we can wait them out until we secure the upper hand."

"Unless, of course, they're already in position to watch you," Ted said, giving William a questioning glance.

"Either way, we're going," Tyler said. "Leastwise I am."

"Me too," William said.

"In that case, I've brought two men along who work for me. Their pasts are a little shady, and I know they are familiar with this area and some of its hideouts. They've proven to be good men, despite their past—and I'm certain you can trust them to be useful. I'll send them with you, and hopefully they can help you find your way through the area."

"My guess," William said, straightening, "is that Carissa's captors won't be worried about covering their tracks out that far. With any luck, we can get to the rendezvous point and trail 'em."

Brandon came into the room just then. "Seems I'm destined to be late to meals and meetings."

"No problem. We're just discussing our strategy," Tyler answered.

"And you're sure you want me to stay here?" Brandon asked, looking from Tyler to William and back again.

"We'll need the women to have protection here. Since Laura can't be moved yet anyway, I figure you're the best one to stay behind," William replied. "You and the others will make a good show of strength. It'd be just like Lockhart to use this money drop as a diversion to get to Hannah and the others."

"Well, they'll have to come through me," Brandon said. "And I don't intend to make it easy."

"I'll send extra men here, as well," Ted volunteered.

"The sheriff and his men are going to ride with us," William continued. "They're just waiting on us to gather our things."

Ted nodded. "Come on outside, and I'll introduce you to Reggie and Dave."

They followed Ted out the back door and into the area by the pen where the men had congregated with the sheriff. "I see you fellows are getting acquainted," Ted stated. "Reg, Dave, this is William Barnett and Tyler Atherton. I think you boys have met before, but you can get to know each other better now. I told Will that you two know that area west and south of Fort Worth from the old days."

The men nodded, although from the looks of their ages, Tyler was certain the old days couldn't have been too long ago.

"We want to get out there and use the night to conceal us," William told the men. "Do you think you can help us to navigate the area?"

"Sure thing," Reg told him. "Glad to help."

William nodded. "Good. Then I guess we'd best saddle up and head out. It's a long ride."

"I wanna come, too," Andy said. He looked to William. "I can help you . . . I know I can."

"You can help me most by staying here. In case this is some sort of a trick—and believe me, Lockhart is full of deception—you may well find your hands full right here at the ranch."

Andy's brows knit together. "I never thought of that, Will. I'll stay. Hannah and the others will be safe with us here."

"Good. I knew I could count on you. Brandon and Berto will give you directions if the worst happens. Listen to them. They've had to fight through ambushes before."

"I'll listen, Will. I promise."

⤶⤷

Carissa looked at the empty bowl beside the bed. It had been days since Lockhart had offered her any food. The last thing had been a small bowl of grits, and Lockhart had never bothered to even retrieve the bowl. In fact, he'd been pretty scarce of late. She wasn't even sure where he or the other men were staying at night, because most of the time she was alone.

Her vision blurred when Carissa tried to sit up, and weakness from lack of eating left her too feeble to seek that position for long. She checked the water pitcher and found it dry.

Falling back against the small pillow, Carissa watched the dizzying spin of the room. She knew she'd angered Lockhart with her comments about how he would fail. To punish her he'd left her alone for most of the time. Maybe this was his way of killing her without having to do the job himself. He'd just let starvation and thirst consume her.

She tried to pray, but her mind was beginning to play tricks on her. She thought she heard voices from time to time and didn't know if she was losing her sanity or if the men were standing just outside the door. Twice she'd awakened to find Lockhart standing over her. The last time he'd made some comment about the affair soon being over.

Carissa had lost track of how long it'd been since Long Knife had first taken her, but it seemed like an eternity. She'd seen nothing of any of the other men since Lockhart had dispersed them to their various duties, but she couldn't help but think that if Long Knife had been there, he would have seen to it that she had food to eat. He seemed more compassionate than the others.

Sleep overcame her again, and when Carissa awoke sometime later, Lockhart had returned and was seated at the table.

She couldn't tell what he was doing, but it looked like he was writing in a book. Maybe he was keeping a journal of all that had transpired. He looked up and found her watching him and closed the book rather hard. Getting to his feet, he crossed to the bed and looked down at her.

"I see you're still alive. Maybe next time you won't be so quick to voice your opinion. I have a great many ways to punish you that don't involve my having to put a bullet in you. Just remember that."

"Water . . . please," she managed to speak. Her mouth was so dry it very nearly choked her.

He looked at her for a moment longer and then checked the empty pitcher. "I suppose I can do that. Of course, I will expect your full cooperation from here on out."

Carissa didn't know what else she could do. She was far too weak to engage in a sparring match of words, so she nodded. Lockhart picked up the pitcher and left the shack for several minutes. When he finally returned, he held only a small tin cup.

"I'm afraid you'll need to let the dirt settle to the bottom. There's not a lot of water in the creek. Dry time of the year, don't you know."

Carissa didn't care. She reached for the cup, desperate for something to drink. Lockhart only laughed. "Drink it if you like." He walked away.

A wave of hatred gave Carissa momentary strength. She ignored her dizziness as she sat up and reached for the cup, but found she lacked the strength to lift it. Tilting it toward her, Carissa put her hand in the muddy water and pulled a handful to her lips. It was gritty, and she was barely able to straighten the cup before growing quite faint.

When she opened her eyes next, the room was once again deserted. The sky was dark and the room chilly. She thought several times that she heard someone talking, and she found herself wishing whoever it was would come and speak to her. If she were dying, she didn't want to face it alone.

You're not alone, Carissa, a voice sounded somewhere deep in her mind. *I will never leave you, nor forsake you.*

She knew the words were somehow from God. Peace descended over her like a comforting quilt. An image of Gloria's face came to her, and she smiled. With Gloria, Carissa could see that the sufferings of the past were not without reward.

She thought of how much she had wanted to provide Gloria with a father. Maybe after she was dead, Laura and Brandon would adopt Gloria and give her their name. Carissa hoped they might. She knew that Tyler would continue to visit them and that Gloria would see him from time to time. She hoped that he would tell her stories about how he and Carissa had met. She hoped Tyler would tell Gloria how he'd saved her mother's life.

Thirst consumed her and Carissa strained to pull herself to the side of the bed. She reached for the cup on the floor, hoping the sediment had settled and that clear water could be had. With all her strength, she forced herself to sit. It felt as if someone else were directing her limbs, however.

Grasping the cup was difficult. Carissa's hands didn't seem to want to do what she needed them to. She wanted to cry, but instead she concentrated on the task at hand. Water was all she wanted. Water was what she desired.

Finally her efforts were successful. She put her hand in the cup, and this time drew out water that was fairly clear. She sucked it up from her palm, then brought the cup to her lips. She tipped it and could feel the liquid slide down her dry throat and hit her empty stomach. Then the water seemed to cause her stomach to spasm, and Carissa teetered for a moment on the side of the bed, feeling as if she would vomit. Without thinking, she dropped her hold on the water to steady herself and the cup fell to the ground. The last of the water quickly soaked into the dry floorboards and disappeared, leaving only sediment behind.

Carissa gasped and tried to reach down as if to somehow save some of the water. The room spun and darkness engulfed her. "God, please," she whispered, her throat still too dry to function properly. "Please help me."

❧

Laura sat in bed with Daniel asleep on her lap and Lucas doing likewise in her arms. She still marveled at the two sons God had given her. At one time in her life she had despaired of ever finding a husband and then Brandon Reid came into her life. The boys looked just like him.

"What's that smile all about?" Brandon asked, entering the bedroom the Barnetts had given them to use.

Glancing up, Laura met her husband's sweet expression. "I'm very blessed. That's what the smile is about. I feel like I'm touching the sky."

He smiled and sank onto the bed beside her. "So you aren't sorry you married me."

"Never," she said, feeling close to tears from sheer joy.

Daniel stirred, and Brandon got up. "I'll put him to bed," he said, lifting the small boy in his arms. He carried Daniel to the opposite side of the room where his bed awaited, then turned to Laura, who was gazing down at Lucas.

"He's quite perfect, Mrs. Reid. I don't believe I've thanked you for him."

She smiled. "You thank me every day just by loving me." She carefully stood and placed the sleeping baby in his cradle and covered him.

Laura wasn't surprised when Brandon came behind her and took her in his arms. "Laura, I don't want to ever be separated from you. I know events will cause that to happen, but I'd rather spend the rest of my life at your side."

"I feel the same way," she said, lifting her face to his.

He rewarded her with a passionate kiss before lifting her in his arms. He placed her carefully on the bed and pulled the covers up to warm her. "I need to check outside, but then I'll be coming to bed. Do you need anything while I'm up?"

She shook her head and sighed in contentment. But once Brandon had gone, Laura couldn't help but grow worried as she thought of Carissa. Was she cold? Was she being cared for? The ransom note promised to set her free, but these were evil men. Would they keep their word?

Night after night she had prayed for her sister—Brandon too. Poor Gloria cried so often for her mother that Laura felt compelled to join her. It seemed so hopeless at times, and yet she knew full well that there was always hope with God.

A light knock sounded on the door. "Yes?" Laura called softly.

The door opened to reveal Juanita. She tiptoed across the room with a glass of milk. "I thought you might like some warm milk. I know these days are very hard for you," she whispered.

Laura smiled. "You're so kind, Juanita. Thank you."

Juanita nodded. "You are worried for Carissa, sí?"

"Yes. Very worried. She's been through so much in her young life—first with her husband, Malcolm, and now this. I worry that she'll lose her faith—that she'll give up hope."

"Your sister is a good woman. She has grown in the Lord, and she knows His faithfulness. You should not worry. No matter what happens, God . . . He will watch over her."

"I know," Laura said. She sipped the warm milk. "But God watches over a lot of good people who still find themselves in peril—who die. I just don't know how I would bear it if . . ."

Juanita put her finger to Laura's lips. "You no speak of it. Your sister . . . she is in His hand, and His grace will be enough. Now you finish the milk and I will take the glass back for you." She smiled in a motherly fashion, and Laura did as the older woman instructed.

"Thank you again," Laura said, giving the glass to Juanita.

"You are welcome."

Juanita turned back to the door and passed Brandon as he entered the room. He looked at her with a worried expression, but she only smiled. "I bring Miss Laura some milk," she whispered. "Good night."

"Good night, Juanita." Brandon closed the door behind her and came to the bed. Sitting, he pulled off his boots.

"Is everything all right outside?"

He nodded. "We have men on watch. Lockhart would be a fool to try and get in here."

Laura waited for Brandon to ready himself for bed, then pulled back the cover and relished his warmth as he pulled her into his arms. For a long while neither said anything. Laura could hear the beating of Brandon's heart and his even breathing, but she knew he wasn't asleep. "I'm trying so hard to be strong," she finally said.

291

"I know. But just remember, you don't have to bear this alone. I'm here, and so are the others. We all love Carissa, and we will continue to do whatever we can to bring her home safe."

"But what if she doesn't come home?"

Brandon didn't so much as move a muscle. "We will deal with that if it happens. No sense planning for the worst at this point. There's no reason to believe Lockhart won't set her free."

"There's the matter of them not taking the ransom money," Laura answered.

He tightened his hold on her ever so slightly. "I didn't realize you knew that part of the plan."

"I overheard you men talking. I think it was the best decision, but I know that it won't bode well for Carissa if William and Tyler aren't able to capture the men who took her."

"William had a good plan, Laura. I think he can pull it off. The sheriff thought so, too, and I guess we'll know soon enough. The money is supposed to be in place for pickup tomorrow."

She nodded and felt him relax his embrace. She wanted to believe the plan would work—that Carissa would be safe. But an overwhelming sense of worry would not be stilled.

I'll go ahead alone. You keep watch, and if anyone shows themselves, do what you need to do," William told Tyler. The men had carefully staked themselves around the area where the money was to be left, and now the time to see the plan through had come. Tyler looked at William and shook his head.

"I still think you ought to let me go."

"Lockhart wants me . . . not you."

"But if his plan is to have us leave the money and return to the ranch, there might not be anyone here."

William tugged on his hat. "That's always possible, but I know Lockhart. He's not going to let sixty thousand in gold sit alone for long. He won't know until he checks out the site that there's no gold, but I know he's not far away. That's why I need you to keep watch. You're the best shot here. If things start going poorly—you'll know what to do."

"I'll see to it." He put out his hand, and William took it. For a moment they shook, but then William embraced Tyler.

"You're like a brother to me," William told Tyler. "Promise me . . . if anything happens . . . to me . . . you'll see to it that Hannah and the children are taken care of."

Tyler pulled back and nodded. "You know I will."

William nodded. "Then let's get this done."

He mounted his horse and headed down the path. Tyler watched from his position for a short time, then set out to parallel William and get as close as possible to the rendez-vous point. He had been one of the most skilled soldiers at sneaking around battlefields and staying unseen. More than once his ability to scout forward without being discovered had helped his men to avoid ambush. This time wasn't that much different; even some of the same men were keeping watch over him. Sidley had Tyler's horse and watched with a spyglass from a safe distance away. Tyler had only to signal the man to move in and he would bring the mount, but for now Tyler was on his own to crawl through the grass and use whatever means to hide his movements.

Finally, after what seemed like forever, Tyler reached the clearing where William was to leave the money. He could see William standing to one side of his horse. He scanned the trees with an expert eye and Tyler did likewise. Then without warning, a man came riding in from the far side. The man spurred his mount and rode fast and low until he reached William and the clearing. Then just as quickly as he'd ap-peared, the man reined his horse back, causing it to rear. The animal gave a harsh whinny and settled back to the ground, but not without stomping the dirt in protest.

"Where's the money, Barnett?" the man asked.

"Jesse Carter. I should have known you'd be at Lockhart's side. You always were his lackey." The men's voices carried well.

Carter grinned and pushed back the rim of his hat a bit. "I ain't no man's lackey, Barnett. That's why I'm here. I've come for the gold. I saw you comin' from a mile away, but I didn't see no lock box."

"That's because I didn't bring one. Instead, I brought men. Men who have you in their sights even now. You're surrounded."

Carter frowned and gave a quick glance around. "I don't believe you. I would have seen."

"Well, it doesn't much matter if you believe me or not," William replied. "Tyler, you wanna join us and show this man we mean business?"

Tyler took the cue and cautiously moved into the clearing. Carter's eyes widened and his jaw clenched. Tyler stepped forward with his rifle leveled.

"Throw away your gun and get down," William ordered Jesse. The man didn't seem inclined to comply. William pulled his pistol. "I said disarm and dismount."

"Lockhart will kill her if I don't come back with the money. You aren't the only one with men on the watch, you know. He's got a small army to help him in this. I ain't the only one."

"Whether you are or not, if you don't climb down from that saddle right now," William ordered, "you'll be the only one with a bullet hole in the leg. Having experienced that, I can tell you it's excruciating, and if care is delayed, it's almost certain to mean amputation."

Tyler saw Carter glance down at William's leg and then nod. "Suit yourself." Carter reached for his revolver, and Tyler raised his rifle for emphasis. Carter carefully tossed the pistol and held up his hands.

"Now climb down."

Carter did so and stood completely still. Tyler stepped forward. The rifle was now level with Carter's heart. "Where is she?" he demanded.

The man grinned. "You ain't got a chance of findin' her. We know these parts better than anyone."

"We've got a couple of men who are pretty knowledgeable about the area," William said, reholstering his gun. He turned and retrieved some rope from his saddle and came back to where Carter stood. "Put your hands together."

Carter hesitated, and Tyler set his sights down the barrel of his rifle, ready if the man actually attacked Will. But finally the moment passed and the man complied. William tied him up and then pushed him to the ground.

"Now we're gonna have us a little discussion," he told Jesse.

Tyler knew the best thing to do would be to bring the boys down to join them. He worried, however, that Jesse might very well have men in hiding, so he delayed. Surely if the men were nearby, they would do something to rescue Carter in the next few minutes. Lowering his rifle, Tyler tried to strike a more casual pose, hoping that if any enemy were watching, he would believe Tyler and William had grown lax in their vigil.

"I was supposed to leave the money and go. I presume you were supposed to retrieve the money and take it back to Lockhart. Do I have it right so far?"

Carter spit and looked up. "He'll kill her if I'm not back by midnight."

"But you made mention of coming to get the money for yourself. Seems you're not too worried about what would happen to Mrs. Lowe after that."

He shrugged. "The woman don't mean nothin' to me. If you stop me from takin' the money to Lockhart, her blood will be on your hands. I know that you bein' an upstandin', law-abidin' man . . . well . . . you'd find it harder to live with. So if you don't let me go now, Lockhart will kill your friend and it'll be your fault."

Tyler was unnerved by the man's nonchalance. He wanted to knock the man in the face with the butt of his rifle and see how calm he was then.

"How many men do you have out there and where are they positioned?" William asked.

"Enough to get the job done. Fact is, one of them is probably already riding back to let Lockhart know we've been taken for fools. The woman is gonna be dead as soon as he knows."

Tyler hit the man with the rifle, just hard enough to get his attention. "You wanna answer the questions?" Tyler asked.

Carter eyed him with great hatred. "I'm not tellin' you nothin'."

"This is futile," William declared. "Signal Sidley's group to join us and we'll track Carter's horse. I doubt he was any too worried about hiding his trail."

Tyler gave the agreed wave, knowing Sidley was watching him through a spyglass. He then turned to William. "What about him? He coming with us?"

"I ain't gonna go anywhere with you. If they see me ridin' in your company, they'll shoot me, too. They won't know it's me."

Tyler smirked. "That'd be a real pity."

William considered the situation for a moment. "I'll tie him to his saddle, and we can take him with us. If he's so concerned with getting shot, maybe he'll keep us apprised of the situation and where those other men are located."

Tyler shouldered the rifle and reached down to yank Carter up by his shirt. "I'll get him on his horse." The man grunted in protest, but in one move Tyler dropped his hold on Carter and slammed the rifle butt into his belly. Carter gave a whooshing sound as the air went out of him and he doubled over.

"Guess we can do this the hard way if you want," Tyler told him.

Carter looked up and tried to straighten. "It'll take you a long time to track it. What say we make a deal? I didn't take the woman. If I had, it would be your wife instead of Mrs. Lowe that's waiting now. You make it worth my while and I'll show you the way."

"What will make it worth your while?" William asked, stepping to within inches of Carter.

"You let me go after I get you close."

"And what's to keep you from ambushing us on the trail home?" Tyler asked.

Carter looked at him with cold indifference. "Nothin', I suppose. I could give you my word, but I don't think you'd take it."

"You're right there," Tyler said.

"We're getting nowhere at this rate," William said.

It seemed like a good old-fashioned standoff to Tyler's way of thinking. He decided to risk another method. "What about money? If I offer to pay you and pay you well—can we work this out?"

Carter smiled. "I'm listenin'."

"Well, I'm thinkin' that maybe you could show us the way, and once we have Carissa safely away from Lockhart and back to the ranch, I could reward you." It made Tyler's stomach turn to even imagine rewarding this man for his part in Carissa's disappearance, but he was desperate.

"And what makes you think I trust you any more than you trust me?" Carter asked. "What's to keep you from turning me over to the sheriff when I come for my pay?"

"You said you had nothing to do with taking Carissa," William countered. "You're only here to pick up something your employer sent you to retrieve. If you haven't broken the law, the sheriff isn't going to have any reason to arrest you. Look, we're losing time."

Carter said nothing for a minute, and Tyler thought for sure he would refuse. Then he shrugged. "All right. I reckon I don't have much choice. I want a thousand dollars. I know Lockhart figured you to have sixty thousand from the sale of your cattle. A thousand won't set you back that much."

"Done," Tyler said, not even bothering to haggle. "As soon as we're safely back to the ranch with Carissa, I will meet you at the bank in Cedar Springs and get you the money. Agreed?" Tyler figured this would keep the man from attempting to ambush them on the trail back to the Barnett ranch.

Carter looked pleased. "You got a deal. But I'm only takin' you as far as where the guards are posted. They'll shoot first and ask questions later if they see more than me ridin' up."

"Good enough," William replied. "Now let's get on with it."

⸎

Carissa's stomach burned, and her thoughts were muddled and confused. When she closed her heavy eyelids, it felt as though she were scraping her eyes with grit. Moaning, she used all her strength to roll to one side. She saw the cup on the floor beside the bed, and it only served to remind her of the futility of her situation. If she'd had any tears left, she would have cried in agony.

How long had it been since she'd had water? Food? She didn't even know how many days had passed by, but she felt certain that death was near. She had heard Brandon talk once of going for nearly a week without much to eat, but it hadn't hurt him because he had water. Without water, he had told them, a person would die within days.

I'm sorry, God. I tried to make changes and be a good woman. I tried to learn my Bible and pray. I don't know where I went wrong, but I pray that you forgive me all my wrongdoings and that when I pass, you'll take me to be with you in heaven.

She felt at peace with her prayer. There was nothing more to do or say. She had done everything that needed to be done. The panic she'd often felt at the thought of Gloria being without her faded. God would see to it that Gloria had a home and people to love her. Of this Carissa was sure.

Her last thoughts were of Tyler and how she wished she would have told him of her feelings prior to his leaving for the cattle drive. She'd let jealousy halt her actions then. She hoped Laura or Hannah would tell him just how much she'd come to care for him . . . to love him.

Closing her eyes, Carissa felt her strength give out. There was nothing to do but wait for the end.

～

"There are two men on top of that rock on the other side," Jesse told William and Tyler. "They're guarding the entrance to the slough that will lead you to the hideout."

"Just two?" William asked.

Carter laughed. "Yeah. There's a couple more out there, but they're closer to the shack."

"And is that it? Is that Lockhart's army?"

Carter looked rather sheepish. It was a strange look on the normally fierce man. "Yeah."

"How do you want to approach this, Will?"

"If they see Jesse coming with two additional riders, I'm sure we'll be in trouble," William said. "Looks like we'll have to climb over the rock and take them by surprise."

Tyler turned to the man. "You better be right about this." He climbed down from his horse and asked William, "What do you want to do with him?"

William shrugged. "We'll tie Carter up and gag him. We'll have to come back for the horses. Sidley and his boys will catch up with us soon enough and find him. Hopefully the sheriff is already in position."

"Sheriff? Wait a minute—you didn't say nothin' about the sheriff."

William looked at him and shook his head. "No, I suppose I didn't."

"Well, that ain't fair. You said you'd let me go. You said you'd pay me."

Tyler undid the rope and yanked Jesse from the back of his horse. "Shut up and get over there." He pushed Carter toward a tree. "We're losing the light, Will. I figure if we move in and wait until dark, we can sneak up on them."

"I did my part! I brought you here," Jesse protested.

"I agree and like I said, if you didn't break the law, the sheriff won't want anything to do with you." William walked over to Carter and pulled the kerchief from his neck. Tying it snug around his mouth, William silenced the man.

The sound of something moving toward them from the trees caused Tyler to snap to attention. He saw that William had also heard and was moving to cover. Leaving Carter securely bound, Tyler slipped into the trees and pulled his revolver.

Lieutenant, it's us," Sidley called. He stepped through the trees with Reggie and Dave.

Tyler returned the gun to his holster. "You scared about ten years of life outta me, and I'm not a lieutenant anymore."

"Sorry, boss. Didn't mean to give you a scare." Sidley smiled. "We've been trailing you pretty close, and since you stopped, we thought we'd better come in this way just in case something was wrong."

"Carter just told us that Lockhart has men stationed on the other side of this ridge. Will and I are going to climb up that rock face and see if we can surprise them. I've got Carter tied to a tree over there, but I'd feel better if one of you stood guard."

"We can see to that easy enough, but are you sure you won't need our help gettin' those other men?" Sidley asked.

Keeping his voice low, Tyler replied, "The fewer of us the better. No sense in risking a lot of noise. If you stay here with

Carter, I think William and I can get the two men. If there happen to be more, we'll cross that bridge when we get to it."

William returned, bringing a coil of rope. "Ready?"

Tyler nodded. "Let's go."

They took off across the dry grass, crouching down just in case anyone might be of a mind to shoot them. Within a matter of minutes they were in the rocks and heading up the side of the small hill. Tyler knew the climb wouldn't be that steep or difficult, but he feared the loose rock would give them away. He prayed that the men keeping watch wouldn't hear them.

When they neared the top, William motioned for Tyler to go one way and he'd go another. Tyler nodded and moved around to the left. He was almost to a place where he felt he might be able to see the two men when he heard the hammer cock on a pistol.

"Hold it right there, mister."

Tyler froze in place. A man stepped out from a crevice in the rock and pointed the gun at Tyler's head.

Hoping the man wouldn't know him, Tyler held up his hands. "Whoa there, friend. I mean you no harm. I'm lost. My horse and I got separated. I'm trying to find some shelter for the night."

The man looked at him for a moment. "Who are you?"

"Just an old soldier makin' my way west. Do you have a camp I might share for the night?"

This seemed to relax the man a bit. "We got a cold camp. No hot coffee or grub. Nothing in the way of hospitable."

"I'd take a cup of water at this point. I don't have a canteen with me." At least that much was true, although Tyler knew if the situation demanded it, he'd tell the man whatever lie was necessary to save Carissa.

"I can get you water," the man said, lowering his gun. "Then you'll have to be on your way. Boss won't like you bein' around these parts."

"Boss? Maybe I could get hired on? I'm a good worker."

The man shook his head. "Ain't lookin' to hire nobody. Now give me your gun," he said, motioning to the pistol at Tyler's side. "I don't want to be shot in the back for doin' a good deed and givin' a man a cup of water."

Tyler didn't want to give up the weapon, but he figured it might well help his cause in the long run. If the man put his guard down enough, Tyler could get the jump on him when William showed up.

He handed the man his weapon and smiled. "Name's Atherton." He hoped the man hadn't heard of him.

"Folks call me Sage," the man replied. "It ain't my rightful name, but that's such a mouthful most prefer Sage."

"Good to meet you, Sage. I feared I might not see another human bein' again."

He watched as the man carefully tucked the revolver in his waistband. It wasn't the brightest move, but Tyler wasn't going to worry overmuch about it. The hammer on his pistol had been rigged in such a way that it could pull back easily. With any luck at all, the man would shoot himself in the groin before everything was said and done.

A gunshot suddenly rang out, and Sage seemed to forget about Tyler and took off at a run. He ducked and dodged his way through scraggly brush, and when he'd rounded a large outcropping of rock, Sage stopped so quickly Tyler very nearly ran into the back of him.

Seeing William standing ahead with a wounded man on the ground, Tyler did the only thing he could. He threw himself at Sage's back. He wrestled the smaller man to the ground rather easily and managed to get his hand on the grip of his revolver. Pulling the gun from Sage's waistband, Tyler quickly drew it to the man's head and demanded his cooperation.

"Unless you wanna be shot like your friend, you'll do what I tell you to."

The man nodded and went limp. Tyler steadied himself. "Throw your gun over there." He pointed across the camp and waited while Sage gave the pistol a heft. "Good. Now get on your knees."

"You ain't gonna kill us, are you, Atherton?"

"That's gonna depend on you. We're here for Carissa Lowe. We've got Carter tied up below and now we have you and your friend. We know there are only another couple of men, and Herbert Lockhart is one of them. You wanna fill us in on who's left?"

"Just the Indian. Long Knife. He's been watching Lockhart's back and keepin' track of the trail to the cabin." Sage seemed more than happy to relay anything he knew.

"And what of Mrs. Lowe?"

"She's in the cabin. She ain't hurt or nothin'. Lockhart tied her to a bed so she wouldn't be able to run away, but otherwise she's fine. He wouldn't let no one put a hand on her."

"That's good," Tyler said, narrowing his eyes. "Where is this cabin?"

"Just up a ways. You go back down on this side," he said, motioning his head toward the road. "Go along that way into the wash and up and around the bend. There's a clearing. It ain't much, but there's room on the rock where someone put up a shelter. That's where she is."

Tyler looked to William and then back to Sage. "Who's that on the ground over there?"

"Roy. He and I been partners for a long time. Is he . . . is he dead?"

"He's not dead . . . not yet," William told the man. "He's shot in the hip and bleedin' out, so unless you want to end up just like him, you'll give us every detail of what awaits in that canyon."

"I'll help you, mister. Honest. I don't wanna die."

It was nearly midnight before the sheriff and his men caught up with William and Tyler. The deputies took over the care of Carter, as well as Sage, but it was too late for Roy.

"We'll take him in for proper identification," the sheriff told them. "I'm pretty sure we have a poster on him. I know there's one for Carter. Maybe for that other one, too. For now, though, we'll leave 'em here and go after Mrs. Lowe. You and Tyler can wait here and keep an eye on them."

"We're going in," William told the sheriff. "Carissa is important to both Tyler and me. Reggie and Dave can wait with Carter and Sage. After all, this really isn't their fight."

"Well, if it's all the same," Sidley said, stepping up, "I plan to go with you and Tyler. I like Mrs. Lowe and wanna make sure I do what I can to help get her back safely."

"It's still a matter for the law," the sheriff said. "If there's trouble, you'd best let me and my boys deal with it."

"We'll do our best," Tyler said, mounting his horse. "But I've never been all that good at waitin'. If you don't mind, I reckon we've done enough of that."

William nodded. "I agree. Let's see this thing through."

The men rode into the dry wash as far as they felt they could without being seen. When they dismounted and tied off their horses, Tyler was more than a little apprehensive. It was difficult to see anything very well. The moon was only about half full, and the indention of the ravine further distorted the light. He'd dealt with similar situations in the war, and those feelings came back to haunt him now. He could imagine himself back in the middle of battle—waiting and watching for the enemy.

They traveled the last half mile on foot, slipping in and out of the rocks much like a lizard might. When they noticed the light coming from the cabin window, the sheriff motioned them to come together.

"Looks like they're either stayin' up late waitin' for the money, or they're on to us. My boys will go around to the back and sides," the sheriff told them. "That will leave the rest of us to take the front. Agreed?"

"Agreed."

They moved out with the utmost care. To give themselves away at this point would only increase the risk to Carissa's life. Tyler prayed as they crept ever closer to the cabin.

Circling the cabin took only a moment. It was a small building, hardly big enough for one person. With no indication that anyone was aware of their lurking, the sheriff moved right up to the door. He gave a nod to William and Tyler, then kicked in the door. They rushed into the cabin, guns drawn.

Tyler could see that there was no one in the room. The crude table and chairs sat empty, save a single lamp that had been lit and placed in the center of the table. On the far side, William and the sheriff were already exploring the kitchen area where a small stove sat cold and unwelcoming.

Then Tyler's glance went to the other side of the room where a small single bed had been positioned against the wall. At first he thought it was empty, but stepping closer, he could see that someone was shackled to the frame.

"Carissa," he whispered and knelt by the bed. "She's over here," he called over his shoulder to William and the others.

The sheriff and William crossed the room to join him. Tyler pulled back a cover and revealed Carissa's small frame. She was deathly still and he feared the worst.

"I'll go back and get the horses," Sidley told Tyler and quickly left the cabin.

"Is she breathing?" the sheriff asked.

Tyler put his hand to her lips. "Barely. Carissa?"

She made an attempt to open her eyes. A hint of a smile touched her lips and was gone. "She's alive," Tyler said. He looked to William. "Help me get her out of this shackle."

"Well, to do that you would benefit from the key," a voice called from the doorway.

Lockhart stood just inside the room with a tall Indian behind him. He held up a key and grinned. Tyler wanted to rush the man and beat him to death. Seeing Carissa so sick and helpless brought his rage to the surface. He started to get up, but the sheriff held him fast.

"Stay here." He moved in front of Tyler and William. "Lockhart, you know why we've come. You're both under arrest."

Lockhart laughed and raised his gun. "I'd say you would be hard-pressed to arrest me at this point. Long Knife just killed your deputies. Slit their throats and never made a sound—unlike you and your men who made enough noise to warn us well in advance." He stepped to one side to let Long Knife move into the room. The Indian filled the doorway.

Lockhart looked past the sheriff to William. "I don't know what you've done with my other men, but it's immaterial. I want my money." He paused and his expression turned purely evil. "And I want you dead. All of you. Long Knife, take their weapons."

The Indian had only moved a fraction of an inch, however, when a rifle shot rang out. Long Knife looked stunned, then dropped his knife to grab his chest. He slumped to the floor, blood spurting out from the gaping hole.

The sheriff grabbed the opportunity to pull his own weapon, and when Lockhart turned with his revolver, the sheriff fired a single bullet, hitting Lockhart between the eyes. As he fell to the floor, Sidley came to the door with his rifle leveled for action.

"We've got them, thanks to you," the sheriff said, looking at Sidley. He blew out a heavy breath and shook his head. "Now, if you'll excuse me, I need to go see to my men."

"Let me help you," Sidley told him. He grabbed a lantern that sat beside the door and lit it from the lamp on the table.

Tyler turned his attention back to Carissa. Her eyes were open, and she watched him as if trying to decide if he were real. Her lips were cracked and dry, and her face was so pale he feared she'd never make the ride home.

"Carissa, don't you die on me," he admonished. "I intend to make you my wife."

William came with the key and unfastened the cuff from Carissa's wrist. Tyler immediately pulled her into his arms.

"Do you hear me, Carissa Lowe? Don't you think you can get out of marryin' me. I won't stand for you dying now." He brushed back strands of the shortened blond hair.

"Give her some water," William said, handing him a canteen.

Tyler held her against him and brought the water to her lips. "You need to drink this," he commanded.

Carissa took in a small bit of the water and nodded a tiny weak nod. Tyler continued to help her to drink, fearful that they were too late to do any good.

"She's not going to be able to travel tonight," William said. "I'll get a fire going and find some food."

Tyler said nothing. He was far too concerned with the woman in his arms. He didn't care what it took or how long, but he would not let her die.

❧

Carissa thought nothing had ever felt so good as the feel of cold water sliding down her dry, gritty throat. She wondered if she was dreaming . . . only this time when she opened her eyes, Tyler was still there and the water was still just as sweet.

It seemed an eternity before she could speak. She saw the worry in Tyler's eyes and wanted only to reassure him that she was strong enough to make it through.

"I . . . I'm . . . fine," she whispered.

Tyler looked at her strangely for a moment. "Yeah, I can see that."

She smiled and nodded. "Good."

She faded back to sleep, but not before she heard him whisper in her ear. "I love you, Carissa. I love you."

❧

When next she woke, the aroma of food made Carissa feel something akin to nausea. She hadn't eaten in so long that her stomach was wont to cramp and churn rather than take on food. Even so, when Tyler came to sit beside her and spoon-fed her a gruel of grits and honey, Carissa tried her best to keep it down.

Carissa had no idea how long Tyler and William had been there. She slept off and on, never quite strong enough to fight the grip of exhaustion, but when she finally felt her senses returning and her head clear a bit, she noticed that Tyler was in desperate need of a shave. He dozed beside her bed, seated on the floor with his head resting on the mattress. Reaching out, Carissa touched his face. He immediately woke.

"You need a shave," she murmured.

He grinned. "And you need a bath."

She nodded. "I've needed one for about a month now. At least it feels that long."

"Well, it hasn't been quite that long, but it might well be by the time we get back to the ranch. How are you feeling?"

"Better," she admitted. "Guess it didn't do me much good to learn to shoot."

He laughed. "You have to have a gun in order to shoot. Not a lot of ladies carry them to the outhouse."

Her cheeks grew hot in embarrassment. "So you heard about that."

Tyler nodded. "Of course. I demanded every detail. I was going to need to know it all in order to find you."

"I remember so little these last few days. How did you find me?"

"It's a long story," he said. "And I'd much rather talk about other things."

She looked at him in curiosity. "Such as?"

"Such as you and me gettin' married. I realize that it might seem like I'm rushin' things a bit, but frankly, I'm learnin' from my mistakes. Seems to me when the moment presents itself, a fella ought to take advantage of it."

Carissa searched his face and found such compelling love and devotion in his expression that she wanted to cry and laugh at the same time. Then a thought came to her and she frowned. "You might not want to marry me when you hear what I did."

He surprised her by roaring with laughter. "Good grief, woman. You nearly got yourself killed—isn't that enough?"

"I bought your ranch," she said hesitantly. "I bought it for you . . . for us."

"I know." He grinned.

"And you aren't mad at me?"

He shook his head. "You're still delirious. Go back to sleep. When you get strong enough, we'll discuss when you want to get hitched."

Carissa closed her eyes and smiled. "The sooner the better."

W e are here this glorious October day to celebrate the marriage of Tyler and Carissa," the pastor said as the clock in the hall struck eleven.

He smiled at the small gathering of well-wishers, then looked directly at Carissa. "Joining two people together to make one is like trying to tame the wind. Focusing on the wrong thing can be useless and even destructive. So rather than trying to tame what cannot be tamed, look to God to teach you how to use the wind—or in this case, the marriage—to benefit you both."

He looked to Tyler, and his expression seemed to grow rather stern. "Marriage isn't always easy, and you two will have to work hard to keep from letting Satan defeat you."

Carissa heard an "Amen" from Marietta Terry and smiled. She glanced down at the simple but beautiful dress of white Indian muslin over yellow cotton. It was nothing like the fashionable gown she'd worn to marry Malcolm Lowe, but she loved this dress far more.

The pastor continued. "Satan wants to strike at the very heart of what God has made holy. If he can destroy marriages and families, Satan knows that it will weaken the faith of man. So I'm telling you both here and now that you need to follow some very simple rules. First, the 'nevers':

"Never let the sun go down on your anger. In other words, clear the slate before you go to sleep at night. If you hold a grudge, work it out. No matter how hard."

Carissa looked up at Tyler and smiled. No doubt they would have their share of arguments. Tyler winked as if reading her mind.

The pastor continued. "Never say anything you don't mean. It's easy to let your mouth spew all sorts of ugly words, but you can never take those back, whether you mean them or not.

"And lastly, never give up on each other. It's easy to grow weary in life and lose sight of what brought you together in the first place. Giving up will seem reasonable at times, but hold fast. Never give up—your love is worth fighting for."

Carissa wished she'd had such advice prior to marrying Malcolm Lowe. She smiled to herself, however, knowing she probably wouldn't have listened.

"Now for the 'always' side of things," the pastor said with a broad smile.

"Always bear one another's burdens and work together. Like two horses in a harness, if you each try to go your own way you won't get anywhere. Likewise, it's easier to carry a load with two sharing the weight.

"Always treat each other with the same amount of patience, mercy, and tenderness that you want for yourself. If you wouldn't appreciate being treated a certain way, then don't treat your mate that way.

"And last, always—*always*—look to God for direction and hope. God is love, and therefore no marriage can survive for long without Him. For true love, love that lasts forever, is born in Him. It's nurtured in God's love, and it's there that love grows strong enough to weather the storms of life. Always love."

Carissa brushed away a tear and pushed back the emotions that threatened to overwhelm her. She recited her marriage vows and felt a sense of wonder as Tyler slipped the ring on her finger. She found it almost too much to believe. After being sure she would never love again, Carissa had fallen in love and married a man unlike any she had ever known.

"You may kiss your bride," the pastor announced, and before Carissa could even react, Tyler had turned her in his arms. He gently tilted her chin up and covered her mouth with his. The kiss was tender yet searing. It was the perfect way to seal their vows.

They turned toward the small group of people, each one dear to Carissa. Even Hannah, who'd given birth to a beautiful baby daughter only the week before, put aside the doctor's wishes that she remain abed and had insisted William allow her to attend the ceremony. For this reason Tyler and Carissa decided to hold the wedding at the Barnett ranch, and William finally gave in. He struck a deal that Hannah could quietly sit and watch the wedding, but could not remain for the reception. She smiled from her seat, with Marty and Andy on one side and Robert and William on the other. Baby Sarah slept peacefully in her arms.

Juanita and her family were there, along with Tyler's men and the Terrys. Laura and Brandon sat with their children, and Carissa couldn't help but remember how Laura had cautioned her against her marriage to Malcolm Lowe. She was more than happy now to see Carissa marry Tyler.

But perhaps most important to Carissa was the presence of her mother and father. She hadn't always felt that close to either one. Her desire for independence and to control her own life had damaged their relationship, but nearly dying had given her a great desire to mend the gulf between them. She had waited the extra month to wed just so her parents could be present. Turning to face them now, she noted that her mother was dabbing her eyes with a handkerchief, but joy radiated in her smile as she gazed at her daughter and new son-in-law.

Gloria took that moment to jump from her grandfather's lap. She came flying toward the newly married couple and wrapped her chubby arms around Tyler's legs. Carissa had spent considerable time prior to the nuptials explaining the wedding to Gloria and telling her how Tyler would now be a part of their family. Gloria made it quite clear that she understood.

"Now you're my papa."

Tyler lifted her and rubbed noses with the child. "I will always be your papa."

Gloria clapped her hands and planted a big kiss on his face. Everyone laughed, and Carissa herself couldn't help but giggle at the sight of her daughter's enthusiastic love. She felt the same way, and had protocol allowed for it, Carissa might have clapped her hands and kissed Tyler with the same excitement.

They celebrated with Juanita's Mexican wedding cake and a luncheon of roasted pork and beef, corn on the cob, fried potatoes, and dozens of other dishes. The hours seemed to fly by, and when Tyler announced that he had a surprise for her, Carissa couldn't help but be curious.

"Your mother and sister have promised to take good care of Gloria for a few days," he told her. Leading her out to a waiting carriage, Tyler pulled her close. "We're going to have some time to ourselves."

"Truly?" She could scarcely believe it. Since Tyler had rescued her from Herbert Lockhart, time to themselves had been scarce.

Even after she'd left the Barnett ranch to return to Laura and Brandon's home, it seemed that the events of life and daily affairs had kept each of them busier than they would have liked. Tyler wouldn't always tell Carissa what he was doing or why he was gone for so long, but she focused on helping Laura to complete improvements to the house. She reminded herself that soon enough Tyler would be with her every evening.

Now as he maneuvered the carriage down the drive, Carissa couldn't help but wonder what Tyler had in mind. "So where are we going?"

"I thought you might like to see your ranch," he told her.

"It's yours now—it's always been yours," she said, smiling.

"Ours," he corrected. "It's ours, and I intend to make it the best home you and Gloria have ever known."

Carissa took hold of his arm and put her head on Tyler's shoulder. She had never known such contentment or peace. She felt she could finally let go of the old and embrace the new. For quite a while neither one said a word.

It wasn't all that long before they turned down a long, narrow road. The landscape was lovely, with rolling prairie turned brown and yellow. Longhorns grazed, mindless of the carriage traversing their feeding grounds. In the distance, Carissa could see a line of trees. That almost always indicated water—usually a river or creek. As they approached, she could see that a small wooden bridge spanned a narrow stream. The banks weren't all that high, but the width of the wash was far wider than the little creek needed.

"When it rains this all fills up," Tyler said as if reading her mind. "Usually the water runs fuller, but we haven't had much rain."

"Who built the bridge?" Carissa asked.

"My father," Tyler replied. "He built it when they first came to take this land. He said he knew it would be almost impossible to accomplish what he wanted unless he secured the bridge first. He and my mother camped on the other side and every day my pa would work on the crossing. He made it to last. He usually made everything that way."

They passed the line of trees, and that was when Carissa saw the burned remains of the ranch house and outbuildings. The charred pieces of the Atherton family dreams served as a haunting reminder of the inconsistent state of life on the Texas frontier.

"I didn't know it was . . . like this," she said, looking at the destruction.

"That's what you get for buying the place sight unseen," he teased.

Carissa couldn't help but imagine that coming back here was hard for Tyler. "We don't have to be here if it's too painful."

"It's not," he told her. "I love this place. There are a lot of good memories here, mingled with the bad. I was out here prayin' one day and it came to me that this ranch is a lot like you and me."

"Like us?"

"We had tragedy in the past that nearly destroyed us. We're like these burned-out buildings. We've seen death and grief, and we've carried those scars all these years. We'll always have reminders of the past, but if we allow God to work, I think we can make a much better future."

Carissa met his gaze. "We just need to clear away the debris."

"Someday we'll clear all of this out," he told her. "One day, I'll build you the most amazing house. But for now, I'm hoping you won't mind living in this little place." He brought the carriage around the old ranch house to reveal a pleasant-looking little building about twenty yards away.

Carissa looked from the house back to Tyler. "Did you build this?"

"I helped to enlarge it. It was already here from when Osage and a couple of other men took care of the place during the war. Along with help from William and some of the other men, we managed to extend it a bit. When you delayed marryin' me until your folks were able to get here, I knew I had to do something to keep myself busy." He reined back on the horses and set the brake. Throwing her a grin, Tyler jumped down from the carriage. "Come on and let me show you around."

Carissa moved to accept his help, but instead of letting her step down, Tyler swung her into his arms and held her as he might do with Gloria. She wrapped her arms around his neck and smiled.

"You look mighty pleased with yourself, Mrs. Atherton."

She giggled. "I must say that I am, Mr. Atherton. Mighty pleased indeed."

He laughed and carried her to the door of the cabin, stopping only to open the door. Carrying her across the threshold, Tyler finally allowed Carissa to touch the ground. She looked around the room in pleasant surprise. It was larger than it had seemed from the outside. A kitchen stood at one end of the long room and a fireplace was positioned at the other. In between were pieces of furniture that gave the place a very homey look.

Carissa moved away from Tyler and went to touch the upholstery of a wing-backed chair that sat on one side of the fireplace. The burgundy and brown material seemed quite fitting for the cabin. On the other side of the hearth was an oak rocker that would serve her well for rocking Gloria and any other babies that might come along. And Carissa silently prayed that there would be many children in their family. She very much enjoyed being a mother.

"Do you like it?" he asked.

"I do." She went to the window and fingered the beautiful curtains hanging there.

"Hannah made those for you. She said a place just wasn't a home without curtains at the windows and rugs on the floor."

Carissa turned and noticed the homemade rug that stretched in front of the fireplace. "I suppose she made the rug, as well."

"No, Marietta did that. She also gave us the quilts on the beds. Do you wanna see?"

She couldn't help but laugh. "Of course."

"This is Gloria's room," he said, opening a door. The small whitewashed room had a bed decorated with a yellow-and-white quilt. Yellow-checked curtains hung at the single window and beneath it was a small dresser.

"It's perfect," Carissa said, looking in wonder at the arrangement. She could already imagine Gloria playing on the wooden floor.

"I didn't go to the trouble of puttin' up wallpaper, 'cause Hannah told me you'd probably want to pick that out yourself."

Carissa smiled. "I'm sure anything you would have chosen would have pleased me. I didn't even know we'd have this beautiful little place. In fact, I wasn't at all sure what to expect for our future living arrangements." She shrugged. "I kind of purposefully avoided asking for fear of making you uncomfortable."

"I hope in the future you won't keep things like that to yourself. We need to always be free to discuss our concerns. Promise me you will just come to me with your worries."

She nodded. "I promise I will."

Tyler took hold of her hand and led her back into the main room. He opened the second of three doors. "This is our bathing room. Your sister told me that you're quite fond of a hot bath, so Will helped rig a tank on the other side of the wall. We'll keep it filled with water and most days it will warm right up under the sun. Then you can just pump it right into the tub," he said pointing to the small pump handle. "It's like having indoor plumbing."

She laughed and marveled at his thoughtfulness. "You went to so much trouble. Thank you for all of this."

"But we aren't done yet," he said, pulling her back out of the room. He drew her to the last of the doors and opened it. "This is ours."

Carissa stepped into the bedroom. Great care had been given to this room. There was a large four-poster bed and a matching chest made of cherry wood. A beautiful double-wedding-ring quilt in pale blues, yellows, and greens graced the top of the bed and matching shams trimmed out the pillows. Carissa couldn't help but run her fingers over the material.

"I got the bed in Dallas. Do you like it?" he asked, coming up behind her. Putting his arms around her, he pulled Carissa back against him. Tyler placed kisses on her neck, causing Carissa to shiver.

"It's beautiful. I love it," she said, feeling her emotions starting to get the best of her. "It would seem this house has everything we could ever need."

Tyler turned her in his arms. "So long as we have each other, we have everything we need. I'm gonna work my best to make you happy here."

Carissa sighed and placed her head on his shoulder. "You won't have to work too hard, because I'm already as happy as a girl could ever be. In fact, for the first time in my life, I feel whole."

He lifted her face to meet his and smiled. "Me too," he whispered. "Me too."

Tracie Peterson is the author of more than ninety novels, both historical and contemporary. Her avid research resonates in her stories, as seen in her bestselling HEIRS OF MONTANA and STRIKING A MATCH series. Tracie and her family make their home in Montana.

Visit Tracie's Web site at *www.traciepeterson.com*.

More Adventure and Romance from Tracie Peterson

To learn more about Tracie and her books, visit traciepeterson.com.

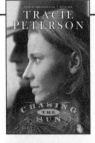

Bound by need but divided by their dreams, Hannah and William form an uneasy truce. In the face of unforeseen challenges, can the blush of first love survive?

Chasing the Sun
LAND OF THE LONE STAR # 1

As the lives of three women are shaped by the untamed Alaskan frontier, each must risk losing what she holds most dear to claim the new life she longs for.

SONG OF ALASKA: *Dawn's Prelude, Morning's Refrain, Twilight's Serenade*

When Deborah Vandermark meets the new town doctor, conflicting desires awaken within her. Is it the man—or his profession—that has captured her heart?

STRIKING A MATCH: *Embers of Love, Hearts Aglow, Hope Rekindled*

Bestselling Series from Tracie Peterson and Judith Miller

To learn more about Tracie, Judith, and their books, visit traciepeterson.com and judithmccoymiller.com.

Romance and intrigue abound on beautiful Bridal Veil Island. Amidst times of change and disaster, two couples struggle to find hope. Will their love—and lives—survive the challenges they face?

BRIDAL VEIL ISLAND: *To Have and To Hold, To Love and Cherish*

When three cousins are suddenly thrust into a world where money equals power, the family's legacy—and wealth—depend on their decisions. Soon each must decide what she's willing to sacrifice for wealth, family, and love.

THE BROADMOOR LEGACY: *A Daughter's Inheritance, An Unexpected Love, A Surrendered Heart*